Telling My Love Lies

By the Same Author

Taking Cover, 1982

Foreign Affairs, 1985

Popular Anatomy, 1995

Bad Trips (editor), 1991

Worst Journeys: The Picador Book of Travel (editor), 1992

As For Me and My Body:
A Memoir of Sinclair Ross, 1997

Keath Fraser

Telling My Love Lies

A Book Club's Collection of
Stories and Comments

by

Geoffrey Denton, Lorin Mae, Anne Tanice Reid,
T. S. Saini, Jim Constance, K. Ives, Robin How,
Stevie Platzer, Mavis Terwiel and Patricia Melmouth

With a Foreword by

Patricia Melmouth

The Porcupine's Quill

CANADIAN CATALOGUING IN PUBLICATION DATA

Fraser, Keath
    Telling my love lies

ISBN 0-88984-179-9

I. Title.

PS8561.R297T44 1996   C813'.54   C96-931548-1
PR9199.3.F62T44 1996

Published by The Porcupine's Quill, Inc., 68 Main Street, Erin, Ontario N0B 1T0, with financial assistance from The Canada Council and the Ontario Arts Council. The support of the Department of Canadian Heritage through the Book and Periodical Industry Development programme and the Periodical Distribution Assistance Programme is also gratefully acknowledged.

This is a work of fiction. Any resemblance of characters to persons, living or dead, is purely coincidental.

Represented in Canada by the Literary Press Group. Trade orders are available from General Distribution Services.

Readied for the press by John Metcalf. Copy edited by Doris Cowan. Typeset in Ehrhardt, printed on Zephyr Antique Laid, sewn into signatures and bound at The Porcupine's Quill.

Cover image is after the oil painting, 'Disappearing Diva #3,' 1993 (80" x 30"), by Kathryn Jacobi. Courtesy of the artist and the Diane Farris Gallery, Vancouver.

For

The only form of lying that is absolutely beyond reproach is lying for its own sake, and the highest development of this is ... Lying in Art.

— Oscar Wilde

Deliver my soul, O Lord, from lying lips and from a deceitful tongue.

— Psalm 120

Contents

Patricia Melmouth

Foreword

ARROGANCE. Fear of extinction. This collection of stories rises from ignoble roots.

Our reading club couldn't agree on a single book, having dug itself in over titles for the coming fall's reading list. In the last season we had stumbled from one month's meeting to the next on compromise choices, pleasing no one.

The nutty fun of our early years had more or less faded into bland discussions. Nothing out of left field, no more insights off the wall. As readers we'd become predictable. Instead of opening us up to new experiences, fresh symmetries, our critical exchanges were commanding boredom.

We knew one another too well.

We believed this.

Deadlocked after five years and with summer now at hand we wondered if we ought to disband. We were sitting over drinks beside Anne Reid's duck pond, the ten of us, debating our survival as a group.

Our host clearly had no intention of convening a wake. In desperation, as she later admitted, Anne proposed that since we couldn't agree on which books to discuss we should try writing our own book. Reinvigorate our reading, by each of us trying to write a story.

We smartly kicked around reasons why we couldn't, shouldn't, wouldn't be so foolish. To our host's credit, she persisted:

Forgive me, intrepid guests. But if it's true no author writes before she reads ... maybe it's also the case she never understands her reading *until* she writes?

We were drinking gin slings. Mellow by now. A curious will to prolong the evening made the rest of us actually want to agree with this impracticable suggestion to become the source of our own bookish enrichment. So everybody said sure, okay, why not? Some of us probably meant it.

Ironically, this casual willingness to keep going held a death wish. For we also agreed, maybe to help lick the self-doubts of closet writers, maybe from shyness at the thought of sharing any stories we might pen, that should any one of us miss a deadline then the group would be allowed to dissolve. We were that suicidal. We *expected* to fail.

Here's how we decided to proceed.

We drew stems of timothy to determine in which of the next ten months, starting in September, each of us would distribute for discussion copies of a story written in rotation for the collective. We could write any kind of tale we wished, of any length, with the proviso that our semi-rural world should somehow figure in each. The common ingredient would be here, where we lived – and so, though we never spoke of this, who we were, why we mattered, etcetera.

A crutch, obviously. But we needed a crutch.

By the following winter an odd thing had happened. No collapse. The early contributors all commented on how much farther their stories had taken them than they'd expected to go. As readers we'd evidently underestimated our imaginations. We'd never appreciated how much fiction writers *made up*. For some reason, before, a story had always seemed to us truer to a life lived than it probably really was. Or so concluded Keefer Ives. *We had had the unfortunate tendency to credit experience and debit make-believe.*

Surprised by each other's work, especially by stuff we knew was grounded in lies, we were frankly troubled at how such unexpected stories had come to be written by fairly conventional people. By people we knew. It was unsettling. Robin How, the eventual author of *Foster Story*, said it felt like jealousy when somebody in your family becomes famous. She told us her twin brother had once jived on a muscular dystrophy telethon in white bucks, lipsynching a Pat Boone song called *Bernadine*, raising thousands of dollars along with several invitations to a televangelist meeting in Taiwan. She hated him. Patently *un*true. But winningly infectious because

Robin didn't expect us to believe her, only to agree to be held like some resident stranger with a counterfeit foreign note.

Accordingly, we began to honour the transformation a writer underwent in composing a story – if transformation it was, and not a richer dream life than the rest of us could have guessed. (After reading Geoff Denton's story, *Argentina My Voice*, I remember wondering if anyone could have guessed the peasant background of Giuseppe Verdi was ever subversive enough for *him* to have gone on to write the other-worldly music of *La Traviata* ... Geoff – he won't mind me saying this, to show how prejudice likes to categorize – is a real estate agent of impeccable pedigree. His father too.) No, it didn't look like we knew each other after all.

We were slowly learning to value imagination for its own sake. It in turn was beginning to consume us. To Mavis Terwiel imagination seemed, in discussing her own later *Sturgeon*, like a compound interest rate, feeding off itself as the balance of details built up in her account. The experience, enriching, encouraged us to act as we never had, becoming what we'd never been, mysterious to one another, a community of readers. It did seem odd that in remaking us as strangers, fiction also had this curious capacity to bring us together.

And cause us sadness, too. Lorin May asked, Was it Baudelaire who said beauty makes you sad? Terry Saini, a big fan of country music, suggested it could just as well have been that other long-hair voice of sad, Patsy Cline.

Sadness seemed to lie in our growing realization that the solitary imagination was stubbornly resistant to any discussion of it. Because. No matter how much we pulled, prodded, paraphrased, we could seldom if *ever* express what we felt to be the essence of someone else's story, no matter how simple seemed this story or how willing its author to avail our curiosity.

Stevie Pratzer was soon testifying to his growing belief (though his story of a war criminal wouldn't appear for another four months) that the 'flower' just can't be botanized and *stay* a flower. To stay beautiful, a flower needed mystery. Same as a song, agreed Terry, like 'Why Can't He Be You'...

We hadn't thought of mysteries *or* flowers in this way earlier, believing insights previously denied us came from inadequate language – either cheerleading and repetitive, or critical and pointless. Stevie's 'bouquet' approach was meant to replace such botanizing and to remind us of another agreement from last June: that we should have no objection to members borrowing from each other's stories in order to jumpstart their own inspiration. Point being our best discussion was another story, another flower, the bouquet's appeal growing in ratio to its arrangement. Our community of stories required this kind of inter-narrative acknowledgement to return in kind what had been borrowed in the first place ...

We had agreed to rename Sherwood Meadows something other than Sherwood Meadows, to give us the liberating leeway of an invented world. Jim Constance, who sometimes travels in Kerala starting up legal aid groups, remembered a town inland from the Malabar Coast, with small farms hugging a dry riverbed as wide as the Sherwood, and surrounded by mountains recalling coastal peaks back here. For fictional purposes, 'here' thus became 'Perumbur'.

A guide book to the larger estuary describes Sherwood Meadows, dairy farms beside the river, a tiny Holland, where whole sections of marshland were once converted to farmland through a twinning reclamation project with the Netherlands. Immigrant Dutchmen had helped bolster our local dikes after the great flood of 1948, staying on afterward to farm.

(This municipality, now protected by the Agricultural Land Reserve, includes dairies, scruffy acreages, blueberry farms. A marshland polder provides sanctuary for birds at the south end of the largest freshwater tidal lake in the world. And on fine days looms a snowy volcano, south of the border. Happy Valley? How safe are things as they *are* here? The village of Sherwood Meadows, on the other side of the highway, is becoming a strip with hardware outlets from Carthage Mall.)

We worry our district is doomed to lose its life on the edge here, poised between wilderness interior and port metropolis. Our fields, as flat as Dutch paintings, fill up with mist from marsh and river. Picturesque, sure, but they're also attracting the flotsam of a mobile population. A young woman died last summer when her boyfriend ran his muscle boat – stuck throttle – into a dike, flipping it high into the air and landing her in a farmer's field.

Wilderness does extract the price of wanting to keep it. (I know, I'm writing this from jail: contempt of court, logging blockade, hidden slaughter of one more watershed.) For now, wilderness remains immanent. Coyotes still plunder our hen houses. The lake upsets canoers and they drown.

* * *

When the others approached me about introducing these stories – as a consolation prize, I suppose, with present circumstances preventing me from joining their discussion of my contribution to the season's last meeting – I discovered not all members thought injustice *had* been served by the author's absence, although most seemed agreed, from reading my elegy, I needed cheering up.

An autobiographical fallacy, admitted Keefer Ives.

He himself was against any notion that my sad tone could *only* have arisen from self-absorbed incarceration.

Which I suppose is why Lorin Mae, staring at my prison togs, suggested everybody should contribute their own authorial *Comment* to the book ... You know, so readers can appreciate for themselves how different a story's seed is from its blossom? What'd be the *point* of pretending to refine ourselves out of the collection like retiring little Flow Bears?

So they charged me to tell our collective story, immodestly urging our experiment upon other groups clustered across the continent. (Is discontent rife out there, you other groups?) Thousands of reading clubs like ours, composed of similarly diverse backgrounds, and just as indifferent to artless language and disposable light: this anthological nudge of ours as a reminder that a literary universe ought to feel no less fresh than the neighbourly Internet's.

Its name?

Polly, moved Geoffrey Denton. After a hoary word accidentally turned up by his young narrator, the farm lad with the ditzy cousin. Geoff, a frustrated musician, had confessed to us how he was looking up *polyphone* when he came across *polyonomy* ... the use of several different names for the same person or thing. The name has since gathered in our collective mind to describe what lies at the petal-heart of stories – the essence of their louche and layered perfume.

COMMENT: *Argentina My Voice*, if I'm going to be truthful, arose from my recent interest in the collective noun for ostriches. I'd bought a breeding pair of hobby birds from a transplanted South African in Aldergrove, and hoped to retire young by selling the offspring at several thousand dollars per chick. With one hen laying up to two dozen eggs, the price of breeders wasn't outrageous when I considered the profit to be had from even the smallest ... flock.

But 'flock' was wrong.

I phoned back the vendor and got his daughter, a no-nonsense child with an obvious distaste for her old man's klutzy birds. She was a big bluffer, with flair. 'Flock?' she said. 'Crock.'

Her manner reminded me of someone else's, a girl I met the summer I turned ten. My first crush. And suddenly she was there, the character for my story. I sensed I could shape a story around the way she talked and not betray my realtor's instinct for accountability.

Even when sisters surprised me by showing up out of her mouth, I felt safe. Her little masterpieces of mendacity, as pathetic as they were, seemed to persuade me of a world just as real as my narrator's.

(A 'wobble of ostrich,' by the way, convinced my current live-in I was dreaming if I expected to turn our hobby farm into an egg factory.)

Geoffrey Denton

Argentina My Voice

CONNIVANCE, FINALLY, had us listening to her sisters as if she *had* sisters, except this is how she wanted it, from the day she arrived bossing them around like a ventriloquist. Talk, talk. Sometimes she inveigled Merrilee into retorting, sure, but never Phoebe.

The hot May her mother died my cousin came to live, and missing home she moped and slept and cried. Her new mom, my old one, rolled dough for her and baked it light. Long hair stuck to the girl's cheeks, you found strands in the porridge. Her skin in the tub rubbed through the door, you heard it, skin and tears. Hair there too, our house was full of hair. Under her arms it grew as fine as corn silk, and as red. Scrubbed and limp she reclined on the veranda with nothing to do but grieve. Pollen fell from the anthers, comic books curled in the sun, our senses had the feel of blond, bulging withers. On tropical evenings we watched the sprinklers – and aboard a wooden ship, look, floated out to view them.

'That's water for fodder, isn't it? You'd mourn your corn if it wasn't, I'm sure. Wouldn't you?' Rhyming, she spoke brazenly. 'My tears are over, Rover, so are my teeth.' I looked at Daddy. My cousin looked at me. She meant the sugar lacing Mom's pies. 'How can I sing with rotted teeth? Don't *you* think I should sing-a-ding-ding?' I thought she should check her marbles. 'Well,' she said. 'I might.' Her name was Argentina. That summer, at sixteen, she outlived first one, then both her imaginary sisters.

Daddy did some singing himself, a weekend western singer whose band was also our hired help. Mom said he hired help on purpose from ranks of unemployed musicians. Quinn and Ivar and Tulley preferred dance halls to fields. So did Daddy. On Saturday night he put on a white satin bowling jacket with a string tie and pineapple toggle, wore cowboy boots and a lemon shirt. The rest of

the week he practised in the cornfields with the high tenor voice of
Slim Whitman and sang Slim's big hit, 'That Silver-Haired Daddy
of Mine'. I listened through the stalks. After intermission, after
lunch, he always tried Slim's first hit, 'The Indian Love Call'. It
never worked for Daddy, he couldn't yodel. He practised yodelling,
had been practising since puberty: first Judy Canova, then Wilf
Carter, at last Slim Whitman. By the time Slim came along my
father was a silver-haired daddy himself.

He sang at dances to make ends meet, forced his talent and
growled at his farm. In a flood plain between mountains and river he
grew silage for dairies and sweet corn for tins. Because he hated
Perumbur, and to soothe his strained cords, he gargled baking soda
to lift his soul.

Talk about a character.

My cousin couldn't have shucked ears for apathy. She just
bathed and sulked and let in flies. In bed Phoebe, her youngest sister, made love to a Coke bottle. She was the laziest sister, looked
dead, like spat-out gum bleached into asphalt. She wasn't happy,
languishing every evening on the veranda. This imaginary Phoebe,
her pores, smelled like corn leaves up your nose, prickly and
suffocating.

Argentina spoke out at the falling darkness, maybe as a way of
forgetting where she was and why. 'It's a daisy being lazy,' she said,
lying late on the veranda looking wide-eyed and distracted. 'If I had
a horse, of course ...' No, no telling where she would canter. Her
eyes strayed to my hoed-out hands. 'You're a worker,' she said, 'I'm
a shirker.' I said I thought rhyming was for kids. Mocking me she
said, 'You're learnin', Vernon,' as if a name were hers to trifle with.
You also became Irving, Sheldon, Euple, for her swerving, well
done scruples.

She had the rhythm and eye to attract an uncle. Giles was
Daddy's stage name, and his real one, he'd never changed it. For
Saturday dances he blackened his hair with shoe polish and was
picked up looking as young as his sidemen. They all drank and came
back late dancing in their headlights. Humming in her room,
Argentina slipped downstairs to greet Giles with a smile and the
aspirin tablets to stop his headache Sunday. She handed him a glass

of water. Mom slept soundly till the imaginary Merrilee died. Fat Merrilee died suspecting evil.

You could tell by the way Merrilee sat at meals Argentina was poisoning her. Sat with her fat back sideways, sat that way on the veranda too. Disturbed was not the word for this weight squatting on her soul. In the hallway upstairs she finally opened up and called her sister disgusting. The older girl replied that Merrilee was done for. 'You fat bat. Your belly's jelly and you think dink!' They quarrelled loudly, Argentina doing both their voices, the ventriloquist hounding herself as well. Merrilee's skin blotched like red dots in a comic book, tears blistered on her cheeks. Nothing could have saved her from the choking weather, the mugginess. She bawled her eyes out.

'I'm a fan,' said Argentina, 'of your old man.' She'd have said anything for the chance to sing with his band. She smiled to hide her teeth. Yodelled in the tub, paraded herself with ears curled around the chatter of Daddy's sidemen in the fields, asking questions about tassels and suckers but mainly lyrics. I listened. Daddy listened. 'Giles smiles,' she claimed, on her.

'The way to succour grief,' said Daddy, 'is take it dancing.' Grief wore a cowboy hat and kisscurls stiffened with Vaseline, and she and he sang duets. According to Daddy she was as slick on stage as dolphin skin. His band's business picked up – church basements, community halls, parties elsewhere after bingo. Phone calls trickled in from up and down the valley. 'A girl singer's the novelty a band needs,' he said.

Maybe Mom knew what Merrilee knew, something was making Mom's moustache grow, the heat maybe. Tackiness kept us all awake the Sunday morning Argentina came home in the moonlight laughing, to whip the cat with corn tassels. At breakfast she said gin punch, funny, made your head go crunch. She couldn't eat her porridge. Eating porridge year round was a bad family trait, but eating it in summer was like putting on longjohns. She said it was no wonder Phoebe turned to Coke, no wonder she was rotting. Merrilee ate porridge with the despair of a fat person. Her blubbering became June's voice of grief. It sounded worse than May's, since it seemed no longer to be accusing Argentina of betraying a dead mother – just a live one.

GEOFFREY DENTON

Ivar, the banjo player, foresaw Merrilee's departure when he retold the story of Tulley's tremors on steel guitar. 'Diagnosed whatchamacallit up here,' he said, tapping himself quietly between the eyes. He too was conniving. Argentina mimicked him with the painted fingernail she was shaking dry. 'So he give it up,' said Ivar.

Merrilee's giving up was easier and painless. I found her in the closed garage with dried tears on her cheeks – I can see her still, a comic in her fist. She's sitting in the back seat, waiting. Our Packard is out of gas and the fumes all leaked away.

To humour the girl Mom laughed, then she wailed, remembering her own sister's funeral in Perumbur's little church. She doubled her baking to soothe her grief. She dribbled in the shortening. 'The genes that give out,' she said, flexing the fingers of an unstable family skeleton. She missed the flatter, plainer prairies of her girlhood.

To make matters worse Phoebe could not, or would not, eat anything. Would not lay one hand on cutlery and passed hunger by. Merrilee's death had bequeathed dresses that hung on her like grain sacks. She wore a new one every afternoon for a week, then nothing. Refused to climb out of bed, lay stretched out on a worn cotton sheet, biting her lips coral.

Argentina braided Merrilee's dead, cutoff hair, calling it a grieve-weave. She pinned it to her own piled-up bun. Her own hair went up and down like hope. Mourning became her, and she cultivated the tempered airs of sorrow. She gazed off the porch like Our Lady of the Sea.

You could have drowned in corn. In the heat the fields seemed wet enough to fish in. The kitchen too, we could have used a punka. Mom baked pies and cakes and jam rolls. But not for Phoebe. That sister lived for Coke and the pleasure of exercising the bottle's lip, its thicker glass. Mom's steadfast worry caused Argentina to warn us her sister had never eaten beans. Beans, said Mom, is what she needs. 'In case she's got worms.'

Conniving. Conniving.

Before Phoebe died I had fat dreams, fattening her up with Old Dutch sprinkled on cookies to bleach her insides. Yet who could have been chaster than a fourteen-year-old making love to eel-soft

⟨ 22 ⟩

glass? After Merrilee's death she closed the door and to see her you watched through the wall. What a dear sweet cousin, what a bonerack. In her wide double bed she hardly moved and her scalp shed hair worse than the cat. In corners you found bales of it. Mom never noticed, she kept house like a trollop.

By the time husks started fattening, Phoebe had lost consciousness. Ivar studied me like he thought I'd stolen her food. 'Didn't you even try to talk to her?' he asked. Embarrassed, I plugged the hole in my wall with Spearmint and hoed harder in the world outside. 'Who named these girls?' Ivar asked my cousin. 'They're stupid names.' But Argentina didn't care. She took her sister up a glass of whole milk, Merlin vitamin pills, a piece of fresh raspberry pie. One afternoon she found Phoebe as spent as a used match. From the veranda she called, *'Mom comme!...'* It sounded like a railroad junction. *'Mom-comme! Mom-comme! Mom-comme!...'* her voice losing music to nonsense and, at last, hysteria. We came. The thing was, with Mom in the kitchen, Argentina had run right by her.

The doctor fretted over Argentina but Phoebe never woke up. Grieve? For Argentina, Phoebe's death now made a chain of death. She made us feel the niblet factory was like a beach we were cultivating sand for, it seemed that pointless. Nobody mentioned creamed corn to her, nobody joked about popcorn. Mom even stopped baking. The band made its way through the sweet corn singing mournfully. Daddy kept shaking his head till Argentina lost her voice.

'Shock,' said Mom.

Three deaths for Argentina, three arrows in her heart. It amounted to a curse.

A disease. The doctor, returning, called it aphonia. 'Sympathetic aphonia,' he told us. Daddy figured it was not that she couldn't talk, but wouldn't. He approved of bed rest ordered by the doctor and resigned himself to singing solo. But he got bored reaching for notes higher than he could scale. It threatened the band.

'This cursed family,' said Mom, lingering aimlessly in sweet rows of depression.

Poor woman, lubricating her adopted daughter with molasses and pills and love, handing Daddy his Cow Brand in a glass of water, clucking Ivar to attention when his eyes roamed south to hair in this girl's palms.

As the corn gained weight my cousin, just like Phoebe, started losing it. Her grieve-weave in Merrilee's memory fell apart in her hands. With her own hair she wove pony tails, horse tails, gawky manes. She was like the ugly sister with hair that never pleased her. But it never fell out, she didn't lose her hair as she did her voice. Her singing now no more than a larynx scratching linoleum, she spent days in bed fiddling with brush and mirror.

I watched her gargle the heat. I opened her window and closed it and opened it, bringing her molasses and smacking flies with a rubber glove. Once I pulled the glove over my head like a toque. She stared, then smiled. She showed me my image in her mirror: the red glove's empty fingers waggled like a rooster's comb.

Said I, 'I'm a rooster booster.'

This tickled her, and for a moment she forgot herself. Said I, 'Combs roam. My comb, your comb. Look in the mirror, dear.' This nonsense, copied from her, spilled out. 'I've got masses of molasses, right?' She hated molasses and her smile disappeared. I showed up with ice cream. 'To help you dream,' said I.

She licked the spoon. She was still a child, had temples with the hollows of a child's, and her round shoulders stuck out naked from a little girl's nightie. Rhyming, I fanned the heat off with a pillow case, a jester in my cousin's court. She had not spoken since she lost her voice.

In August the band fell apart. Nothing to do with Argentina, it was Tulley, he and Daddy quarrelling that month over Daddy's share of the take. All Daddy did, said Tulley, was sing four or five songs, then leave the others to play the dance. Daddy came home on his own, complaining of tonsillitis. After Tulley quit, Quinn, who hated the cornfields anyway, said it was crazy to try to play dances without a lead guitar, and he quit too. The lazy way he brushed his drumskins had made him a perfect country drummer, and Daddy went begging. He could not go on without a drummer and a lead guitar. Just Ivar was left, and what could you do with a banjo picker? Still, Daddy was careful around Ivar, needing him for when harvest started and, if he ever got one going again, a band. Ivar tapped the vellum and plonked tunes with finger picks on five wire strings. 'Pingatore,' he said, 'daddied this little instrument.' He knew everything about things and very little of bodies. Ivar dressed the way a squirrel dozes spread-legged and stomach-down on a branch, with no thought of style. 'But I play good,' he said. We sat on the porch at breaks. Daddy, white hair in his ears, had stopped singing in the fields. Mom said there was no way *he* had lost his voice, just his self-esteem.

One late night in August I heard a noise upstairs, then nothing. I had come down for a glass of milk. I let out the cat, locked the screen, washed out my glass. The air was still and sticky. Taking a cookie I put out the light and moved up the stairs. Outside Argentina's room I stopped to listen. I tried her keyhole, saw blackness, listened some more. Just the usual sound of dreams scratching for a voice. Also some groaning in the gloaming, I thought, chewing my cookie.

Gloaming, looking it up two days later in the dictionary, I found on the same page as *gloppen*. I remember gloppen because nothing I could think of rhymed with it. Just the word I needed that night when I walked into her bedroom.

When I walked in I gloppened Daddy. Startled him.

'*What? What do you want!*' he hissed. Gloppened too, I dropped my cookie on the carpet. He rushed at me in the dim light cast from the stairwell. '*Have you let out the cat!*' he hissed. '*I've been talking!*' he fumed, disappearing down the stairs.

Turning on Argentina's lamp I saw the rucked-up bed, smelt the shoe polish. Awake, tears in her eyes, she was licking the tip of her nose.

I wanted to ask if my father had bitten her.

Instead I cleared the hair off her face and whispered, 'Rest.'

'Chest,' she said.

I wondered if she was hurt, pained into utterance. I put my ear to her breast as to a conch shell. Listened for the rise and fall of a tide, our river, some reason for her voice. Her heart seemed clocked to give nothing away but its regularity. Chest, I thought. Rest.

Gently I placed my fingers on her to acknowledge the word. Ashamed, I turned away to look for my cookie.

Down in the kitchen Daddy had gone out and let in moths. I kicked out the cat and locked the screen. Stood before the open refrigerator in the stifling night.

Instead of ice cream I found seven dill pickles in a cold jar, so I took these to the table and ate six. The seventh I kept for rubbing on the lump where Daddy'd socked me. Imaginary Merrilee must have known everything. You could still hear her boohooing. I felt sorry for Mom. I felt sorry for Argentina. No word could I think of to rhyme with Argentina – not Indonesia, not Guatemala. Home was not where my heart was at all. Around us, cooling down, the old house released the sun, shuddered on its wooden raft, expired and fell asleep. The pickles were sour.

Next morning Mom said if her niece had said a word she would like to know what it was, thank you.

'Suitcase,' I said.

'Suitcase?' She put her cup down slowly. 'Is she thinking of leaving us? Did she find her voice after three weeks just so she can leave?' She turned to Daddy who was stirring his eyes in his porridge. He looked like he'd slept in the barn. 'She's only a kid. She's an *only* kid. We can't let her run off!' Her face was less alarmed than I expected. 'She's in no condition to travel. Where could she go?'

Daddy ate his porridge not saying anything.

'I'll have a word with her,' said Mom. She served Daddy his toast and wiped her hands on the tea towel. When Ivar arrived, toothpick in mouth, Daddy vanished into the fields. Ivar stood there letting wire laces slowly, imperceptibly, tear out the eyes of his boots. 'Whatchamacallit,' he said. 'Try some.' He meant bran, the elixir of health, Ivar's health, the All Bran he called Little Logs. 'They work for me every time,' he said, delighted at the mystery.

Mom came back down. 'She can't talk. I don't know what you're telling lies for. I didn't see any suitcase.' She went to the cupboard. 'Here. Take her up these molasses. And try her on porridge and cream. If we don't look out, she'll follow Agnes.' Mom looked like she might follow Agnes herself. Her eyes drooped over large dark bags as she slumped down with her tea.

Ivar told her she should start in baking again, that he wanted to see her wrist wriggling the cookie-cutter some more. He didn't mention her last cookies were stale. He shuffled across the linoleum and went out the door.

When I went in to Argentina she was sitting up with her hair all over creation. A blue-bottle, the beggar, was buzzing it. She pushed away the tray.

'Tired?'

She looked at me. A little huskily answered, 'Mired.'

I tried again. 'Hoarse.'

'Force,' she whispered.

'Glide.'

She came back, 'Lied.'

This was therapy like ping-pong, ping-sing I thought, one-note conversations batted back and forth over logic's net. You lost a point for half rhyming the ball, or not trying at all. If I was tired from hoeing, I'd take in the dictionary.

'Gloaming.'

'Roaming,' she answered.

'Doleful.'

'Hoe full.'

Some days were worse and she struggled in despair. At night I kept an ear tuned for Daddy prowling like the cat. I listened outside her door. I listened outside his own door for a set of snores from him and Mom. Giles and Rhoda. Nothing except the soda Rhoda fed Daddy's tonsils rhymed with my mother's name.

By late August the corn had grown near the sky, the river had dropped to its lowest level in half a century, and Daddy had taken to the sheds to prepare his machinery. He meant to punish me. He kept me hoeing till my hands swelled and the blisters popped. Even the ocean, miles west of Perumbur, the thought of setting out across it Kon-Tiki fashion from a beach in Vancouver, had begun to make more sense than being used as a joeboy.

Looking up *joeboy* I found *joskin*.

'Saucepin,' she said.

Saucepan.

Mom herself must have wondered at what she heard. I told her I was getting somewhere and not to despair. She would've needed a bright imagination where I was concerned to think of concupiscence – an unrhymable word I was saving up. Her ear at the keyhole, a lobe I loved, would have been more startled than her eye.

PAWKY	LUPINE
YOUNKER	TROPE
ROCKY	SUPINE
CONQUER	DOPE

My cousin and I shared the dictionary and served up unrhymable words like *gloppen* to win a point. She had no memory of sentences, they left no impression when I spoke them. Words by themselves made her listen.

Phoebe.

Merrilee.

Lonely words, stupid names. Characters without voices.

By late summer I had begun to feel words as substances. In the past, heat and voices were humidity you suffered through, excused one another in the middle of, or drowned in hating. A bad family trait. Now when you spoke them in our baking heat, words moved on the tongue lighter than pastry.

That year Indian summer was as hot as real summer. Copper days, golden corn: dent, sweet and a hybrid flint corn of Daddy's confection used for fritters and popping. When the cobs glistened, when the dimple in each grain showed the soft starch dried out, when a dark dot appeared at the cob's tip, two hundred acres were ready for harvest. Ivar drove the Finning that pulled the thresher that cut the stalks, blowing the whole works as silage into a trailing wagon. Daddy harvested the sweet corn with more refined machinery.

No songs that year, just work. Loading and unloading wagons, weighing corn by the bushel, by the ton, telephoning wholesalers and arguing with dairymen. Perumbur dairy farms depended all winter on our corn rotting sweetly in their siloes. School for me was out till the harvest was in. A news photo in the paper showed Nikita Khrushchev dwarfed by the champion cornfield of one Roswell

Garst, in Coon Rapids, Iowa. The dictator was mad they hadn't let him visit Disneyland.

From Ivar I learned corn had more uses than his tractor. Husks for dolls, stalks for paper and wallboard, cobs for charcoal and solvents and pipes, grain for dextrose and booze. All these were the wider uses he said Daddy never bothered with. Daddy only sold corn for silage and canning. His concession to Lacey's cinema hardly counted when you figured out the price of popcorn and what they paid him. But he liked the Odeon because its manager showed Gene Autry singing as he unwound fencewire. Daddy must have counted on singing again himself, if only in his fields, when I wasn't around to remind him of what I knew.

Argentina agreed to come down at last and sit on the veranda. It was sweltering that evening and she had on a dress. I sat in the rocker beside her, moving like a fan, talking softly. Her interest in therapy had worn off as the heat wave kept on. To each of my words she seemed content to offer only half a rhyme. 'Bosky,' I might read. Her reply, 'Lusty.' If you pronounced *polyonymy* with a careful and tricky serve, she batted it away with *dummy*.

'Fetter?'

'Brine.'

Mom had no idea what we were talking about. She sat off a ways in a wicker chair listening to notes Ivar was picking on his banjo. She could not understand how, if her niece could say separate words, she could not speak in sentences.

The next evening I tried the hardest word I knew. 'Argentina.'

The others sat waiting too.

She gave no answer. Just sat there watching the mountains receive the copper sun.

In the morning she was dressed and down to breakfast. She had brushed her hair till it shone. Taking her chair she asked for waffles, done on the griddle till they crusted, please. A sentence delivered in lumpy phrases that held the texture of her voice without resonance, or rhyme. The sound of it stuck to our ribs. Its request caused Mom to give thanks to the saints, walk to her stove and begin baking again. Waffle batter.

Deceived, I decided my cousin's aphonia, like her rhyming

before that, her ventriloquism and hyperbole, had only been ways to get noticed. Now she no longer spoke in rhyme. She spoke crisply of her sisters' virtues, mellowness and assent, and refused to finish high school. She borrowed Daddy's guitar. Determined to become a singer she dressed up in cowboy boots and sequins. She put on weight, where it counted, she claimed, and yodelled in the bath. She dreamt of capped teeth. Unwilling to chip her nail polish, she turned down housework and chores with the cheek of a princess. The perfume she wore set the cat purring on her shoulder.

The way Mom found out about her niece and Giles was the same way I had, more or less. Except it happened one afternoon, after harvest, when Mom was shopping and I was in school. She'd come home early and found them together in bed. She never said what they were doing, never even said where she'd found them. But her face had turned as white as flour. The staff of life, wheat of the world, she survived a vanished moustache and cheekbones fallen to a lower place.

She quit baking and cried in the corn like Ruth.

Argentina packed her suitcase and was gone by the time I got home. On the sheets of my parents' bed I sniffed Lily of the Valley. Daddy claimed he didn't understand anything that was happening and swallowed a chaser of Cow Brand. He growled to deflect the vast front blowing in upon us and just gaped at the thunder. It rained regularly after that for years. In the spring my cousin wrote to me once from the home of other relations. She had forgotten some lyrics in our sideboard drawer. Truly Yours she signed off, but I never believed it, I never found her songs.

In time, as they came out, my father learned 'Cold Empty Arms' and 'At the End of Nowhere', off Slim Whitman records, and sometimes talked, not of rebuilding the band, but of retiring under bougainvillaea. Florida was where his hero Slim was born, had worked in shipyards and joined his first band. Ivar joined a band called the Rhythm Sons, up the valley near Chilliwack where I saw him once at a dance. My mother, like her sister before her, ruptured an aneurysm and went to an early grave.

On the radio I would listen to a talent programme for new country and western artists, but Argentina wasn't the name of any girls

introduced. Their songs weren't 'The Indian Love Call' or any others you remembered. Protest, war. Alien voices creeping into popular songs, and it may be she found consort in this newer music we
normally, habitually, tuned out.

COMMENT: I'm not ashamed to admit I grew up poor by today's standards, forced to watch my ma 'do' for others what others wouldn't do for themselves. She was a fat woman, yet could, with the stylishness of some super mom in lemon chiffon, play *Amazing Grace* on her vacuum cleaner. I always wanted her to play *Stupid Cupid*, instead of demanding of me Maclean's Method on foolscap with a nib.

When Geoffrey Denton gave his story to us in September, I thought of Connie Francis and what she'd suffered in the aftermath of a shocking experience that affected her voice. I used to be a groupie, kind of. I was always the shy one at band. I could empathize with the piccolo.

When a shameful experience happened once to my ma at the municipal hall where she cleaned in a faded cotton frock, she never told us what it was, but for a long time I thought I would die for the hurt. I knew she was somehow marked after that. I was marked. It was the mental equivalent of leaving my zipper open at a sock hop. I wanted boys to respect me and they ignored me out of joky habit.

– *L. M.*

Lorin Mae

Damages

I AM GOING TO CONFESS something libellous. Can you sue your-self for libel? Am I liable to myself if I reveal this lamentable thing? The reason I hesitate is I wonder if it's worth my while confessing or would I be better off keeping quiet. I guess I like the contact. Like lots of women when I talk I risk losing a settlement against myself. It's not fair. By telling the truth I'm punished for indiscretion. I know the best defence against libel is to prove it's true. You see what a position this leaves me in. I could lie and say blackberry thorns really hurt me in the pleasure of filling my pail. But they don't.

The stars know this. They risk libel every night they turn on in the hills. The stars are foolish and who notices, who suffers? We do. Their watchers do, we suffer for them. We read libel in their glitter. We make a to-do about the showboaty stars and it gives them plea-sure. Not till morning can we trace our scars, their scars, with our fingers. The skin declines to lie.

Take just one star. Look at the things Connie Francis has had to face. Bobby Darin. A gun, her father came after Bobby with a gun, so that was the end of a potentially huge romance. Bobby married Sandra Dee, not her. Bobby died. Then her brother was murdered. Her two, three marriages fizzled out. She miscarried. One husband beat her. She had typhoid fever and bled from the ears. A perfec-tionist about singing, she just made her pain worse. Lost her voice, attempted suicide, became psychotic. It got gross. She travelled in and out of clinics like a laundry van. A court found her incompetent to look after her own affairs. Twice. By the way, it was the mob in New York City who shot her brother – in the driveway of his New Jersey home. He was a racketeer.

These facts are part of our public record. I think it would be wrong to repeat them at all if magazines hadn't reported them, newspapers, if she hadn't told us herself. It's all true. Kicking a policeman, the lithium treatments, problems in her fourth marriage. Everything. I have watched her growing darker, I must admit, watched with more than wonder.

Take, for example, when a knife-armed stranger broke in and raped her in a Howard Johnson motor lodge, I too experienced a loss of self-esteem, failed to recover my usual good nature, and little by little lost my pitch till I *whrrrred* like a pheasant with strep throat. I couldn't have sung to save my supper.

'Something eating you?' asked Mr Delmore, not looking up. 'That ... uh, tenant still troubling you?'

Nerves in need of the sun I told him, since it was December by then.

'Feed a fever,' he suggested. 'Starve a cold.'

After the lawsuit she tried comebacks. She lipsynched on the Dick Clark show, I watched her on TV, and she flew home from L.A. feeling like a fraud. She who had sung for the Queen, sung in Carnegie Hall, been chosen Female Entertainer of the Century at Expo 67. She made herself go back to finish an engagement at the Westbury nightclub where she was singing the night of her rape. But nothing soared. She couldn't repeat the past. She was already passing into myth.

You felt it was all going to come out: barricading herself inside her house, inside her bedroom, where her wretched change of voice seemed to echo the men who'd violated her. A father who pushed her, husbands who left her, the stranger who raped her and was never caught. She herself blamed it on air-conditioning. On the effect of air-conditioned rooms on her throat, after surgery to narrow her nose and the operations afterwards to fix up the first surgery's leftover scar tissue. It's hard to say. You admire vanity.

But who can write off the gagging fruit of evil?

Listen. *All* her hits came before the rape, before the marriages, before she found out her brother, rubbed out for squealing, was a crook.

> *Right to the end, just like a friend,*
> *I tried to warn you somehow ...*

I don't know who wrote that one – my father once said it was an old song, a real poco andante. He'd sniff his Dutch-Reform sniff at the Hit Parade, at how it sparked, then doused its stars. He was right. The stars flared, went shooting, died out. Frankie Avalon, Neil Sedaka – her father tolerated those two though he hated Bobby Darin, who went on to become a bigger star than either of them. Frankie befriended her, Neil wrote her songs. Such songs, even one song could have made her a star. Isn't it your memory of a song that stays constant when the flame that inspired the words is gone?

I could show you the river where Bernice Hailey and I were sitting in her father's Mercury when Tony Bellis sang a song on the radio that should have become a bigger hit and never did, not really, *Robbing the Cradle*. Or where I was when Ricky Nelson gave me the answer, 'Uh huh', in a falling third to every question asked of me for a week, from his big hit *Poor Little Fool*. I was at Mrs Kabush's kicking the slats out of used lettuce boxes for her stove – not a thing in neighbourly conscience I could dodge, stocking her kindling.

'I'm in your hands, dearie!' she would scream. 'I'd freeze and starve both without you!'

I just bet, I thought.

'Hold on, dearie, I'll turn up the radio!'

The old have ways of wheedling life from the young. What is dignity?

When I reported the record settlement for negligence against Howard Johnson, in the millions, to Mr Delmore, he only stared out the window at passing traffic and said lawyers were so many farts in a closet. I think he said ten. He should know, he wrote the book on fustiness. Darkness. Not that litigation has ever threatened Mr Delmore, he's too wary. I help Mr Delmore to manage Stay-A-While outside Lacey. We're the last resort for travellers who, because of indifference or just bad timing, are unable to reach the coast before nightfall. They come out of the Interior, over passes, down the Canyon, before making their mistake. Our highway isn't the Trans-Canada but a secondary route down the north bank of the Fraser, veering off at Hope. 'Typical,' mutters Mr Delmore. He's been trying to sell out for years. Powerlines buzz overhead and remind him of electric chairs.

He's an aging man with gas-station sideburns and a need of blunt pencils. He'd rather go to jail than mark anything, a cheque or crossword puzzles, with a pen. The nearness of an eraser encourages in him the conceit of retraction and the second chance. Around me he prefers to listen rather than comment, so I prattle, and dust lightly. He has no love for people who wear him down and all of us do. His face at the counter resembles the slumped side of an old boot, propped up at the chin with the heel of his hand.

When I say help him 'manage' I mean changing sheets, vacuuming carpets, Cometing sinks. The things a wife'd get stuck doing for free to help her husband in any one-man operation of ten units. Mr Delmore has that many peeling cabins around a weedy driveway and seldom more than four occupied per night. Nobody stays longer than a night. The Datsun trucks and Suzuki motorcycles all pull out by eight, eight-thirty, in the morning. Good riddance to the grumps. By noon yours faithfully is on her way home.

Except once. Just once in twelve years have I had to enforce noon checkout and I was not a success. This was when I first started. I was new and hating the job, my morale was rock-bottom. A young man with dirty yellow hair who hadn't bothered to close his blinds was still in bed, on top of it, in underpants. He groaned when I knocked on his door to explain who I was and what time the clock said. I heard nothing till he fumbled open the door, just enough to reveal a mole-sprinkled face and skinny chest. I looked away. He wasn't telling me anything, he muttered, if he was to tell me he thought he might drop dead from wild oats. He didn't look sarcastic so much as hung over.

I had to knock again, this time sharply with my broom handle. I walked to the window and rapped there too. He slowly guillotined my view with a downward pull of the blinds. So I walked over to the office and reported him to Mr Delmore. Mr Delmore looked at me, said it was nothing to get upset about, and pencilled in No. 9 for another day.

'What if he ups and leaves without paying?' I said. 'Look, Mr Delmore. I haven't been here long but I know a smart ass when I hear one. He'll just out and away on those parked wheels.'

Mr Delmore raised his chin to window level. 'Got his Gibson.'

Casually, he pulled out some baggage from under the counter and unzipped a canvas bag to show me the smart ass's guitar. A shiny, expensive instrument.

'He give it in for safekeeping.'

'Who's he afraid's going to burgle it? Other guests?'

Next morning I discovered the blinds still down and the same motorcycle on its kickstand. The licence said Saskatchewan or Manitoba. I knew how to wake the lazy ones by rattling my key in their locks to remind them it was time. This time I pushed forward and ran into the nightchain. Into the unresponsive gloom, wondering if I ought to shout through the crack, saying I was the cleaning lady. I tried.

The only rough part of the little episode was Mr Delmore, finally, who had to come and lean in with a hacksaw across the chain. The minstrel in underpants offered no more resistance. We prodded him, God knows we tried to get a rise out of him ...

As it happened he *had* dropped dead, and of course I felt shock as well as grief. I really did. What he died of Mr Delmore didn't bother to phone the RCMP back to find out, after the ambulance took away the body. The heart, he guessed, gummed up with drugs. To the police he neglected to mention the guitar when they took away the motorcycle. Mr Delmore is like that. Guests can do what they like to mess up, even exit their rooms in bodybags, so long as they pay in advance and I'm around to clean up.

That afternoon I think he came near to firing me when I refused to enter No. 9 and he had to scour it himself. But he kept his tongue. If he found a syringe he kept that too. He was liable for nothing so long as no evidence of neglect surfaced to threaten him. Negligence of the heart didn't count. Such hopes as once beat in the dead boy's breast didn't concern Mr Delmore. And he was safe from reporters. Our guest had become no star. Had not in all likelihood, coming west, even managed to see salt water for the first time in his life.

In the Carthage shopping mall that Christmas I listened to a choir carolling 'O Holy Night' around the ears of K-Mart customers. It reminded me how run down and depressed I felt. My spirit was taking a beating, my lungs felt padlocked, my priorities had been misplaced somewhere along the way. Where? How very pissy the future looked. At twenty-eight that year I was still living on a dairy farm with my parents. You didn't need a little bird to tell you when you had a crisis on your hands. In the presence of a cat, barn swallows can drive you bughouse.

Tonight, looking back, I'm thinking of stars who peter out too. Who can't see themselves till too late to stop the damage, the libel of dying larger than life. I bruise easily in August, but I see farther. I see how we have three ages: young, not young, old. I see that the abiding age is the middle one. We are not young most of our lives. An evil age because we learn what decay is and face it sometimes with bad grace. I did. I understood history then without understanding the stars. The stars who flail longest against any intrusion of this knowledge and fade badly.

Aren't I a peach at hindsight? I could run a clinic for guests at Stay-A-While. As a matter of principle, I've stayed far too long myself since those days when Mr Delmore's sideburns were still brown and boys carried guitars.

I was sure about the sun then. I believed in it, yes. But spring failed to renew me and made Christmas seem by no means the lowest I was going to sink. Whiny, I moped a lot. Mr Delmore was dying to tell me to take a powder.

At home I behaved like a schoolgirl with no responsibilities to the parents who'd wheedled her into staying. I was to come into their farm – but who wanted a farm? I went silent. Noises gave me a headache. I couldn't pee without clenching over water. For someone who liked to talk, I was so far off the beam I was in danger of flying smack into silence. I made up my mind to fly south.

Club Med in Guaymas, Mexico, on the Sea of Cortez, is an Indian pueblo village above a lagoon with the dry Bacochibampo mountains behind. When I saw the violet hills and cactus desert I thought of our own BC Interior with the same Mediterranean climate that attracts stars to southern California, along with reptiles and greasewood. I might as well have been in California, if you counted the swimming pools, tennis courts and restaurants.

I'm not athletic but was willing to make an effort. I played volleyball, bocce ball, ping-pong. I horsebacked into the desert, rafted on the Yaqui River, tried deep-sea fishing and caught a sunburn. I visited the quaint town of Santa Rosalia, ate too much, above all *talked* to anybody who would listen. I was determined to reacquire cheerfulness. Finally, in the evenings, I snuggled up to the mesquite fire listening to singsongs. I love songs. I love the way a singer trusts a song, the way she trusts a stamp not to poison her when she licks it. I listened closely those nights. Stretched thin, my throat wasn't up to flight.

Those were my two weeks on the surface. Black and white, cut and dried. No great fissures. My two weeks underneath are another story if this trip south isn't to sound distorted, even a lie. They say the greater the truth the greater the libel – the worse the libel they mean. I want to be brief.

I was talking so much, to anybody who'd listen, because of what happened after landing and busing in to the club. This I was trying to put out of mind. All Club Med bungalows are based on double occupancy, so if you go alone you end up, unless a single man tumbles for you in the plane or airport bus, sharing your room with another woman. The odd thing is I ended up in a double room of my own.

The other girl assigned to this room opened the door, looked at me, coughed, and backed out again with her luggage. I thought she had the wrong room – what she wanted me to think, in her straw Stetson. I was hanging up my dresses. Then it happened again, a second girl looked in, hesitated, vanished. Maybe her lip gloss needed freshening. Who were they looking for, Linda Ronstadt? Who was I, Linda Leper? Downstairs the G.O., a camp counsellor for adults, a French boy with lean tanned cheeks, introduced me to a third girl, from Wyoming. 'No,' said the girl. You see she was expecting a ponce friend to show up any minute now. You like a lie when it's well turned.

I went back up pretending nothing was the matter. Pretended I was going to have a very nice time. Made up my mind to it. Pretended I was not an unattractive young woman. I kept busy, as I mentioned. Kept talking.

I talked to people in a breezy way and refused just because it was popular to shy off a kissy face. I took lessons in scuba diving to be included in a group: that group, any group. People were polite and this hurt. At meals no one shunned me, but no one lingered.

My room on the second floor was right below an identical room on the third, with a moonlit view of the Bacochibampo, where I'd hear two men at night, and sometimes a man and a girl, depending on who was changing rooms and shacked up with whom. Atmospheric conditions in a Club Med are randy, there's no other word for the weather. Swapping has lots of singles on the hop all night.

On the last night I woke up with a body pressing down on mine and smelled cocktails on its breath. It recognized its mistake right away and apologized. This calmed me down. It was nothing to get upset about, *he* wasn't going to get upset, he acted lazy and reluctant to leave. He knew he was an intruder, I knew he was an intruder, we both knew where we were. In that climate you learn to guard your privacy with a little less dignity.

'I think you have the wrong room,' I said, turning at the same moment he chose to slip his hand down the side of my bare leg, under the blanket. In the moonlight I recognized the body as belonging to a Seafirst Bank employee from Seattle, not an unpleasant young man I'd made a point of chatting to on a trail ride to the waterfall. Arthur Perry. Peterson, maybe.

'Holy smoke,' he said, suddenly embarrassed.

His fingers twitched and he looked away, down toward his fingers. In all the moments of my life none has seemed more glacial, more eternal, than that moment. He didn't know what to say in a place that didn't cater much to talking, having to talk, your way out of anything. Like the girls backing out of my room he couldn't think of anything to say. Small talk, anything, might have cheered me up.

Just listen to what he concocted, in this ticklish situation, listen to what this strong silent type said very carefully to me, who was more or less a stranger.

'*So help me . . .*' he began, whispering with real passion.

I thought for a moment he was just trying to make the best of a bad scene.

'*. . . So help me Christ, I could give it to you ten different ways to breakfast . . . do you understand? . . . and have you screaming from every orifice like Tonto in a teepee.*'

Whispering, he was coming on to me like life depended on his performance. He definitely sounded menacing.

'Savvy, sweetheart? I'm saying I could eat your ratatouille like you've never had it eaten before. How would you like right now ... to give me a dish of ratatouille and for me to wolf it?'

He was moving the tips of his fingers over my burnt leg, rubbing it under the covers. He was staring down to where his fingers were misusing my leg.

'Tell me,' he whispered, 'how you'd like to feel the mouth of hunger so bad it gives you spasms for a week. Tell me how you couldn't stand supper from any other teeth. Who wants fast food, hm, when her gravy train is pulling into the station for pork loin buffet? Tapioca pudding? Jesus, I got teeth so sweet for you they're singing in my gums. Listen ...'

He couldn't stop talking like this, turning himself on I figured, getting cruder and cruder like he was making up a libretto for buddies at a stag. Some of his other lyrics I remember are, 'You can wait for it like a mare in heat, sugar, but try kicking me and I'll have you broken into saddle so quick it'll fry your curlers.' And, 'I don't take prisoners. When the sun comes up you'll find yourself either eaten alive or looping the stars. Both.' And, 'So help me Christ, I'm going to stuff you backwards like a Thanksgiving turkey ... Brown juice is going to run out of you so fast I'll need the gift of tongues to lap it up ... and spit it over you till you get down on your knees and thank me to do it some more.'

I may not have this last lyric right, it doesn't have much of a beat. It was pretty disgusting. Circling, he kept on like this for four or five minutes, whispering, watching his own grazing, invisible fingers. I wondered about his obsession. I mean talking like that, hard and voguish, he'd begun to give himself away. His whispering sounded passionate but the words sounded hollow. He sounded like he was lying. If anything, too big for boots, he didn't believe his own threats. I was concerned, but not terrified, the way I would've been with a total stranger. I was tense but not rigid. The point is I was not screaming.

He stopped then. Talking, he hadn't so much as removed the blanket with his hand, but had kept rubbing his fingers in menacing little moons on the skin of my thigh. I could tell he was up against me in an uncomfortable position. But that wasn't his problem.

His problem was anger had gradually got the better of him. Silent, quiet anger. He'd stopped whispering. In the end he was angry to the point of violence. You could have set fire to the silence.

'God,' he said at last. In a normal voice, glancing up at my face, he said, 'You haven't heard one word I've said. Not a word, have you?'

His anger had given way to pity. He removed his hand and sat up.

'*Yes,*' I whispered. '*I have, Art.*'

'No, you haven't,' he repeated, irritated at this licence. 'You haven't heard one single syllable. I pity you,' he said. 'I feel sorry for you, you know that?'

Maybe he was trying to cover up his own tactics, his own violent language, his own embarrassment. His own failure, for all I knew, to think up any more sexy threats. He stood up soberly in T-shirt and bathing suit, then flapped in thongs to my door – his thongs hadn't even fallen off – opened it and went out.

I thought about reporting him to our Gentils Organisateurs. I thought over his dirty talking, what he'd meant by it, just talking like that. And then the disgust, the pity in his venom. I felt sorry for him, for how foolish he was going to feel at breakfast for talking to me that way.

I don't exactly recall the hour that morning I thought I might have it wrong. *Him* wrong. No knife at the throat, no gag in the mouth, had stopped me from calling out. Worse, if I was being honest, I hadn't even felt insulted. This man was testing me, he was putting me on trial, and I just lay there ... *listening!*

I confess I cried after that, for a long time. The moon moved on. I cried for ages and ran my fingers over myself for a long time afterwards.

People at breakfast were nicer than normal because I didn't try to talk to them, and at our last breakfast it made them feel guilty. I must have looked like death warmed over. It was like they knew at last, what I knew they knew. That they were young and full of the future, or so they thought, and I was not. I went out of my way not to glance at Arthur's table, not to notice it, not to acknowledge its existence. I felt raw.

On my return to Canada Mr Delmore didn't look up, but he had about him a generally sympathetic air. Maybe he missed me, laundering for the transient, unplugging their toilets.

'Sounds like your cold's got worse. Wintertime in Mexico too?' Only he pronounced it the Spanish way, Mayheeko, as if his adenoids were paperclipped.

I didn't want him to think I liked working at Stay-A-While any better than when I'd started, but couldn't think of anything smart to say, when he said, 'Here. Take it.'

He was holding out to me the canvas bag with the Gibson.

'Take it,' he said.

With his pencil he returned to a real estate flyer, the heel of his hand covering back up his wealed chin.

I still sometimes take out this guitar and think of the dead boy and wonder if he'd known suffering, and how well he'd played the blues. *'Who's sad and blue ...'* strum, pause, *'Who's crying too ...'* The boohoo strains of a blue guitar. You can never learn the bridges too well.

Like tonight, I sit here in the window on the second floor, strumming, looking out at the fields. Mountains surround the meadows and from up here I can see the river where the brambles grow. A mist this morning was lifting off the mown hay and my father, old and stubborn, was calling in the herd. Bawling like a little sheik. It's a large Holstein herd. He came out from Holland to help drain the polder when this river overflowed its banks in the forties. He thought with his lore of flood plains he wouldn't need to stay in Perumbur past spring to contain the damage. But tempted by offers of cheap land he stayed on to do the Dutch thing and build a dairy farm. He built this house. We followed him, my mother and I, an infant.

The lamentable thing is I'm thirty-nine and still living with my parents. There was a time I would have lied about this. A time when I believed in the right to be free of oppression, that I had a right to be happy.

No more.

Listen, dearie! I can hear myself calling to the young a generation from now ... But no one uses kindling these days. It's the young who blame their parents for the narrowness of age, including their own. The not young withdraw their accusations and settle down to compromise. We insist on paying rent in spite of objections they don't need it, no, they don't need it, please.

Notice how the tempo of my strings picks up to mock revolutionary fervour? The other day in a glossy magazine from New York I saw pictures of Beirut guerrillas modelling the latest fashions in uniforms. These boys, these men, in murderous pose – checked scarves over heads, bullet belts over shoulders. Asses over teakettles. I could have screamed! The myth of the young is their belief in the right to be free of oppression. What right is this? Who gives it?

Fashion's who. That tyrant of our age. The guerrilla as top dog, character of history, supreme individual. Listen, Mr Fatigues, in your oversized boots.

What about me?

I often want to love and can't succeed in loving. I seek my own defeat without finding it, and am forced to remain free.

Like Elvis. Fattened on junk food and drugs, he fell off his toilet in the ensuite bathroom of a mansion where his heart, with no more room, lay enlarged and surrounded with fat. Bloated, beatless, his body needed fourteen mourners to carry its casket. Today it lives on in T-shirts and mugs. Is this dignity?

It's the stars who go to parties wearing the glass facsimiles of diamonds in safes at home. The false stones make those real stones look bigger than life. It's the same with the stars. To be bigger than life they leave their real selves at home. It makes them illusions like stars in the sky, glittering, long after dying into holes. Their light takes so long to reach us, so long to matter, sometimes we forget we're looking at history! Glitter has become its opposite: a dwarf, blackness, vapour: Time run out of gas. It's only distance that makes them appear to throb with life, poor things, unable to face death, condemned to be young.

This morning when I phoned Mr Delmore to excuse myself from work he just grunted. Leery of being horsed around, he'd have to mop up, scour, sweep on his own. But he won't. He'll leave the dirty rooms for me as though I'd never missed a day. In real estate, as Mr Delmore knows from long experience of trying to sell out, the three important things are location, location, location. In the case of libel I sometimes think they must be detail, detail, detail. Tomorrow all the rooms will be dirty and I'll be hard-pressed to launder so many sheets. If you knew that sometimes I leave the unsoiled ones, stretch them tight over mattresses to look unused, would it shock you? The next guests never notice.

In spring the dike along the river protects us in these lowlands, an earthen wall of grass with a small road running on top, a trail, really, for the cattle. It stretches miles and looks natural. The river comes out of the lake. The delta comes before the sea. Where the river runs into the sea we learn, slowly, to read the sand dollar as a microchip of evolution – fossils implanted in its shell like scars in our own. Skin. Soul, it's the same. When your soul meets history you become liable for the damages. And they say you cannot libel the dead.

Some nights like tonight I accompany myself back to life, fret marks in my fingers, the memory of this song my deepest, no, wildest pleasure.

COMMENT: I think Wallace in my story has bought into a myth that isn't his. He can never satisfy his own imagination. He's based on a dead underwriter I once engaged to insure my knees when I rowed Olympically for Canada. I rather warmed to my character, but then all writers say this.

His daughter, the heroine, came about this way. I felt Lorin Mae had been a bit hard on his woman in *Damages*, though her dirty little jaunt to Mexico reminded me of how often Canadians try to disarm depression in a warm winter place. I saw how light was going to enter my story, but not yet where it was coming from. (Disney World, it turned out.)

Resorts began to interest me. If a southern resort satisfied our Canadian requirement for change (a warm sky with a little fruit) I decided Americans liked nothing less than a utopia. Utopias require vigilance and compliance, don't they? Resorts sunscreen and complacency. So which was the oasis.

When poets describe a yearning for peace they'll usually eulogize the failure. You know, mythologize the conflict. Storytellers are much more melodramatic. Frankly, my own interest in *The Girl with the White Light* was domestic squabble. I could just imagine the bathos for a poet. Patricia put it very sententiously when she said soap opera is the supreme fiction because its politics are local. I think I knew immediately what she meant.

– *A. T. R*

Anne Tanice Reid

The Girl with the White Light

— A SOAP OPERA —

WHO HAS EVER TRAPPED the sun? Seen it, the thing as it is.

'This is what having brains amounts to?' complained her father. 'A whole new ball of wax?'

Life as it was not. Squinting into their daughter's bright lights, Wallace and Elsie decided if she was on to something they guessed they were willing to tolerate a little tampering with their leisure time to help iron out the wrinkles.

'Maybe our wrinkles,' said her mother, hopefully.

Her father said, 'She doesn't miss a trick, that one. And if she's paying rent who am I to squawk? Tell that to my big mouth.' He said this to reassure himself his word still mattered in his own house.

For hours a day his daughter was flooding their rooms with artificial light, experimenting with refuge, unshadowing the air's overcast blue. It wasn't natural. Quite a change from their sixty-watt bulbs, these sunlamps and fluorescent tubes, the house sucking at Hydro like a fish on an udder.

'I'm supposed to feel good, but I don't feel a snip different than normal,' Wallace said. He preferred things as they were. He wasn't somebody to sit still for music or even science. No dosage of unnatural light was going to improve his moods by levelling them all out and then lifting him to a higher plane. 'I wanna watch hockey and I can't see the bloody screen,' he groused. 'Why *us*, Holly?' No inventor alive, she thought (be her discovery tonic, purgative, or someday even profitable), could hope to get away with bleeding the living colour from the Great Gretzky and still dream of cooperation from her old man. She understood this and let him alone on these playoff nights in May.

By sitting down and staring regularly into bright white light, she herself had come, in an accidental way, to believe in its healing power. In herself she felt less sad now, less lethargic. She speculated that depression in her father was a season she could also alter – that light served up beforehand, instead of supper, could settle him down during a fight on ice, curb his boasting when the Great One scored, keep him from falling into vindictiveness when the team he opposed scored one goal upon another. What disillusion when his team lost! He sat incommunicado. Sank lower than low, couldn't stand the disappointment. Any disappointment.

The welfare state knew this and had given up on him ever applying for a job he didn't like, and he liked none.

Her mother knew this and had given up hoping for happiness.

The seven children knew this and were leaving home just as soon as they found jobs, lovers, or get-rich schemes after high school graduation. (Before, if possible.)

But this spring her father, compared to the last twenty years, including Holly's earliest memories of him, seemed less dolorous, and she quite sensibly put it down to the therapy she'd discovered. Practically a breeze to administer: plug in and get her mother and him to sit down and stare into the resultant white world. Evaporation of gloom and depression would sometimes lift their whole house into a sweet temper. Wallace would float in and out of rooms like a bubble. And without *him* carping and dragging her down it was natural for Elsie to cheer up too.

The idea was such a simple one Holly had almost missed the link between changes in her own moods and a plain sunlamp she bought last January to keep her tan from fading.

Life from receding.

'Holly Bright,' Wallace had taken to calling her, the way he used to when she was a high school ace in another century.

– 2 –

Last January, despondent at rain on the river, at low cloud on the surrounding mountains and the lack of any colour in her world at all, she was trying to remember a two-week vacation to Florida, won off a cereal box, and from which she'd just returned. Jet lag had left her feeling stoned. She knew without looking, the moored log booms were chained to the black bottom of a bottomless river. Flat on her mattress, her eyes carelessly open under a sunlamp, she felt unresponsive to any light at the thought of her failed marriage.

At seventeen she'd married a boy from Perumbur and left him thirty-two months later when the weather in her brain would not stop raining. She had wanted to be happy and love a man who liked change, talked with inflections, even liked to travel. But it transpired that Rupert Kupe could never escape his cows. He was a bad story. Oh, how she'd sobbed in desperation at the prospect of living at all, when the predictability of their life together, thirty years on, might surround them like this junk-filled orchard of her parents'. Detritus without end, never lessening the burden of their unlived lives, never lighting up the prune-coloured sky. Deluged too soon by night.

Lying here four months ago in her old room, who knew for how long under that sunlamp, she began realizing her mood wasn't so dejected after all, given the letdown of her homecoming from the south. Something was making her feel that the sky was about to blow itself into a very blue world, and even after she'd pulled the plug, put on her clothes and gone out for a winter walk in the rain, these mountains she couldn't see for prunes were standing out with the sharpness of a morning in May.

Maybe she dreamed this. The sound of shotguns on the river, dogs sweeping toward her up the dike, mallards hanging like scalps from three armed hunters, who muttered: 'How do.' She said to them, as she and her family always said to duck hunters, she wished they'd stop shooting their weapons, because people lived around here. Politely, she pointed to her house. They ignored her, as duck hunters always did, with their sullen antagonism to peaceful coexistence.

In her newly tranquil mood she'd gone on, letting the drizzle soak her hair. She thought she could smell shooting sap and ripe quince. In the middle of winter. Later, returning to her parents' tarpaper house, she went up to her room and shone the sunlamp some more in her eyes. She wanted to stay carefree. Like a junkie, forgetting what day it was, she was back lying in the Floridian sun without clothes.

She was hooked. Before dawn she plugged in the lamp again. Felt slowly beatific in the white light's gradual accretion on her retinas. It was the same after supper. Florida was more real again than Perumbur. It had to be the light, what else could it be? She saw the Gulf of Mexico from a balcony framed by palm trees.

In that one-bedroom condo in Sarasota, where she'd stayed her second week, was a guest book. It held a snapshot of its owner, a fat Philadelphian, who'd recently entered his own comments. *Great weather and fun times with our friends Shana and Andy. This year installed chandelier over dining table, polished brass stereo stand, hung the new pix in bathroom. Tacked shells to bedroom ceiling for kinks. The laid-back approach!* (Not seashells, she observed, handgun shells, in a uterus-shaped mosaic.)

Strangers, the paying guests, had commented on other stays. Errol and Eleanor Logan from Bethlehem, Pa., said the accommodation was *Absolute bliss. Good work, Jack. What a lovely place to spend our honeymoon. We'll come back for our 'second'.* Herb and Alice MacLeod from Hamilton, Ont., found the weather stinky, although No. 209 had helped soften the rain. A potter from Troy, Tennessee, attached her card and wrote a page. A Welsh couple from Mumbles found fat Jack Upland's condo, the beach, the weather, absolute heaven and worth every mile they'd come (32,000, they claimed) via Singapore in a Liberian freighter. And it was Serendipity! for Eugene and Wanda Randall of Prince Al, Sask. – the Ultimate! in condos – *We're crazy about the unit. You interested in selling? Many thanx for sharing it with us.* As if they weren't paying a fortune for the privilege of squatting here. *Just like home without the pressures. Great!!* (Walt and Traci Boyd, Morris, Man.)

Holly Harker hadn't written anything. She could've written she was an Air Canada/Disney World contest winner. *Hey, lucky girls don't deserve all this lux! You have a great place, Mr Uplands!* Slob. The heaviness of Americans had surprised her and her first week at Disney World was without thrills. Fat families, inflated fantasies: grotesque. She preferred solitude at the seashore, which is where she spent her second week, in Sarasota, enraptured by clear skies and warm sea, sunbathing on the pool deck. Maybe it was too good to be true, these places like heaven and not as they were.

— 3 —

Yes, last January she even wondered what guests here at her parents' house might write in a similar guest book and whether, after a little sunlamp therapy to pamper them, their own view of the world might shift.

Looking from the window of her luxurious penthouse room, she saw the rank orchard full of gutted cars, dented stoves and leafless tables, flotsam of all sorts including a wringerless washer, rusted mag wheels, a rowboat with its ribs showing, the carcass of a Ski-doo, somebody's discarded duck blind, a nest of tires that had once promised to breed more, two or three inoperable Rototillers, a cap-sized doghouse, chicken feathers from a fresh fox kill, blown-down laundry pole, a tractor without engine. Etc. 'Ed Settera,' her father would joke, pitching another piece of junk to this mythical dealer called Ed. 'He'll buy anything! His profits cheese me off!'

Her window had a sock stuffed in the pane. The floor sloped, the ceiling leaked and the air smelled mouldy. *Loved the adventure, hope #4's available same dates next winter!* Tom and Mary Strud, Spuzzum, BC. She replied, *Dear Mr and Mrs Strud: It was a pleasure to welcome you to our guest farm. This is to confirm your reservations a year hence. By then we hope to have in operation further new concepts in light-hearted rest! Ta ta till next year. Yours faithfully, Elsie and Wallace Harker.*

'It don't reflect bad on us,' her father might say. 'You putting us down. Putting us in a bad light like.'

His nine acres of blueberry bushes, planted when rubber tires fell through and long since grown wild, survived in spite of neglect and undrained fields. The same extended family of East Indians came on spec every July to fight through Wallace's jungle with plastic pails and emerge five weeks later with enough fruit to supplement his welfare cheques. Her father did nothing to earn it, except weigh their berries daily in the barn and try to fudge their poundage on his notepad. Every year he complained how clouds of starlings swept in low, settling down on the ripe fruit like locusts to rob him silly. Wallace was full of excuses for the meagre return on his untended bushes – mostly excuses to do with birds. Birds got him down.

They also afforded him a rare source of cheerfulness.

'Okay, here's my latest idea, listen to this beaut. Listening...?' He'd be drinking a Labatt's Blue in the kitchen.

'These local blueberry czars've tried every kinda weapon known to man, right? Rotating cannons that upset folks' sleep. Fancy Dan handguns that fire them shriek shells at about a buck a shot.' He'd throw up his hands, whistling through his remaining teeth with the sound of an incoming mortar. '... Listen, those starling beggars don't hear nothing!' He belched and laughed.

'I heard of this one guy, up the way like, built himself a rotating metal tower with whistles on a wire. *His* idea, see, was to whirl his whistles in big circles over bushes to stop birds landing. Scare them crazy. Failsafe, he figured. Was going to set up a whole field of these towers in strategic positions. Doomsday machines.' Wallace hooted. 'Real mutual deterrents! Trouble was, when he switched on his motor, pulled his switch, turned his key, whatever, he had so much weight to whirl, unfolding arms and metal wires, gantries and that there, his engine burned up inside four seconds!'

Wallace went right down the list of deterrents his neighbours stood for. He laughed at their scarecrows, shotguns, noise-makers. He especially mocked blueberry farmers who strung nets, claiming they wouldn't pay for these in twenty-five years, when they wouldn't last ten. ('And *you're* so clever, aren't you, Wallace?' her mother would taunt.) He'd laugh at, mock and abuse his neighbours' muscle-flexing, and every summer complain the reason he made so little profit from his own blueberries was because starlings were eating him alive. Not to mention that shyster tire-farmer, Bill Sauvage, the neighbour who'd betrayed him once over the chance to open up his land to tire-dumping and the big profits to be made from sitting back and doing nothing. Now all Wallace had were headaches from enemies and pests.

'My plan's to get a hawk. An eagle. Bird of prey who hates the guts of starlings and the beggars know it.' He guzzled stubbornly with a glint in his eye. 'When I was positive this hawk was starving and mad enough to jump the dog I'd tie a three-hundred-foot piece of twine to his leg and let him loose. Get the picture?' He'd laugh so hard he'd spill his Blue, making wings of his hands in pursuit of starlings to the end of a tether. *Whhaaaaaagh! ... Squaaaaawk! ... Thump!*

By now, usually, Max and Eva would've vanished to their rooms with homework.

Her father reminded her of a schoolboy, recounting a Road Runner cartoon with accompanying sound effects, dreaming up absurd strategies for his life that excused his ever having to take part in it.

'Yeah,' he'd tell the welfare officer, on the phone to Wallace about a possible job. 'I heard from that outfit all right. You'll shake your head when you hear what they wanted me to do, with *my* back. Pack cheese! Cheesewheels, one apiece on either shoulder! Nosir, I told them. I explained to the gentleman, I was a man of fifty-four with a dislocated back. Don't believe me, listen to this ...' And he'd hold the receiver against his neck and give his double-chin a sudden crank sideways with the heel of his hand. It made the sound of twenty knuckles, cracking. 'And whatnot ...' he said soberly, into the mouthpiece. 'I don't like to think about it.' He was a short stocky man who believed thermal undershirts gave him support, and that braces were the legacy and curse of Lester Pearson. He wouldn't wear them.

He talked about Brezhnev behind his back, as he did everyone else. Only the Great One was immune.

Thanksgiving last, depressed about his family eating him out of house and home, Wallace had hinted just how strongly his thoughts were running in a mercenary current. Holly, not long removed from her husband's house, apologized for her thoughtlessness and offered to pay what she could for board, till she found an apartment in Lacey, where she was working part-time in a real estate office. 'Oh, I didn't mean you, honey,' her father said. 'Don't think I want money from a guest.' He did, though, relent when he found out how many weeks she might be home, and accepted her money as he had when she was a teenager working at

A&W. 'I'm becoming a bloody landlord,' he said in fey disgust.

'Fascist,' whispered Max. To Holly, behind the old man's back.

The decline of their father, once a master electrician, had imbued her younger brother with dread of freeloading at an age when other teenagers had still to lose callowness. Max feared the loss of his after-school job at Overwaitea as gravely as he might his passport inside some consulless country of punitive law. He was determined to make ends meet, dismissing dependence on the state. Like all her siblings, Max was precocious. Like their mother, he was also submissive.

Despondent last October, Holly would've welcomed the chance to talk about her failed marriage, but Eva and Max were always busy and her parents really didn't like to hear. For better or worse you got married and stayed married, and Elsie and Wallace Harker were the living proof that worse wasn't so bad when you still had each other after thirty-plus years. So instead she had let herself be drawn into yet another diatribe against birds.

She interrupted him. 'Why don't you arrange a catastrophe?'

'What?'

'To get rid of the starlings?'

He looked at her, balefully. 'I thought you used to be Einstein at school.' Wallace swallowed his beer, his Adam's apple a cork, making it easier for him than other men to talk when this cork appeared to float clear of his esophagus. 'Catastrophe? Sounds like utopia.'

'What would happen if the starlings never produced any baby starlings?'

'That's a catastrophe? I'd be a wealthy man.'

Her mother chortled. 'Then you'd find out what you really deserved, Wally. Crop in decline, not because of birds, but your own laziness.' She sometimes wished he could at least keep up the pruning so their bushes would produce real crops instead of just enough sucker berries to pay the pickers every year. '... The pickers practically make more than you do,' she told him.

'And so they should,' replied Wallace. 'I don't do any of the picking.'

He for one didn't mind the proliferation of Pakis and ragheads moving into Perumbur: nimble-fingered, respectful, they worked a damned sight harder than cannon-shooters and net-stringers. Of course he didn't mind admitting to bilking them if he could, denying the swindle if any complained. In his own defence he'd say, 'They rip *me* off, smuggling home berries to sell on the black-market! Worse than the birds!'

Max would roll his eyes.

'Horsebuns,' Elsie would say. 'Maybe they take a pail or two home for pies. Nothing more.'

Her mother knew about pie-making, indeed how to prepare blueberries for every season, in some recipe or other every day. Fresh, curried, jammed ... For soups and quiches and muffins.

'It's enough to overdose a Ukrainian,' said Wallace.

'You want sockeye,' answered Elsie, 'catch us one.'

'At least,' admitted Wallace, 'the berries keep you loose.'

The children snickered. Their parents were always up and down, back and forth, like the river beyond the dike. 'What's there here but weather,' said Wallace. 'What spirit have I 'cept it comes from the sun?' This saying of his rang true to Holly's ears. It sounded poetic.

She shrugged, exhausted. 'I guess if you could stop them breeding, in no time flocks would be down exponentially.' Trying to keep that Thanksgiving conversation going.

Wallace turned away from her. Talk of breeding made him uncomfortable. He looked around for a crust to chew on. 'That one of them fancy words? Ain't natural. Are you gonna scare them so much they can't breed? Next it'll be vasextumies.'

Holly laughed, dutifully.

He said to her, 'Pronouncing it right don't change the drift of my argument. The natural inclination is to shoot first, not sterilize 'em.'

'Well,' she answered, 'maybe there's some way you could sterilize them with electricity.'

At this, Wallace the master electrician perked up.

She was remembering a documentary from school, on tse-tse flies in the Serengeti reducing herds of cattle to skin and tissue. She now told him a scientist had come up with an electrocuting machine to radiate the male fly. Male flies were attracted by a captive cow's breath. This allowed them back into nature where they bred without actually fertilizing any eggs.

Her father pondered this.

'Any idea how much a billion times a billion zaps of radiation would cost? That there is a great example of counter-cost efficiency. A country like Africa is better off with fly swatters.'

Pleased with himself, he asked Elsie to pour him another Blue. 'That's my analysis. From an alcoholic brain.'

Holly, biting into a stale Cheezie, shook her head. 'You wouldn't sterilize every fly.'

'Couldn't do it.'

'There's the unknown factor in the equation.'

'You bet there is.'

'Oh Wally,' said Elsie. 'Leave the girl alone.'

'Eventually,' said Holly, 'the tse-tse flies would decline in ratio to the number of zaps. Theoretically, over his lifetime, one sterile male could account for billions of unhatched eggs.'

'Poor bloody women flies,' remarked Wallace. He allowed his mug to be topped up, before saying to his daughter, 'Sounds like you wasted your time on math 'stead of biology.'

He was enjoying himself. She was still his little ball of fire. Holly Bright. And anything related to hockey – deterrence and threat, war and reprisal – seemed worthy of debate. The clean give and take of electricity (what had got him into the electrical profession in the first place, the lack of manure under his fingernails) appealed to Wallace.

'It's a great idea,' he said, giving himself a push in his rocker. 'Mind you, I don't think the birds would cooperate.'

She had closed her eyes. In her own apartment she wouldn't have to talk if she didn't feel like it. Maybe she could work up enough hours at the real estate office to let her escape this dump by Christmas. Then, whiskers tucked, she could sleep all weekend if she felt like it.

'Still,' said Wallace. 'Wouldn't it be something to patent a deal like that, seeing as you're throwing out your idea for general conversation, get outta the berries and make a fortune selling electrical knowledge to dodoes plagued by enemy aircraft and willing to pay me good money to get rid of them starlings, zap, once and for all?' He chuckled. 'What is there in life 'cept your own ideas, eh?'

He sounded expansive, radiating confidence by inventing an electronic field to annihilate the plague of birds in a jiffy. As a decoy, he was willing to offer up his entire crop next summer, provided he was compensated by the goddamn farmers' co-op for his sacrifice in the name of strategic sovereignty. Wouldn't pick a berry, birds could gulp every last berry, so long as the beggars passed through the eye of his revenge.

'Zap!'

He felt sadly certain the species would prevail, however. These birds got him down. The more Blue he drank the more baroque his disappointments got.

'What's for supper?' When her mother told him, meatloaf, he got mad. Meatloaf took an hour to bake and she'd hardly begun. 'Besides,' he growled. 'This is Thanksgiving. Where's the turkey?'

'We'd see your patience roasting then, wouldn't we, Wally, waiting on a turkey.'

Eva came in and Wallace barked at her to leave her smelly wool coat outside. She ignored him and spoke to her mother. She approved of meatloaf, it beat wieners. Eva, following in a family line, worked at A&W on the highway. Upon the public demand for Baby, Mama and Papa burgers four sisters had bought clothes, pierced ears and financed underwear – autonomous actions arising from a family of buns. Now in the eleventh grade, Eva couldn't wait to move out too.

Wallace turned to his son.

'Listen. Stop masticating so much and bring me that bowl of Cheezies.'

'*Wallass!*' whispered Max.

Holly had crept up to her room and lain down on her old mattress. October and already monsoonal. She could hear drops of rain hitting the crumbling duroid shingles, held in place by moss. Was anything more oppressive than coming home to live? Should she have hung on at Rupert Kupe's until she could afford a place of her own? Or, better, persuaded Rupert to lend her money? Walking out on her husband wasn't going to bring in a nickel.

The day after Thanksgiving, at her job, she'd mailed off a request for information regarding seed packets from a company promising personalized pouches of forget-me-nots for real estate agents interested in 'cultivating' new clients. As secretary she got all the jobs. She also remembered to mail a boxtop.

When an unexpected call in November came through from Toronto, Ontario, that she'd just won a trip to Florida, if she could answer the skill-testing question 'What is two plus two squared?' it released her from lucklessness and offered freedom from the darkness of approaching winter. It was as if she'd answered the question of relativity.

The tarpaper house was in heaven for a day. Max and Eva, Wallace and Elsie, nobody could believe her good fortune. 'That's the thing about taking risks,' said Wallace. 'If you'd stayed on with Rupert Dupert, being happy with things as they were, you'd never of thought of Walt let alone dreamt of cosying up in Disney World!' A cereal box! Cereal Wallace himself had provided!

He overlooked his disapproval of her failed marriage in the drama of this exquisite, triumphant moment. Had they friends her parents would've phoned them to bask in the reflected glow of their daughter's success. Instead, they had to satisfy themselves with calls to Holly's older sisters and their unfriendly husbands in Surrey and Chilliwack.

Holly had wanted to share news of her lucky stroke with Seth, her older brother, but Wallace claimed Seth was living in a van, that she'd never locate him. 'Might as well give up on Seth,' he warned her. Elsie said baloney, their son was working for an investment house in Vancouver, and phoned *her* whenever he thought his father wasn't home.

'Funny thing is,' answered Wallace, 'I'm always home.'

It sure felt like it, agreed Elsie. But, no, she didn't have Seth's number either.

So Seth didn't even know his sister had left his old friend Rupert Kupe – actually, Seth had warned her about Rupert's dedication to cows – nor, when she finally went away to Florida, did he find out that for Holly Harker the wheel of fortune had finally budged. That year he didn't come home for Christmas.

If Holly had seen the light, who were Wallace and Elsie not to go along with her suggestion and help her test it on themselves? Look at her, happy in wintertime! At first they put it down to the residue of tropical leisure, except the aura of her trip had faded with her suntan. She herself was still expecting to fall back into seasonal gloom.

That gloom with the depth of a wine-dark river.

Of course, the treatment began to appeal less to her parents when she had them up before the hens, treating them for their persistent funk, shining light ten, twenty times brighter than roomlight in their eyes.

'A whole new ball of wax,' said Wallace. 'It really stinks.'

Between January and May she brought home bigger and brighter lights to shine in all their eyes. Savings she should have hoarded were now given to hardware stores in Lacey and shopping malls in Carthage. She reasoned that if she could experiment with the body's rhythms, use light to recycle these in times of darkness and hibernation, she might, through regular treatment, relieve irritability and depression in others just as she was doing in herself.

At five a.m. she would bring the tarpaper house into a white warm glow, and only Max and Eva, who said they needed their sleep for school, were allowed to stay in bed. She didn't really understand how a false dawn could approximate summer's, which always woke you in a good mood, but it did. She made Daylight Saving Time come early, until the black house greeted real dawn with equanimity. Irradiated, the pall of winter lifted.

After her sessions Holly would bicycle miles to the office actually looking forward to typing up Agreements to Purchase overpriced acreages, contacting evasive vendors, seeding forget-me-nots in the fig planter. Similarly energized, Elsie and Wallace trashed morning TV in favour of radio hotline programmes, an acknowledgement of their alerted minds. And they no longer overate.

By dusk, often rained-in and beginning to flag again, Holly and her parents sat down for another big dosage of light. They sat on the worn-out chesterfield, heads resting on drab filigree doilies, staring into the white, white light.

'This is for quacks,' grumbled Wallace, not unhappily.

'You stay put,' Elsie told him. 'It gets better every day.'

'Ta dum!' he said. 'Me and the light are one.'

Max and Eva, fingering the Cheez Whiz jar, figured their sister was bananas. In protest, they wore sunglasses and begged alms from these suntanning tourists.

Holly had never forgotten the winter she turned sixteen and nearly threw herself in the river out of the blackness in her brain. Teachers had told her not to squander such a good brain, but she couldn't shake the darkness. Only Rupert Kupe, sympathetic to dumb creatures, seemed to promise the restful blankness she desired, a world of cows moving sleekly, fragrantly, through emerald fields. Touching them, wiping their udders with wet flannel cloths, and tipping milk from one pail to another: she could survive by caressing these crusts of shape. Couldn't she? Marriage would give her sunshine.

Instead, it had put up shutters, as though anticipating the storm. Months, then years, went by and the wind grew. Shut in and afraid, she doubted her courage just to stand up and walk out Rupert Kupe's door. Some inherited disorder lurked like a virus in her body, waiting to spread under cover of darkness. She sometimes wondered if depression, like the common cold, was less common in sunny countries where the living was harder. A reason why the starving and destitute in India, or so she imagined them, didn't commit suicide.

Each married spring had arrived with winter's jackboot toeing hopes, until her perennial sadness would lift with the advent of May. This is what she seemed to recall, a better world in May. In May, Rupert's herd disappeared into clover, blueberry fields blossomed, the peaks gleamed with melting snow way above Perumbur's flat meadows. The river rose, dikes held, she relaxed her huddled brain. Trees in leaf hid nests of starlings, red-winged blackbirds, even hawks. Marsh fowl scoured the sodden, undrained fields of the upper polder for emergent bugs. In May, the sun finally bore its responsibility to these higher, neglected latitudes, sparkling in compensation with an overabundance of light.

Light, she was now recording in a scribbler, made you more bird-like. She read over her winter notes on wattage. On pulse rates, retinal dilation, appreciable changes in the dispositions and sleep-wake cycles of her parents and herself. She had to conclude that artificial light at the day's edges altered something deep in the brain, her brain. She felt chirpy. Even if the elation of peace didn't last, conflict felt deterred. It was a scientific method of sorts to give her hope.

Eat your heart out, Jack.

In January she had assumed May would mean an end to such dedication to artificial light. In May, as she remembered May, the light flooded in your window at five a.m. and washed you with vigour for the coming day.

But, no, her parents insisted on getting up even earlier and trailing downstairs to prostrate themselves before her bank of white light. Wallace, without admitting he needed a fix at all, grew noticeably irritated when he missed one, as he did on hockey nights in Canada. Otherwise, sure, he didn't have anything better to do than contribute his mornings and evenings to lying around on the sofa for Holly's sake, having his pulse taken and looking into her eyes. The attention took his mind off holes in his shingles, cracks in his life. A bum back.

And so it was, that spring, she happened to be looking out her window and had seen her father's old barn in a new light. That night she dreamed of opening up a resort, a light centre, dreamed she'd actually gone ahead on a wider spectrum than she ever imagined and challenged disappointment.

Right, Wallace told her in the morning, go ahead and use his barn, but he didn't have any money to help her fix it up.

'Nosir, no capital whatsoever.'

However, for a share of the profits he'd help her rewire the place with outlets and spot lighting – 'the whole concert hall', he said, not for a minute believing he'd ever have to. Conceding that if this light business worked for the average Joe (he was thinking of himself, but more as manager than janitor) it might have commercial possibilities.

'Hey, you should get cracking on it, honey.'

Really, such a long shot that she'd ever get his barn cleaned up, let alone finance the clinic she was dreaming about, Wallace could afford to offer his support without much risk of having to roll up his sleeves. He was feeling expansive again. His team had just won the Stanley Cup.

'Go ahead,' he encouraged her. 'Make my day.'

— 5 —

In the beginning, her dream went well owing to an unexpected boost from her older brother – the black sheep, Seth – who seemed to bring out the competitive spirit in their father. Seth was smart. They were all smart.

He had driven his van out to 'old Perumbur' one afternoon in early June on an unexpected visit. He was wearing a blue suit, only a little rumpled, and tasselled patent loafers. He smelled of Dentyne. He didn't mention Rupert Kupe, but he must have guessed.

Filling his family in on city life, he told them all he got up with the birds, earlier than other businessmen, and accordingly felt done in by suppertime. The high life wasn't all it was cracked up to be.

'Up with the birds,' repeated Wallace. 'Around here we're up before the birds. The bloody birds are still dreaming when we appear.'

Seth ignored him. 'Stock exchange has to open same hours as in TO and the Big Apple – those guys keep bankers' hours compared to us. My outfit's trading at seven a.m. in Toronto, New York, Hong Kong, Tokyo ...'

'Your outfit,' repeated Wallace, 'is a penny-ante outfit compared to Midland Doherty, one of them outfits.'

'What's penny-ante?' asked Eva.

'Ask your bigshot brother. Means living on the street like a panhandler, since you can't afford anywhere else.'

Elsie told Wallace to cork it.

Max asked Seth if he really lived in his van. The younger brother was noticeably impressed with the red sunset, painted on the side, the dark bubble windows, and, inside, shag-carpeted walls vented by speakers. There was even a little chandelier hanging from the ceiling that must have chimed when he drove.

Seth denied living in his van. But Wallace bet Max he'd find a cook stove under the spare tire. And dirty laundry in the wheelwells. He was the determined voice of truth, broadcasting over bluff and the disinformation of a stock trader.

Tired, Seth drank off a cup of black coffee, and told Max of his attempts to start up his own company on the exchange.

'Penny stocks,' snorted Wallace. 'Lose your shirt in a berry bucket to Heaven.'

Elsie made sure her eldest son stayed for supper, and it was at the table over calves' liver – 'should of told us you were coming,' she told him, 'we'd of punched a hen' – that Seth learned of Holly's big idea.

He turned to his sister, offering to pass her the ketchup. 'A kind of resort, like?'

'That's right,' said Wallace, jealous. 'Here,' he said, handing a dish of peas to the other end of the table. 'Take your pay outta that.'

Seth passed the dish on up the other side. What sort of lights? All these fluorescent things lying around? How much equipment would she need to get it going? Could carpenters really turn that owl's nest of a barn into a warm space?

His entrepreneurial snoopiness got his father worked up.

'Big shots,' muttered Wallace, 'brass me off.' He changed direction, and passed the carrots the other way. 'Your team' – meaning the city hockey team he presumed Seth supported – 'went nowhere this year. With them canary-coloured uniforms, what d'you expect?' Wallace laughed. 'B-all next year, too.'

But the prodigal son, to his father's grief, didn't follow hockey and had no idea what he was talking about. Wallace might as well have been talking ballet.

Accepting a cup of Salada her brother loosened his tie, undid his collar button, and, probably to irritate Wallace, started tapping his signet ring on a Jell-O spoon.

He said to her, 'It might be just the vehicle I'm looking for.'

'Just the vehicle he's looking for,' repeated Wallace, bumping his teeth on a bottle of Blue. 'Listen, Seth, this isn't a tractor, this here's a structure we're talking about doing over. We're not interested in triflers. That's what we say in real estate. No Triflers, get it?'

With daylight lingering in the west, and the sweet evening air to beckon them, Seth invited Holly for a walk on the dike. Bear lumbered after them, black tail swatting air as if to propel his shaggy fuselage above these gravitational fields. Grass on the dike deepened in colour, and brother and sister strolled through it in supernal light, toward the sugarloaf mountains.

Seth confessed he loved this river. The city had nothing like it. 'Not the gulf. Not even night clubs.' He had his suit jacket over one arm and pant cuffs rolled. He said this river ran into another one that ran into the ocean. He mentioned his surprise on learning at school rivers weren't supposed to be tidal. He asked her if she remembered them waterskiing in the lake, with Rupert Kupe and Fin Sauvage.

Fin, she responded, had phoned her last month to say hello. He was living in California now.

'He's queer,' said Seth. 'So was Michael.' Michael had drowned.

Seth said he wasn't surprised to hear about her leaving Rupert. 'About the only exciting thing Kupe ever did was buy a speedboat.'

'I remember,' said Holly, 'you two stole logs. From the booms tied up in the river.'

'*Salvaged* logs.'

Aspects of his past were definitely behind him.

'Hey,' he said, stopping. 'You serious about this light and depression stuff? I mean isn't it just a joke to keep the parents happy, or what?'

'Sound weird?'

'Would the public buy it?'

She shrugged. 'Wallace thinks it's the mental equivalent of inventing the wheel.'

'Sold, is he? That's a start.'

'If it isn't abused, I guess it could help change people's feelings. Recycle their moods. It recycles mine.'

'Dynamite,' said Seth. 'What kinda music would you pipe in? You'd need music with all that light, otherwise wouldn't it be boring, just lying around? Unless you had dancing. With strobe lights?'

She supposed music wouldn't do any harm. 'Guitar,' she conceded. 'Blues.'

He considered this choice of instrument, doubtfully. 'Well, I suppose you could sell it as something to help you feel better, like a hurtin' song. Myself, I can handle sad music, makes me feel better.'

She wondered at this, at ennoblement in the face of oppression. Maybe what a lousy marriage needed was a man with a blues guitar.

'Where'd you find out all this stuff, by the way, about depression and that? Cycles. *Scientific American*?' He reached over and patted her brainy temple.

She protested. 'The light's just something that struck me.'

By now they'd walked to the end of the dike, to where the river disappeared round a bend, and they turned to watch the setting sun. 'Hey,' said Seth. 'It's just like my van.'

They needed no shades at this hour to stare right into it.

The fields to their left were slowly bled of the sun as it disappeared behind her brother's hidden city.

'Look,' he said. 'Think you could write me up a prospectus? Something I could sell to anybody interested in underwriting something like this, a resort, say, if they could be persuaded it might make them some money?' He picked a long blade of grass and tore it carefully near the middle, lined it up between both thumbs and offered it to his lips. There was a lot of air when he blew.

'Otherwise,' he told her straight, 'you can dream on, if you're thinking of going public. With an idea like yours, what you need is investment capital.'

– 6 –

So this was how her dream got listed on the stock exchange in the city, no longer a dream but a happening, a thing, like light in a mirroring of mountains.

Not long after Seth's visit a large man in a black Riviera drove out to visit her, smoking a Dutch cigar. He said it was a Dutch cigar, rolled especially for the low rollers like himself.

'This the Harker residence?' he asked Elsie at her door. A rich bass voice, not unfriendly. Sethy-boy had sent Mr Roth around for a look-see. Elsie introduced Mr Roth to her ingenious daughter.

Holly took him out to the barn in his grey suit.

'Say … You ever think of selling this property? What's that, a river over there? Mountains…?'

Wandering through the dilapidated barn, two-stepping rotten floorboards, puffing on his cigar, he couldn't resist letting Holly in on his business dealings, even where he lived and where he might someday live.

'I'll be candid with you, Holly … you're somebody with brains, you know these things. It's a lot of money, for what? The view is nice, sure. But the guy beside you playing his stereo at three in the morning? Who needs it? Ask him to turn it down he tells you he paid a hundred seventy-five thou to play his stereo whenever he feels like it – what are you going to do? I ask you? Not his fault. Not your fault. It's the lousy building's fault, bang bang bang, one condo after another … like living in a chicken feeder. Go figure. I asked this fellow – he was a very nice man, I've got nothing against him trying to sell me one – I asked him what if I don't like the condo? What then? Can I turn it over for the same money or am I stuck with it? At a hundred seventy-five thousand you aren't going to do a fast flip – who wants to live next to stereo speakers? Who wants to take the chance? He was very nice. I'll be frank with you, Holly, I liked the place. Only I didn't want to be stuck in the middle. This fellow was very honest with me. Said we're building more up above, on reclaimed mountainside … same view, even better. I told him I'd think about it. You understand? I'm a businessman, right? Like your brother, Seth. In the end I gave him two thousand dollars to hold me a condominium on the end, the corner, so I'd have the view both ways across English Bay. I figured it was worth the investment to see what kind of job they do. I'm not committed. I can get my money back any time. We like the apartment we're in … It's my wife though. I worry about her not meeting people in the building. She needs to be in a place with people. You know?'

He glanced up to the rafters, draped by doilied dirt. Cats peered down from the darkness. They had no enemies but the owls, no prey but the mice. The place smelled like a fishboat.

He stepped outside and peered into the silo – except for chickens it was empty.

In the orchard, finally, he gestured grandly.

'So this here is going to be the garden of Eden, is it?' He puffed smoke and Holly said boom all – which is how Wallace later summarized her failure at these negotiations before Mr Roth got back in his car and made the window glide down. He said, 'It's an eye-for-an-eye world, Holly. Believe me. Stay away from the nihilists.'

Then he snuck into reverse and his tires bit down on the tarred gravel road.

She'd thought her dream was finished before it began. Until abruptly, money started coming in, as though her project had suddenly become an indispensable arm of national security against false promises like the nihilism Mr Roth had decided to warn her about.

To her surprise, to everybody's surprise, Wallace ended up doing more than wiring the barn. In July as the project took shape, she noticed a change come over her father, a deep competitiveness emerging to replace his Road Runner fantasies. Upon such a flimsy theory as her light shield he seemed willing to expend an inordinate amount of energy to see it through. Lame Hephaestus at his forge. And she, remembering grade seven socials, his Venus.

Sunlight Control Centre, with its initial offering of seed shares only to private investors, and then an offering of two hundred and fifty thousand Sun Con shares at forty-five cents a share to the general public, was listed on the stock exchange after underwriters and lawyers rewrote her prospectus and quibbled over sentences. The seed shares were purchased at an undisclosed cost by Seth and others, underwriting the cost of rebuilding the barn and getting their new company registered, financed, listed. Among the one hundred and fifty public shareholders, as required of a listed company, were Holly and Wallace, who were to retain in equal partnership twenty-five thousand shares. They received these from Seth, by registered mail, with the name Sun Con printed in bold type on very expensive paper. They noticed a good deal of fine print on both sides of these securities.

Accountants phoned them, asking to speak to Mr Harker and

Mrs Kupe. Seth phoned them. They were to redirect all construction bills to the box number he gave them in Vancouver. It seemed amazing just how fast her company had grown, even before the barn had been finished or the lights installed.

'Something's fishy,' said Wallace. He distrusted fish stories and had no appreciation of poetic licence. These entrepreneurs were all poachers.

When Seth phoned back to say the best way to get things really rolling was to list the company in his, Seth's name, Wallace called his son an extortionist.

'Pragmatic,' countered Seth. 'We'd have a quicker response time.' With Mr Roth he meant, who'd bought up much of the public offering and with whom Seth felt he was better positioned than they to negotiate on their behalf.

'Doesn't mean I don't own the building,' his father stubbornly answered.

Holly didn't care who owned the building, so long as the carpenters, who were hammering and sawing, finished off the structural changes that summer, so she could tell the other workmen what kind of wallboard and carpets she wanted, and Wallace where to wire. Max offered to paint the exterior for a fraction of the cost of new siding.

'Don't know where Seth's getting the bread for all these doings,' said her father. 'I don't think he cares if we finish the place or not. Just wants us to keep it secret and his stock to go up. It's a scam for him – a hole in the ground.'

The reimagined barn smelled of new paint, Gyprock, wool carpets and freshly unpacked electrical supplies that made Wallace tearful for his old trade. Ballasts, dimmers, switches, transformers, rectifiers, brackets, cable … The cats moved out. In his day her father had lit ballrooms, houses, stages and parking lots. 'Maybe we should think about a reflector spot, too, what d'you think?'

He installed a perch of spots in the lowered ceiling and along one wall. Sealed-beam, ellipsoidal and bifocal spots, and he wished he had an arc light, to mount on a sturdy stop collar, something to really peel back your eyes. Holly arranged couches and chairs, to take advantage of the white light once it began to bloom in her mirrors and open white interior. Stereo speakers, space heaters, a water cooler: bunkered in, she'd thought of everything.

When they returned in a contractor's van for the first time that summer, the berry pickers were amazed at the activity under way. Wallace had tidied up his orchard and scythed the wild grass among the decaying apple trees. The transfigured barn shone whitely in the summer sun, humming with enterprise. Her father even apologized in the kind of pidgin English he used with foreigners, for not having had time to prune his bushes in order to increase the harvest, nor to mow between rows to make their picking easier. Diplomacy was new for Wallace. They appeared to accept his apology at face value. 'New castle,' they said cheerfully, pointing at the unfamiliar structure. Secrecy surrounded the old barn and the flurry within. From now on, he told them, he'd be weighing their berries over at the house.

Elsie seemed proud of her family. Busy people, inspired souls. Not surprising, with everybody so buoyant, no one seemed to require therapy any more. It was the pioneering spirit all over, a time of pulling together against threat of implosion. Against redskins storming in over the palisade.

A big sign delivered by a commercial painter arrived from the city. It arrived on a flatdeck truck and Wallace, when the bearded driver asked where he wanted it erected, told him to hide the tarpaper house so as not to put off the customers. It didn't even hide the doghouse. Bear baptized the sign as soon as posts and bracing went up.

SUNLIGHT CONTROL CENTRE
A New Concept in Stability and Deterrence
Eradicate
Aggression Stress Depression
Call Now

'It's a dead ringer,' Wallace said, 'for free enterprise.'

The Sikh pickers didn't question these changes. They were more concerned that Wallace should keep out 'the refugees', as they called them, a large Laotian family looking for work and making the round of berry farms these Indian immigrants considered their own for the picking. They liked things the way they were.

'They're all refugees far as I'm concerned,' said Wallace. 'Bad for business. *I'm* bad for business.' He was thinking of their new business, the light business. 'Enemies of free enterprise. Next thing they'll be agitating for a union.'

Elsie tied up Bear to stop him scaring off potential customers. The chain collar dug into his old black hackles when he growled at the pickers, who ran out of berries by the third week of August.

Theirs was the bread of time to come.

– 7 –

In the early days of Sunlight Control Centre's operation that autumn, Seth was often on the phone to his sister. Like Wallace he objected to her word 'patients' and asked that she call them 'guests'. This would enhance the image of their centre as a resort rather than a sick ward.

The clients who came with increasing regularity the first eight weeks included Bianca Tse, one of the forget-me-not agents; several older ladies recommended by somebody's wife, possibly Mr Roth's, who together drove out from West Vancouver every Thursday evening in an expensive station wagon for a marathon treatment; a garage mechanic, Victor Soledad, who'd read their ad in the *Lacey News*, and arrived each day after work black in hand and mood; a retired botany instructor, a nice man with secrets; Lawrence Puddle, a square-dance caller, who liked to come before dawn Wednesdays and Fridays; a couple of college basketball players who let the light bathe them like water in a whirlpool, boys too long for the furniture.

Oddly, who also came – or rather came back, and who didn't sign her guest book – were Mr and Mrs Singh, the grandparents of the blueberry-picking family, who returned in early October to 'find peace'.

Wallace warned, 'We'll do bad catering to Hindus. Don't mention this to Seth.'

But Seth, once the company established itself on the stock exchange, lost interest and didn't seem to care how few or many clients appeared, even telling Holly to keep whatever fees she charged since it was her baby. He already had 'a ballpark idea' of how the place would do. He talked of 'white knights', of 'dropping a bombshell or two' and 'market fallout', by way of optioning the future. Wallace figured it was the least his son could do, letting Holly keep the guest fees, but decided Seth must be cooking the books 'if he doesn't care about profits and loss'. The fees received hardly covered the cost of Hydro. Seth must have understood this, because periodically, 'to help defray costs, electricity and such', he mailed them cheques.

'Subsidies,' snorted Wallace. 'That takes the cake. We might as well be living in Russia.' He was determined to up the ante.

When her brother drove out to Perumbur in November he seemed genuinely surprised to discover their operation actually *doing business*. He forced a smile. 'Small but efficient, eh?' It was Remembrance Day and he was wearing a plastic poppy in his lapel.

Wallace, in touch with a broker every week or two, casually mentioned to Seth he'd heard where the price of Sun Con had risen to eighty-two cents a share. He was thinking of selling some. At this disclosure Seth's tone became noticeably confidential. He cautioned his father that the worst thing Wallace could do right now, with their company still climbing, was to sell.

Elsie, pleased to see her son still dressed like a gentleman, was inclined to agree. 'Seth's the best judge of business, Wally.'

'Shyster business, maybe.'

Wallace begrudged his son an on-site inspection, seeing as how Seth had shown so little interest in the actual building of his sister's mysterious project.

'What's the matter with keeping him in the dark?'

'Don't be a jealous old bird,' said Seth.

'Don't you forget who wired all the lights. Think about that component. The wattage.'

'I financed the lights,' replied Seth.

'Dopes financed them,' said Wallace. 'Trying to make a fast buck off what they figured was some Mickey Mouse outfit ready to bomb out. Dopes like Mr Riviera who makes his living from two-bit mining stock. I know about these guys and their propaganda!'

'Well, Wally, you sounded willing to make a dollar or two,' Elsie reminded him.

Holly served her brother decaffeinated coffee in the refurbished silo where her office was. Loquacious in mood, happy in the light, she told him she interviewed patients here – 'sorry, guests' – and confidentially discussed their programmes prior to treatment. If they suffered from stress or sadness, the usual reasons for coming, she probed to discover how badly, whether it sometimes led to aggression, and asked if they were receiving any medical attention. If she thought her light could help them, as it helped her, she offered a choice of treatments to do with length and intensity of dosage. She told them truthfully she worked part-time in a real estate office.

Seth tasted the coffee and put it down. He frowned at the circular wall.

She said, 'I tell them about how our bright lights are going to secrete changes in their brains and make them feel very good. Chemical changes, I guess, who knows what theory's behind it? I just tell them we need to make up for our lack of sunlight in this part of the world. Compared to equatorial calm. And that they have to stay at it. For their body rhythm.'

'Music to their ears,' said Seth.

With manics she admitted caution because she didn't really know what a manic was. Wallace could be a manic, she wasn't sure.

'Wallace is a paranoid,' said Seth. 'If you ask me.'

'I won't take chances,' she told him. 'I start everybody off listening to music, checking their reactor just in case all they need is calming down. Light's the last thing.'

He asked, 'What music?'

'Guitar,' she said. 'Want to hear?' They went a few steps into the barn and she put a tape into the brand new Pioneer, which seemed to hearten him.

Her brother looked vigilant as it played. A city man, he seemed to expect interruption at every turn. But Elsie had popped the last roosting hens into her freezer.

After a while he asked, 'Does any of this so-called treatment ever work?'

His asking this now, after raising so much money, surprised her.

'Well, I don't think we know how the brain ...' she repeated.

'Yeah? No, I guess not.'

'It can feel like a whole world calmed down between your eyebrows. Stabilized by the sun.'

'I bet.'

'Your biological clock isn't an atomic clock,' she told him, handing him the guest book. 'It can run fast and get out of whack. Maybe the length of day and night ...'

'You want to control the length of day and night?'

She shrugged. 'If it'll help, why not?'

Her brother was pleased by the comments he read over. He was nodding. Then he stood up to inspect the rest of the Centre for himself. He lay down on a sofa in the white light and after a while, closing his eyes then reopening them, pronounced himself cured. 'You ought to add a jacuzzi though. For afterwards. *Après* light. People look for that kind of extra. It's like carpet in a van.' And he advised her to buy a white lab coat.

Over supper the talk was of Wallace's war record. He had none.

'I was too young. Otherwise I'd of been over there doing my bit against Hitler and them, you bet. Now we got Brezhnev who needs smartening up and I'm too old. I got this 4-F back. Still, when push comes to shove, I'm with the Poles, I'd do my bit for the Poles same as I'd of done for the Dutch. The Dutch love us, you know that? For liberating them. You only have to wear a maple leaf in the lapel and they'll invite a Canadian in off the street for supper. That's if you're a tourist over there. On Remembrance Day, like today, they take you out for supper. Not like over here at the polder, these Dutchmen care about cows and that's it.'

His allusion might have been to Rupert Kupe, except Rupert's heritage was Polish.

'The Japs love us too,' observed Seth. 'And we pulverized them back to a Bikini atoll. Thanks to the Bomb.'

Max and Eva snickered at their father. He put down his knife and drank straight from the bottle, his beer bottle, not the fancy bottle of red wine Seth had brought. Eyeing this gift he now said, 'We don't drink that around here. This ain't dinner. It's supper.'

'It's delicious,' said Elsie, sipping from a stolen A&W mug. 'It's French.'

Wallace said, 'The Japs respect our strength. We beat 'em at their own game and now they respect us for it. Wouldn't say they love us. I don't imagine they'd go a yard to invite a Canadian in for supper.'

Eva said, 'Pass the chicken, Daddy dearest.'

– 8 –

Except for Lawrence Puddle, who came early in the morning, Holly conducted her treatments in the evening. But already she was wondering if they had any lasting effect, or if people like herself were condemned to artifice. Could the dark monster ever be escaped? She still worked three afternoons a week in Lacey, where the cost of inflation was rocketing up property prices and stampeding people into the mortgage market. That fall, burning up energy at an accelerated rate, she put off moving out of her parents' house, although Wallace reminded her she owned stock she could sell for a nice profit whenever she fancied.

'Despite what Seth claims,' said Wallace, 'ours to do what we like with.'

By the end of November their stock had risen to ninety-seven cents a share and her father was seriously thinking of selling. That's when Eva came to her older, apparently successful sister with an offer to share the cost of an apartment as soon as Eva graduated in June. 'You don't want to stick around here,' she said making a face. 'Do you?' Eva longed to live in Vancouver, by the sea, where Seth clubbed till dawn. He'd been phoning her.

Unfortunately, by December, almost a year since her trip to Disney World, Holly's weekly clientele had settled down to no more than seven or eight guests a session, and a couple who came irregularly and promised to pay when they could. This couple was Grandpa and Granny Singh, who appeared dissatisfied with the way things were in Canada, who loved Holly's white light because it reminded them of the Punjabi plains. She understood they disliked the mountains, the clouds, the rain. 'Catch cold,' muttered the old woman, shivering, pointing back outside where they would appear out of the mist, Grandpa at the wheel of a rusted Dodge. Mrs Singh wore a long green v-neck sweater over tattered saffron pyjamas.

'They're still glum from the blueberries,' cracked Wallace. 'And cagey. Summers they make enough to get themselves on UI the whole winter, but they'll never pay you for treatment.'

He jabbed Holly's shoulder with his fingers. 'Say, d'you hear about the Lotto winner wins three million bucks, spends it, somebody asks him where it all went and he says – Wellsir, the first million I spent on wimmin. The second million I spent on wine. And the third million I spent foolishly.'

He chuckled, expectantly. When she didn't laugh, barely smiled, he got annoyed.

'Now that's funny!' he shouted.

To Holly it sounded more like a parable, the sad accumulated wisdom of her father's half century. She wondered what Mr Roth would say if he could see the way Sunlight Control Centre hadn't, after all, taken off in the public imagination.

'That creep?' said Wallace. 'What's he care? Some faithful underwriter. Undertaker's more like it, the duds he wears. It figures he's a friend of your brother's all right. Got about the same gumption.'

At Christmas, across the turkey, he and Seth quarrelled again over Wallace's desire to sell the family shares.

'Listen,' Seth told him. 'Don't forget who's carrying the mortgage on your barn. Who d'you think paid for the place and the whole shebang inside it?'

He sounded defensive.

'Dopes paid for it,' said Wallace. 'Cat's out of the bag.'

'Yeah? Tell us about it.'

'Sure. My shares are worth a buck six now – what for? I'd like to know who's willing to pay one oh six for a security in an unprofitable setup. Tell the old man, eh? Mind you, I don't care how stupid people are for buying into a business that pulls in a grand total of a hundred seventy or eighty bucks a week. That there is their beeswax. This here's the time to get out with a profit. QED. Take my advice and pay off your mortgage, now!'

Her father was determined to sell his twelve and a half thousand shares, and the two of *them* – Holly and her brother – could do what they pleased. Wallace wasn't interested in containment. 'What is this anyway, a profit-free zone?'

This seemed to Seth to threaten the standoff he thought they'd reached on Armistice Day. By Christmas Day, only six weeks later, he and his father were quarrelling bitterly. Before Elsie could serve her blueberry pudding, her son had walked out of the tarpaper house forever, and disappeared into the sunset. It was overcast and raining steadily.

'He's stonewalling,' claimed Wallace.

Holly's discovery, her hope of ending the slow war of attrition in people's brains, had led to cold war in her own family. Not conducive to an atmosphere of stability in herself, no. She had avoided being drawn in on either side, against brother *or* father, but neutrality seemed peripheral. Bitter winds of change were going to blow away her house of light. She might as well wake up.

Wallace meanwhile had forgotten about light treatment for himself, even though his hockey team was now in mid-season doldrums – 'a slump', he called it, the present condition of his own disposition.

'My back is acting up,' he complained. 'Feels like the Serbonian bog.'

But he cheerfully told the welfare office, when it finally called to cut him off, 'Lots of money in light right now, and I'm glad I got in on the bottom floor, years ago.' He was referring to his old profession as a juice jockey, and wasn't about to grovel. 'These days, madam, if you know how to use energy you can light the world with a candle. My daughter's a big cheese now. The cat's meow, frankly. It was me that told her to go for it.'

– 9 –

In January a shock, worse than electrical shock, came to her father when, turning to the stock quotes in the newspaper, he noticed shares in Sun Con had suddenly plummeted. Somebody, some s.o.b., had sold over a hundred and thirty thousand shares in one day and the company had fallen from a high of a dollar twenty-six to thirty cents. Wallace saw red, then he turned blue.

He couldn't get through to Seth. By the time he located his broker, the next morning at 7:10 a.m., he learned more heavy selling of Sun Con was under way on the floor. The broker said he would do his best for Mr Harker, how many shares did he wish to sell?

'Twenty-five thousand,' said Wallace morosely, without even consulting his partner. 'Only a bozo would hold on to this sinking ship now. Sun Con is sinking, sunk.'

His partner considered her position. She was actually surprised at how little she feared going under. The secret of light was still in her control.

A week later she and her father ended up with a cheque at the post office for $625, an average of two and a half cents a share – which divided in half came to $312 per partner.

'Well,' said Elsie. 'It's better than what Welfare's paying at the moment. Stop complaining.'

'Compared to what I put into Sun Con, my labour and that, it's a ripoff,' Wallace told her.

He brooded, angrily.

He explained to his daughter it was a lesson for her, what Seth had done to them, his own family, what his bad faith and propaganda had cost them. Thanks to Seth they were no longer free from creeping socialism in the guise of welfare. The welfare state was corrupt.

Holly replied that at least the mortgage wasn't their responsibility. The seed partners, whoever they were, were still looking after the mortgage on his barn. Weren't they? And she still had an income from her guests.

'Guests!' hooted her father. 'When the guests hear what's happened to Sun Con, are they gonna keep coming to a two-and-a-half-cent resort? Anyways, how can you keep the barn lit if somebody's pulled the plug? That's like shutting the door after the horse's split.' He called his own son a ruddy swindler, obviously PWU (Present Whereabouts Unknown) because he was living in his van in a nice new location. 'On Easy Street,' claimed Wallace. 'He's living on Easy Street now – laid an egg and sold his own damn family down the frigging river.'

Elsie denied it. 'Ain't the barn been done over? It's a new barn. You own the whole barn, lock, stock and silo.'

'Don't talk to me about stock.'

About title and deed he was unwilling to listen. They had been stolen from him. He wanted to take the architect of this epic catastrophe to court. Ever since his hockey team had gone into a tailspin, he wouldn't listen to reason and was irritable and hostile.

That night Holly went out to the barn – stood still in the darkness – then switched it off. She lay down in the light. The electricity buzzed lazily like flies in autumn air. She wanted to float above despair listening to the guitar, its leaden twang her reason in a storm. The barn was cold and it took time to burn off the chill with glowing space heaters. She tasted phlegm in her lungs. Looking into the lights she felt things slowly lift, like cloud along the river. She did not mind the intrusion.

He entered in gumboots, remembering halfway over her carpet to return and remove them at the door. Padding back he sat down beside her on the sofa, taking her hand in his. His was as soft as a gundog's mouth. He just wanted her to know the worst about Seth, he said, which was why he'd spoken freely.

'I'm a trueblue patriot, I guess. Family comes first.'

His son had fallen in with shady company, been looking for any scheme to make money, of pulling a confidence trick on his own family. 'Your idea was just the foot in the door he needed, honey. Might as well've left this place to the cats. I'm surprised Seth bothered to let us doodad it up at all, before it blew up in our face.'

He added, trying to sound wise but with his voice betraying disappointment and bitterness, 'Sun Con was a pirate's dream. To him this place was no more than a hole in the ground somewheres north of … A silo for silage!'

She drew back, afraid she wasn't very understanding of her father's vengeful tone.

It seemed her new concept in stability and deterrence had begun to resemble the old one of a family standoff. Maybe if you had to live at war, with the hoard of destructions in your head, better to avoid the contamination of unnatural light and false survival. To understand yourself as you are.

Before the spring rains desisted she imagined her dream would eventually darken and retreat from artifice to the gradual reemergence of mice, cats and owls. Her romance with light would fade.

Wallace was going on now about goons. Goons on the stock exchange, goons at the bar, goons in the Kremlin. 'Who can you trust if you can't trust your own family? Our own skin and blood?'

By March her guests would probably trickle away anyway, to just Granny and Grandpa Singh, trying to defeat their homesickness and make of this temperate, intemperate climate their country. By courting the sun, or rather its proxy ...

'No stick-to-itiveness,' her father might put it, when even these guests no longer came. 'No bloody good.'

He caressed her hand. 'Light lets folks appreciate the world by lifting oppression from their state of bloody being. What *is* there here but weather? With this negative thinking today, who appreciates light? Who appreciates the world? Light keeps us ready, tooth and claw. Reagan, the cold warrior, is ready. He calls it like he sees it.'

Her father in the end would doubtless dismiss these remaining guests as freeloaders, telling them he could no longer afford to run the resort. Mr and Mrs Singh would stop coming, be the last guests, without having written a word in her book.

'You get some sleep,' Wallace said, letting go her hand. 'There's a late sports report I wanna look at.' And padded out.

Light by light Holly went around pulling plugs, drawing switches, till her centre fell dark. And cold. She threw away the lights, the defining shadows, whatever stood between her and this shape she was. Moon on the rise, it shared nothing, a pale copy of the sun. She opened the barn door and stood inhaling Perumbur's heavy air to cool her lungs.

Suspicious, Bear sniffed the air as though poised to chase her scent up a tree.

Drawing closed the door she left the stoop and passed into sleep.

— 10 —

Ed Settera returned to the farm. Junk spread slowly through the orchard. Underneath apple trees choked with suckers came the same old flotsam, wet dawns, things as they were. The cats had cats and the grass turned grey.

For the first time in the franchise's history, Wallace's hockey team failed to advance in the playoffs. Not even the Great One was now immune to his wrath. Her father fired abuse at him, claiming the colour of his garter belt was pink.

Inside the tarpaper house, in a darkened room, he sat before a flickering screen watching slow replays and suffering his bad back with the lameness of Hephaestus.

Holly survived her birthday supper.

And the sun frequently returned.

She had promised herself to absorb this sun, tan her body all over to berry-brown, despite the enduring quarrel between father and brother threatening to make her feel worse than Rupert had. Both had the knowledge now to rebuild the core of her idea and threaten each other with a patent or restraining order. Eternal jealousy over a stalemated panacea! Over the intense brightness of its promise, the beauty and symmetry of its market logic!

In theory, yes, father and son possessed the knowledge to make economic depression for themselves obsolete. As she did, daddy's little ball of fire, but she couldn't believe any more in her theory of Nirvana in a rush, halcyon poise, old-age security. Not in removing folks in a flash to palmy atolls, days brighter than the sun itself.

Loved the fireworks, Jack. Great little son et lumière you've got here…

No, the imbalance of light was going to remain as it was, folks still prone among these greyer latitudes to impatience, lies, retaliation. Predisposed in such an inconstant climate to making money and, against their neighbours, war.

Later, when she awoke in the night, the wind was lifting curtains, calendar, her spirits. A new front was moving in, blowing apart the bedroom, tickling her fancy and filling up her mind in soothing waves like the sea. Her whole body expanded to receive the tide. A final atmosphere for now, this west wind lifting up, blowing away…

Thus would she forget by day, except when she chose to see the imagined starling, the imagined May.

COMMENT: I heard a voice. The embroidered voice of a politician, trained to sound as pulchritudinous as possible without sacrificing votes. I felt he must have trained on stage. This is all I knew. Except what *wouldn't* make it into my story, a dead mother's nickname for him, the first word he learned. Honk.

It's hard to account for origins. The way when you squash a moth between your fingers it only ever seems to have been an arrangement of dust. Ditto story. His mother must've died as he was coming into manhood. She seemed important, as if I were planning to arrange his story, his voice, from her ashes. Who was he *talking* to?

Sikh owes something to the pickers in Anne Reid's story. I could see the blueberry stains in their aging pores. Suddenly I wanted to explore the texture of a world that had descended from their poor working one. Almost December and I was in a hurry.

Then I remembered *The Lady or the Tiger?* I didn't have a plot. No matter how high the waves come in, the tide still goes out. So I thought, stick with the waves, let them carry you. What I always notice in a story is its texture anyway. Texture will bear a drama.

– T.S.S.

T. S. Saini

Sikh

SALLY, WAIT. I may be exasperating but am I not worth it? I've spoken freely to the press, true. To those ink-stained wretches I'm a bedizened new airhead, taunted by backbenchers and cursed by militants. They see no harm in quoting my off-the-record remarks, even if they should. In the mail on my twenty-seventh birthday I got a pretty package of ribbon-wrapped dung, probably a dog's, so I know that along with one bloody hanky on the aerial of my CRX, and three ugly phone calls, it's a demand for silence. Hoarse bondage for windy tonsils like mine. Making my maiden speech as the legislature's youngest member, and first of my kind, I'd fallen under the charm of immunity. Now I rise to euphemisms as best I can. Listen, Sally: *I would I were thy bird.* (Do you remember your lines too? How on stage I sometimes sounded like Sylvester's foe Tweetie? So light is vanity.) Please tuck this tape in your trousseau and rethink your snit. I am not a playboy. The press will print anything.

History is my witness, Sally.

My secretary, loyal and brainless, should have put you through right away, not told you I was in committee. Now you refuse to return my calls. And I refuse to take calls from those who threaten me and Debon-Air too. We rest our cases, the world stops. Home for the weekend I turn to this microcassette and its digital counter, which I mail to you in good faith.

You won't be surprised, I should not have been, by what I saw on the road this morning driving to the airfield. I was following a muddy pickup paying it no more attention than any slow crate goading me to follow it, when a sign imprinted like a bumper sticker on the cab's rear window made me peer. Sally, I was looking at the translucent image, slashed with a diagonal red line like the cigarette in the no-smoking sign, of a turbaned Sikh. For less than this they close down restaurants! My constituency grows intolerant as terrorists go on stoking the Punjab, carrying their righteousness to the sky, and punishing fellow Sikhs with shootings in our own province. But is theirs an excuse for more bigotry?

For the nonce I considered pulling alongside, rolling down my passenger window and mailing the driver a thrombosis. Pray, sahib, your attention. Yet how? Why, by pulling my handgun from the glove compartment – for the tire gauge, I thought, would double as a barrel – even better by shooting him a line in the despised sing-song rhythm of my race (racism rooted in the ear of the beholder): *'Excuse me, redneck, is that stink coming from your very bad teeth, or just have you forgotten your shower this month?'* – easing over to give his fender a light hickey from mine, till he drove right into the watery ditch separating this road from Perumbur's hayfields.

I pulled out to chasten his halfton, Sally, to sweep in sharply and cut him off, when I noticed the driver dabbing her eyes with a handkerchief. I flew by then with no more threats, deciding, with the prejudice of a chauvinist, that her husband was the bastard who had stuck that sign in the window, and done her an injury over a bad breakfast of beer cans. He was treating her like some ugly he could slap around the way he would a raghead in the Save-On parking lot. He would have knuckles like peach stones.

Sally, I am on edge these days. Even driving is a balancing act, as delicate as making a speech or giving interviews. Is it surprising you see me so little lately? Extremists keep me engaged with tactics of the middle ground. Despite what you hear of my cavorting in the capital – 'this merry member', wrote one columnist who avoids the narrowness of research – I have no time for a social life and hardly any on a weekend like this to come home and bury my mother. I swear. She has been dead seven years, true, yet in the glove compartment this morning were her ashes accompanying me to the airfield. Delicacy is something that opposing teaches, and if for this reason, Sally, I'm guilty of neglecting you it's because I believe us still to be in harmony – in love! – regardless of my legislative absences across the gulf, those endless ferry rides. Granted I have much to learn about delicate consideration. Yet I beseech you, reconsider our engagement. Come back on side.

I do think the future demands me ... us, Sally. Members are saying I could be party leader some day. You remember how I took over the student body at university, already accustomed to launching as well as breasting the slings and arrows for our debating team? And with you on stage I played a leading role. The student stage has simply grown bigger, Sally – *we* have grown bigger. I will take to it again in a leading role, possibly as premier. You should count your chickens now!

Sally, when I rose in the legislature to speak last week I was wonderful. You would have been proud. I savour the memory, the lift it gave me, the house that hung on my words. At the same time I grow fearful of banishment from this place where I was born, my country, you. Jaded reporters write that rising too fast is hubris. But what do yeastless loafs know of rising? Of real tragedy? And just as fickle are immigrants who call me a quisling and would teach me a lesson. Would prevent the reelection of a cocky white Sikh, Sally, these born-again militants once farm and sawmill workers, who join brotherhoods like Babbar Khalsa – a mob that makes me think of whiskers, crowbars, and plastic explosives, leaving aside cheap aftershave cologne (English Leather Lime), a queer scent given they refuse to shave their faces, grow sweaty beating up the unorthodox who dub them wacko, and hate rival organizations dedicated to the same homeland (their sad and dusty Khalistan), parading around in costumes like seventeenth-century warriors who bathe once a month in the temple tank and cap the smell under starched saffron turbans as tall as beehives. Sally, these Tigers of the True Faith like to peep. They are voyeurs and terrorists too. They love to bomb by delayed charge and enjoy death at a distance. I suggest our security agents should hire ultralights, but am scolded in the press for self-interest. I know precisely where these thugs evade agents south of Aldergrove, to slip over the line with Canadian passports to see them freely out of America ...

Do you remember, bright angel, how you would caution me to slow my lines by fingering the fine gold necklace at your throat? A gesture as natural as your husky-voiced soliloquy to night and me, *So tedious is this day* ..., until word of my death abruptly reached you, and your voice lifted an octave in stricken anguish, as skilfully as any member of Equity's? Our voices were our deliverance from banishment. We belonged to ourselves then. I still confess to quavers of adolescent embarrassment remembering the way my parents, or maybe cousins fresh from India, would bob from their knees in the gurdwara, chanting to thick drumbeats, stretching and flapping their hands, boggling their heads in rhythms ingrained from scripture. Maybe the militants are right to detect in me a deeper grudge than I recognize ... in my early refusal to prostrate myself before the enthroned guru flicking a peacock whisk at his sacred page, or to touch folded hands to forehead, to lay my father's dollar at his feet. I was churlish. I would have kept the dollar. These days, I'm informed, the temple is run under influence of the New Orthodox, self-appointed 'commandos' and 'liberators', their leaders wealthy from real estate flips made in their sawmill years, shorn and indifferent then to the culture they now champion. I mention no names. All of them Singhs, they have better spies than the Capulets, and swifter revenge. I remember two or three from my father's mill, where I worked summers splitting shakes ... Sally, the drivel they now spout! They are worse than cabinet ministers.

My father is orthodox in another way. Did I tell you *why* he went back to the Punjab lately with me in weary tow? I'm ashamed to say in his annoyance at you, and at my flat refusal to let him choose me a wife, he decided to buy *himself* a bride. We returned to his mud-housed village and he professed to be enchanted with it. (It would be like your father returning to a Warsaw ghetto and not telling the truth about his disgust.) No one recalled my mother. Peasants were breathing a hot dusty wind, shuffled barefoot through pinched streets, schoolchildren carried slates – not the scribblers we grew up with, Sally – each entrance to the village was guarded, and fear of terrorists made everybody squeeze inside at dusk and lock their doors. The teacher had already been shot. Relatives and friends had been murdered. I thought I would die ... of boredom, of that grouchy landscape of puddles, riverbeds and ditches. It was so *brown*.

How I admire the green lawns of your own parents' home, the sea and city views from their patio, their shake roof, their beds and shrubbery, their three fireplaces. I promise to fly over your emerald city soon and tip my wings to capital. Oh, Sally (O Canada, the militants would tease, accusing me of disregarding your plumpness, of whoring after whiteness) am I a quisling? Would you be better off without me? Forgive me, you are *not* heavy ... Trust me, Sally. Am I not entitled to feel part of you now, from the inside out (if you will let me say it, say anything), haven't I forgiven your coolness at times, your indifference to what I believe is fairly mine, and those pink striped ear rings, Sally, that resemble cheap jam tarts nibbled by sowbugs? And your way of blowing smoke out the ... But common language saves us. We really have more in common than if we'd been arranged for each other by families of the same history.

Side by side in class, did the Elizabethan tongue not lift us finally to the stage of public lovers, making us chew our lines as the food of indiscretion, digesting them barely, before rushing on to the next? Did we not waggle arms together to warm our blood, unclench calves to loosen our legwarmers, scream to release our natural voices? We soared! Sally, sometimes my jaws ached. Enunciating like metronomes we missed the depth of real love and sometimes sounded wooden. Intoxicated with ourselves we unlocked mere noise. To speak the soberest lines, do you remember, they would insert an Equity player to lend the likes of Friar Lawrence a grave sound:

These violent delights have violent ends,
And in their triumph die, like fire and powder,
Which as they kiss consume ...

Sally, Sally, Sally ... I love saying your name. Saying it is Valium these nights of nerve-racking work, whispering to myself that gruff cawed 'c', Sally, when you first whispered 'cock' ... 'lend me your cock, sir' ... your final exploding consonant a credit to our nasal speech coach, Professor Hill-Tout, reminding me each time we make love (only twice since my election in May?) of the Khalsa's five 'k's' my father drummed in with male Sikh pride, expecting me to adopt the unshorn hair and the drawers, Sally, sword and haircomb ...

My only concession to orthodoxy is this steel *kara* I lift elegantly in the legislature on a brown wrist – worn frankly for fashion and to remind me of risks I court on middle ground – the same way you do your engagement ring. (By the way, will you be returning this ring, Sally? It's a keepsake of dear employment.) I am really the beau of balance. The party whips find the dandy in me trying, while the press hounds me for colourful copy. You know how I prefer clothes with a flair to dull livery. Were I orthodox you'd find me among the avant garde in a striped, nay, a polka-dot turban! (Why is the fight for homeland, my precious, fuelled as it is by religion in Lebanon Northern Ireland the Punjab Palestine Sri Lanka, always so *leaden*?)

My homeland, Sally, my constituency spreads out beneath me whether I take to the air as a politician or pilot. Your pilot. Imagine arriving this morning at my flight school, hoisting yourself into the front seat of the open ultralight – as you have done before, Sally – with me in back. To thwart the screaming engine, trying to shake off its rear-mounted propeller, I've switched on the headset in your crash helmet, can you hear me? Do you recall our checkdown? But this time I will spare you my instructor's jargon, the statistics and length of this grass runway alongside strawberry fields, the expected cruising altitude of our fibreglass fuselage. Just fasten your safety harness, pay no mind to the absence of sides, to that jumpy tachometer, or the glass tube on your left with the unworking float. (No need to know our airspeed because a desperate pilot can read every tremble of these nylon wings, Sally, every gust of wind short of an eagle's fart.) No, don't start asking ... there, I've switched off your little Styrofoam mike. Sit back and enjoy the –

Sally, look how mess, disorder, grunge recede as we go up, how full of symmetry seem these fields and sloughs of Perumbur's flood plain, lake and freshwater marshes, the peaks above. If the whole world only knew, ridge soaring, thermal soaring, is the art it calls out for! Lightness! Lite beer, lite food, lite touch ... It calls out for ultralights, I have no doubt, this business of instruction, sales and service that I invest my father's money in shamelessly (yours too) to buy aircraft, build sheds, hire more pilots ... From an ultralight people rediscover perspective, Sally, they throw away their lines. Only aloft in black Spandex pants and white Nikes do I ever feel

free. Is it any wonder the militants want to bomb me from the sky –
evidently the same way they do the passenger jet drifting in over the
mountains at sunset, descending to the Pacific, its rigid bird's body
ahead of sound, its silver glint in heaven bursting suddenly into
orange, like a marigold in the earthbound maniac's dream? The militants care nothing for soaring free of heavy halftons with their No
Sikhing signs on the trunk roads, the highways, the back roads
below us. They are from another time zone. They go on fighting the
fierce and foolish Sikh Wars of the last century, losing cannons and
their lives like ice cubes in the baking Punjabi plain.

Sally, don't be surprised by the cargo we carry. Water is our destination. Because my father never approved of death, at least not *her*
death, my mother wasn't buried – her ashes collected, yes, but never
strewn over local water in our custom. My new mother is now
younger than I and it troubles me to leave this urn in the same
house with her. The sister, even younger, tried to plant a posy in it!
(Let her beware.) It's I who am responsible, eldest son igniting his
mother's platform of firewood – that very week, by the way, you and
I first met in rehearsal over our playbooks, do you remember, avoid-
ing one another's eyes like chosen ones of different poles? This
morning my farewell gesture (to lift one of your lines) is to kill her
with much cherishing, set her free of my father's house, trail her
ashes in a wake over the widest river. Look below us, Sally, under
the right pontoon three thousand feet. Water ...

> *Can I go forward when my heart is here?*
> *Turn back, dull earth, and find thy centre out.*

... My father's sawmill is one of many that crowd this river most
of the way to Hope. At night driving north you can see their beehive
burners glow, fuelled by bark, butt ends, and sawdust. The river
eddies past in silence, or gurgles round pilings, muddy from sluic-
ing the dirt canyons and dry hills of the Interior, boomed with lake
logs it squeezes beneath, its current cold against the roe-stuffed
salmon, hiding hundred-year-old sturgeon, challenging muddy
dikes when the tide floods upstream from the gulf, miles. Sally,
fishboats plough it, loggers dance across the waves, a monastery

looks down upon it from a mountain, prospectors still grovel in the gravel. I embrace its fertile valley wrinkled with tributaries older than the cradle. Sally, this spreading swale calls me like a lover. Can you smell its reedy clay and sweet alder? Here is where the first Sikhs dreamed of owning the mills they sweated in (my father got *his* working two shifts a day for twenty years), the farms where Sikhs still dream, picking mushrooms and blueberries for pennies a pound, near toxic sprays and starling guns.

Lady, I picked berries and pulled lumber too. I'm not a playboy. I have scars to prove it. Don't tune me out now, pay attention to the silence when I cut our engine, that gust of silence in the cockpit, hear it?...

Sally, listen. It is good to quarrel. I wish our families would – to give us more pleasure by what is denied us, don't you feel? My father doesn't approve, true, but the blessing of one who marries a child matters little. Your family I think deems me a dashing catch. This is very disappointing. Until yesterday you and they were too welcoming, too generous, too accepting. You let me in where I wish you might have treated me sometimes, Sally, as my turbaned forefathers were treated, turned away at the port of entry to this country, stranded aboard a steamer ... But forgive me if I seem to be hinting you were an easy lay! (You were at least a generous one.) Just to tell how long it took to persuade you to meet my gaze at our first meeting on stage, would take more time than this tape, I see, has seconds left to –

So that is what I did this morning, Sally, gliding free of encumbrance and gauging my altitude. Releasing her ashes at last to trail away in the wind, and falling with them a long way, just falling, toward the watery surface of the world in my amphibious craft ... Could I have miscalculated the drift of things once mine? Could it really be, I wondered, we will never meet again? Sally, I wonder if she, if you [*click*]

COMMENT: I'd already written the first two parts of my story, and was wondering how to dramatize the last, when the aerial perspective in Terry Saini's *Sikh* sent my oldest character aloft in a Thai balloon.

In January, halfway through our reading year, I offered the group my story in three discrete parts. (In the last century it might've appeared as a triple-decker novel, a three-generational saga, a domestic epic.) I felt just because I have more than one teller doesn't mean the story can't have integrity, nor be read as a 'whole' story, without a lot of stuffing that goes into a turkey of a novel. I tried to maintain the start of a novel.

True, the work is set outside of Perumbur, but I felt it derived very much from the father's doctorly background *in* Perumbur, where his grandson wonders about housesitting as a way to escape city life and the example of his own father's urbane striving.

As a lawyer, I tend to be more opinionated than other men the same mellow age. My wife tells me this is a death kiss to art. She concedes I've softened since we first met back in the war, and the following exercise, to her credit, was a modest attempt to explore a dictum by one of my favourite authors, Samuel Butler: 'He who knows not how to wink knows not how to see; and he who knows not how to lie knows not how to speak the truth. So he who cannot suppress his opinions cannot express them.'

– J. C.

Jim Constance

Flight

— GRANDSON —

HE FIGURES, why go home to a rented house with gutter weed when the most he gets there is a nice jack-off view of next-door bikinis from the sunroom? But what else can he afford? Numbers, including his own SIN, tease him, although those measuring engine capacity on the trunks of Japanese and German cars do more. They provoke him. He doesn't think. He pinches his house key and trolls it thigh-high along the paint jobs. Korean Ponies get a break, because of their drivers: single women on part-time salaries, he can prove it. But the Saabs he takes a walking tour around.

Give us a B, M, W, S, L, C, R, X ... Yea Team! Most of them tend to replace numbers on their plates with letters, provided they get to the registrar first, or else fudge the spellings. EH-1, JAMEEE!, MACH-2, EPIC 1, PR, etc. Their Italian rubber tires he takes care of with a pistol of sufficient calibre to rattle the chrome numbers as well.

Sure, dude. Go believe yourself.

'D'you know what a robbed house feels like?' he asks his Shaughnessy hosts. 'Like love lost. Someone's cleared out of your life with something yours. It can really spoil a party.' He tells them you need to make the best of a bad surprise when you come home, and hang on for the fingerprint squad. 'Those boys dust the jambs and drawers, as fresh as daisies at two a.m. Their shift starts at midnight.' His solution is not to go home, except he maintains he's going anyway. '... Like the pacifist Catholic, who refuses to wrestle with his conscience.' Arf, arf. He's been drinking, what of it? 'A party takes the load off your back and puts bearing in your balls.'

At four a.m. he claims his artful housemate is saving him a piece of blackberry pie – not a bad time to leave except bus service has withdrawn till dawn. And no other guest is left to drive him. He looks for rolls on the mantel and scrapes the chili pot. He hangs on till seven, eight, breakfast of papaya and herb tea with hibiscus flowers and cranberries. He makes the most of this unsatisfying meal and looks in the fridge for lunch meat: 'All right, you jars, who's hiding the ham?' He offers to send out for pizza, but can't get a response from his hosts, abed since four. (Those parlours for Bohemians and the proletariat have all closed anyway for the night.) He could always ring up for Chinese, what his father's generation used to ring for, his hosts' come to that, as tasteless budding bourgeois ... Give us a DING, huh, give us a HO.

Here's the drill, so listen. But his father is renewing himself with a second family and won't listen. Can't he see what's happening to the world?

In the pool outside he goes for a swim on a hungry stomach. He makes himself open his green eyes and look at his fingernails, between his toes, the blue walls. Inside he expects to find a hair-dryer upstairs, but makes do with a towel job and very little body until his hair starts to revive somewhere around ten, when the sun comes out from behind clouds and it (his hair) sort of puffs out like feathers. The snored-in look is what he wants and would admit to. The party-crashing look. By now this opaque girl who baby-sits for the family is hungry too. She bounces down on the counter a thousand grams of bacon from the freezer. His swimmer's gut coils audibly when ice hits the pan. Fat in the air!

Shit in the fan. Some people's pleasure is another's cross. He hangs around, swimming and napping on the pool deck in his gaunchwear, sending out for pizza when lunchtime rolls around. But when the party looks like it could pick up again, music-wise, the hosts stay in bed, and their kids, taking dutiful turns on the trampoline, look appalled at how one leftover guest can command such tolerance from their folks. He feeds them anyway, including the baby-sitter and her boyfriend – a friendly freshman his own age with no hatred of cars – a number 15 combination. He has one more snooze, with his hostess's pink-dressed breasts in mind, before he goes home on a number 14, transferring to a number 9.

His housemate is out of town looking for a life preserver. Money, what else, to finance a noodle-packaging scheme for pork and chicken Chinese soups. There is no blackberry pie. There is a seventy-year-old wooden bungalow in decay, rented from a land-lord now looking to level it, at which point his friend (who'd offered him a room here when an offshore swine decided to knock over his building downtown) would be expected to cart away his antiques. Even their burglars declined that job. Antique's the upscale word his friend uses for any basement junk of potential value from here to old age. This basement is as rank and neglected by them as the yard is by their landlord, a Portuguese contractor who builds houses, condos, and is wanted by the city for dumping toxic waste, extract of homemade deck stain – only the city doesn't know it's him they're looking for. Phone calls to city hall are not returned. Graft is rampant and capitalism flourishes. You could publish stuff like this: fire off a pamphlet for Hammer Co-op.

The afternoon sun is hot. Ash trees are growing out of the garage, the lawn is kneehigh. A rhododendron has gone berserk, maybe ten years ago, and morning glory snakes through blackberry vines that've suffered the back fence to disappear in their clinging. A cherry tree drapes the whole small yard in shade.

To pretend he doesn't spy on bikinis from the sunroom, he goes outside this Sunday and sits figuring at the swaying picnic table. He's trying to balance numbers and survive. He can still see bare backs through the pickets. They lie in long grass basking, baking, in the fallen seed. Renters proliferate through these houses that landlords decline to keep up, in exchange for moder-ate rents. But the word is out. *Buzzword.* For in a diminishing world of rented houses, rainforested lots, impoverished tenants, it's this word 'renewal' that's become the euphemism for demoli-tion, clear-cutting and eviction. Grass grows in gutters, suites carve up rooms, and pigeons land on roofs as often as pizza flyers on porches. Renewal is no longer an option, but policy. In time their own house will also become the pink townhouse with brass numbers across the alley.

'Hi, there.' Arf. He'd invite the bikinis across for coffee but the Bing cherry's shade doesn't encourage it. So he's left to figuring with a pencil. He doesn't glance up to notice if there are any cherries. They're finished anyway.

What the bottom line comes down to is whether, if he takes up his grandfather's offer to housesit in the country, he can live on welfare cheaper than here. Cheaper, but what happens to pleasure? Vancouver offers pleasures he can't afford, unless he counts richbashing – Bingo! – cars and sometimes hospitality. (Still, he paid for the pizza.) The woman he really desired, with swell nachos in a black sweater, he didn't even get her name before she left the party at a decent hour with her husband. If he had would it've mattered, with such a difference in their ages? He can still feel the stiffening effects of the way her dark eyes spoke to him, as she sipped her husband's rye. Christ, rye. And boiling water made a toddy, he told her, while settling for ice and no seltzer himself, thanks. She poured. With her he could *go* for the bourgeois life of pointy red boots and agree it needn't always be jangly bracelets and love in a cottage. Arf. They could dispute and bicker too.

Still, the bourgeois world is too much with him, and the age of noise bears no mercy. Car alarms bleat in the night, by mistake, maybe not. There are radios now on motorcyles, gas grass blowers on sidewalks, and no mufflers on the lawnmowers. Jets land, they take off – no one even minds the damn seaplanes. The Coast Guard beats up the Bay in a hydrofoil to rescue foolish yachters from themselves. What about tapedecks on beaches, power shovels in yards, and junk calls on the telephone? Main traffic arteries. 'Let's move up the hill,' the upwardly mobile wife will suggest. 'Just as much traffic up there,' comes the answer. 'Yes, but it's quality traffic.' Diesel buses, garbage trucks, articulated vehicles – bellowing, belching, bleating their lungs out in the burden of too long lives.

Should he go back to school maybe? Nowhere to go appeals to him more. He's just nineteen. It is the ultimate escape. There isn't anything he can afford he wants, and nothing he desires has a price. He isn't blind. Having a social conscience unlike anybody else makes him weird in their eyes – they never say why, they never get past his social gracelessness that really is, *he* knows, satirical.

Here in the city, pleasure is about leaving behind an impression of yourself. Burglars, builders, bores are in it up to their hips. The only trouble with self-abuse in the sunroom is it leaves nobody else with an inkling. It deflates on its own. So all the good bad pleasures are about power, revenge, egoism. He doesn't know what the good good pleasures might be. Love, of course, he guesses. Having a good job and no elephant to weigh you down. It's a joke how badly he yearns to be part of the fucking tradition, with a party to go to, an address book full of names, a bank book full of numbers, an old General Motors muscle car. The all-American guy with his girl on the gearshift. He studies his figures. Listen, he doesn't care where he lives. If there is one guy he wants to escape it is the voyeur with the means and nothing else in his grasp.

— SON —

I decided to become a great man. It was in me to be so, the expansiveness, the generosity of spirit, the exhilarating release from obsession and pettiness. It would take courage. I would have to be brave. I was going to change the way people looked at me – insofar as they looked at me at all, this job I have – the way I looked at myself. I would accomplish more in the day's hours than I ever had before. I would be discussed, not always without envy, and I would make my mark on Time.

But this by itself was not enough. It would be enough to delight in my own talents, discover the consistency in my inconsistencies, and live musically. Breathing to the long phrase I would sound melodious, give of myself in a manner not given by me before, and behave with simplicity, compassion, wonder. I would be my wife's lover. I would cultivate my children with the fervour of a man aware of going *pfft* tomorrow. I would adopt an orphan, start up a foundation for dispossessed Haitians, enroll in a Spanish language lab. I would speak at banquets on issues of the day. So help me, I would.

I would address school children, art students, Rotary clubs, whoever in God's green city invited me – executive officers of trust companies (I know some) willing to listen to fairer ways of renewing mortgages without acrimony. I would wake up from my lethargic, sometimes cynical, manner of greeting the future and plan parties in my home. Dinner parties, surprise parties, neighbourhood bashes and garden brunches. Friends, not contacts, were to come first.

My door was to be open at all times, phone number listed, my way with the world frank. I would find the time after office hours to amuse and educate my children, compose a Russian novel, read poetry on my own far into the night. Think up songs and engage a librettist. Sing my heart out in the shower, learn to prosper on five hours' sleep, take piano lessons and certified instruction, possibly, in French cooking.

As much as anything I would discover the value, no, the pricelessness of time, and think of wasting it as the unforgivable sin. Except for very special programmes, I would give up watching TV. I would no longer insist on having supper watching the news. As a family, we were going to converse over meals and share our experiences, anxieties, jokes. I would listen to my children's jokes, try to answer their riddles, learn to interest them in the larger world. 'Why did the little moron eat his shorts, Dad?' I would curtail my opinions. I would encourage them to bring me their homework, help my wife shop for their clothes, take them travelling as my greatness spread.

I would pay the babysitter extra to dress up as Elizabeth Barrett Browning and recite to them *Sonnets from the Melanese*. I would enroll them in tennis, the cello, Japanese. When time came, I would encourage them to borrow the Camry, treat their friends generously to our food and rec room, hold after-grads in their own home. (*Sonnets from the Portuguese*, isn't it?) Before shuffling off this mortal coil I would see them dandled, delighted, and dowried. I would drop the stern way I treated my first son – sour and sarcastic though he was – miss him more and send out a diplomatic mission. I would throw a party of reconciliation and maybe even kill a fatted calf.

In the spring, I would succumb to the lure of gardening and dig new rosebeds for my wife. I would learn the difference between a bud and a scion. I would plant wisteria and prune suckers from the lilacs. I would stop the laurel hedge from taking over my present, uncomfortable house. In fact, why not, we would move up the hill to a split-level view of the ocean from here to Binh Dinh.

What a change!

I would learn to carpenter and build my wife a gazebo for tea parties with her friends. I would encourage her to buy filmy clothes to enhance her softness, take vacations on her own, see herself as a woman of the world. And if she were to take a lover, I would understand and forgive. And also weep.

In my professional life I would be practical and reliable, considerate and unassuming. I would be great without being opprobrious, fractious, or flagitious. I mean abusive, touchy, or wicked – for I would learn simplicity and burn my *Thesaurus*. Those who wished to overcome me by the strength of their personalities I would treat courteously and without indifference. I would listen in meetings for silent cries from deep inside their hearts. The promise of greatness would keep me cheerful, sympathetic, and *wise*. I would command respect when I spoke in natural, winning ways – though my search for oratorical models would always take a back seat to quiet conversation with myself. I would neither natter, flatter, nor brag. I would speak with the deep conviction of having been, sometimes all night, at my desk over minds deeper, more encompassing, than mine. No longer would I complain. I would turn philosophy into action, compassion into deed, and flour into an elevated golden state when I baked bread in the kitchen for my family.

I would feel great in any clothes. At sales conferences and at the beach I would look terrific because of what shone from within! I would accept the religious beliefs of others, not as evidence of their shallowness, or confirmation of their received spirits, but as the benefits of doubt one always must have about impersonal matters of the universe. I would accept their need for religion as I would in others a need for astrology, lotteries, and unions. I would go up on my toes in secret pleasure at my iconoclasm, for I would enjoy sniffing out the radical hydrant of my heart. I would nourish my mettle by facing nothing alone. I would be great because of this willingness and ability to have it both ways.

I would make sacred the secular ways of us all. I would listen to great music, Berlioz's *Requiem*, and have the courage to sprinkle my Desert Island choices with rock 'n' roll songs – evergreen greats, golden oldies – which come from the passionate years when greatness was still a dream. I would practise tithing by giving money to charities (a tenth of my income to strangers is surely a requirement of greatness?). I would tithe, temper, and transform. (I would try to corral my alliteration, when provoked by tenderness.)

I would remember my childhood and go back to visit my parents, laugh at my father's jokes, fall in love again with Perumbur. I would purchase land by the river, build a summer house there, and share paradise with my children.

I would travel within the restrictions and responsibilities placed upon my time, by spending time at home. I would bear my greatness with unaffected lightness, kindness, and popularity. Like La Bruyère I would detect false greatness in the unsociable and remote, the careful and humourless. All the same, I would spurn greatness for the sake of being great (unlike the famous who cultivate fame for its own pleasure), and know that real greatness rests on more than solipsism. I would decline requests for interviews more often than I accepted them. Reticence would prove my distrust of the horn-blown name, my admiration for accomplishment that dared speak its own. I would become less jealous, intolerant, and erratic. Would I ever, would I always. I would stop whining for the world. I would finally grow up.

— FATHER —

'I'm looking forward to this,' says his wife. 'When do we start?' They're standing inside a picnic basket, creaking wicker when they move. A flame above is keeping things warm for them inside the colourful, billowing dome. Who wouldn't believe in Heaven? A champagne breakfast afloat over Pattaya's a long way from breakfast with mallards off the back patio in Perumbur. Country doctor, retired, he checks his watch and fingers a gondola cable, its pulse twitching to be off. 'Once we tip out a little sand,' he jokes, 'we're gone.' But it's hot air that will determine their departure, not sand. Loyally, she acknowledges the joke. His joky style goes way, way back, to courtship in the Stone Age when her hourglass figure first led him into comic sublimation. Over the years he found house calls went off better with a joke. 'D'you hear the one our Ted told me the day we took off, about the pacifist Catholic who refused to ...?' So he gets carried away, so what's pleasure anyway but transportation? By bending over backwards out of their basket, he can read small letters stamped on the balloon's collar, and wonders how this ad could possibly be read from the ground. Convexity prevents him seeing the elephants, but much higher, encircling the whole top third of their present world, are Indian elephants attached trunk-to-tail, plodding lightly, it would appear, around the ethereal elements of silk and hot air. If someone happens to be settling early into a beach chair, that person could probably see the beasts hovering over palms, an illusion of weight, bulk, and seams.

Their mahout, or whatever you call this driver of the Elephant Walk balloon, emerges from the Palace Hotel with a bucket on a stand, two glasses and a wired-up magnum stuck in ice, followed by a white-jacketed waiter bearing a covered tray the size of a small airport, glinting in the sun. 'Yummy, breakfast,' says his wife. To the small sandy-haired man climbing the step-stool with his bucket, she declaims, 'Our life, our soul, our gondolier!' Quoting? 'I wouldn't know,' she says. 'Thought I just made it up.' Doctor looks heavenward in a big parody of tolerance: Fly Cathay Pacific, command the little letters – in case he's forgotten. 'You folks feeling hungry?' An American mahout, by the sound of him, his balloon having flown all the way from Paris, folded neatly in a cargo hold. 'We'll get flying as soon as I ... Hang on, now.' *Whoooooosh* ... Increasing his bottled jet from Bunsen burner to acetylene torch to flame thrower, till the entire heated-up vessel is straining at its anchor, he prepares to cast off by making sure the toy table in their basket is OK to receive the waiter's hot tray. They his first guests or what? Housekeeping seems foreign to him. 'All set for liftoff? Stand by in your places for liftoff.' The wicker protests. But then, look, the three of them rising gently over the Gulf of Thailand, trying to salvage perspective, not drop it, as when passing from one element into another.

He knows immediately now what's been missing since leaving home for their look at Asia, and why, touring Manila, Bangkok, this Thai resort, he chose long ago to turn his back on cities to practise in the country. Very simple, just listen, between these intermittent whooshes when the mahout goads his balloon a little higher ... the silence! It's the silence he values! No zoom of pink-turbaned Sikhs on rented motorcycles, no whining water scooters bouncing off waves, no go-go music from the rash of open-sided bars along Beach Road. Not on your life. Up here the champagne cork pops with the thrilling echo it'd make inside a vast cathedral's dome. 'To us Asian impostors!' she toasts, including their American gondolier, who won't drink on the job – only pour, goad, and pilot them – all set to take the lid off breakfast. 'Look,' she points, 'there's our hotel with the sunburnt prawn!' The emblem arches high over the Regent Marina's sign. She's balancing her effervescent glass by its stem, in the mood for a good chatter, despite a cold. 'Why do we say swimming pools are kidney-shaped? Are they, really?' He's distracted by a – doesn't answer till she – 'Yoohoo! Will the real doctor please stand up?' My dear one. 'You think,' he tells her, 'the makers are going to sell any pools to the cocktail set by calling them liver-shaped? Suck 'em up!' Is what Don Ho used to tell them in the fifties, sixties? on their first ever extraterrestrial hols. After the floorshows they'd watch 'To Tell The Truth' on a black and white TV in their room, looking down on Waikiki ... Voyeurs! 'Lookit, I'm going to put my pistol in your holster and cock it,' he would tell her with a Mai Tai under his belt. 'Get ready to die, bad girl.' Undoctorly of him, that.

'Go ahead and use the floor of the gondola,' says the gondolier. Their life, their soul, their mahout. Gary Moore in a brushcut. 'Good idea not to drop anything out of a balloon, you never know.' Not even Kleenex, for she's blown once, twice, to rid herself of phlegm picked up from gusts of Hyatt air conditioning in Tokyo. And she's blowing to make her ears pop, since the balloon has risen faster than a – Maybe her middle ear's infected. With a cold she's been lucky, not having to hear Asian din the way it's meant to be heard, not in Guam anyway, where, for goodness' sake, they found themselves on an unscheduled refuelling stop, except they ended up on the ground for ten hours, and *she* didn't need the earmuffs offered at the shooting gallery they were taken to, where the range-master at the Wild West Gun Club – who ran the show for Japanese tourists – handed her a .44 magnum, compliments of Cathay Pacific, and told her to live out her fantasies with the paper men straight down range. The one in the middle was sitting on the fence when she got to him with a live, if less than full charge, *blam*, Son-of-Sam sound, blowing the barrel cool at her lips, and with her cold she couldn't smell the cordite. Better up here, where she thinks she can smell the salty northeast monsoon. He sniffs. His nose packing up or what? Either aging membranes or the champagne bubbles have succeeded in corking it. So he gazes instead. A country club has spread out below them as they drift inland, and the view makes up for his loss of smell. He feels like swinging. 'You have a course at home,' she says, 'you never use. You're a member.' *Whoooooosh* ... Man in charge gives them a goose to arrest the inland drift, and then uncovers her steaming eggs for breakfast. He *can* smell after all! Microwaving, like the neutron bomb, seems to put the heat where it belongs without cracking the china.

'Stand over here,' she says, 'and have your breakfast by me, Doctor. I have a woman's ailment I want to complain about.'

It's like being in a beer commercial over the Canadian prairies, when a helicopter camera circles the balloon, and we see a waving couple, wind bearing them in the direction of foothills. Except a chinook would be blowing from, not to, the foothills, so where they'd really be heading with a Molson was Hudson Bay. She wants a cuddle. Can he cut his sausage and pat her bottom at the same time? Chew gum and have a gander? Time was they used to paint each other with the little tautologies of tongues, and have the world to themselves. Well, don't they still? Good breeding ignores a mahout. But what of the invisible cook who prepared their breakfast – could *he* possibly prove intrusive? Who knows any more? Hairnets, plastic gloves, face masks *de rigueur* in the Rajneeshi commune for couples relaxing into missionary positions – and Safeway, where food comes from, today sounding like a condom factory! President Suharto, whose country's health clinics are next on their list, has the biggest growth industry in the Third World. *Should* they look for his condom factory on Java? All the President needs to get into now, for sustained growth, is razor blades.

'D'you hear the one about two rubbydub dope addicts sharing

the same needle?' he asks their mahout. 'Social worker asks them if they aren't afraid of contracting AIDS. The older one says nah, they're both wearing condoms.' Arf, arf. The gondolier laughs like their Ted in Perumbur. A sardonic sound, but it's a jungle everywhere these days; you need *some* kind of camouflage for self-protection. Take the last time they went for a walk in the city, they saw a seal rolling in waves along the seawall, dead. Plugged by a fisherman and brought in on the tide – or victim of a toxic breakfast afloat in the wrong element?

She can't finish her omelette for coughing. In fact the cold has sunk to her chest as they've risen. To release the phlegm and bring it up requires a patient hacking. No picnic for an *old* couple in a balloon, even when you can afford champagne instead of lager. What if one of them has to pee from it? From the champagne? The gentleman farmer in him spies the champagne icebucket melting; but would she use that? A bucket? Possibly Kleenex. How did the raj once pee in baskets atop its imperial elephants? With a very strict – Nah, barely a one-arfer that one. He draws her attention overboard again to the parachute beneath them, rising from the beach, a man in harness towed by a speedboat: the apple of God's eye. 'Yes,' she replies, choking, 'had *we* not drifted by hitched to a silkier apple.' Their balloon's swung back for the ocean now, rolling down Beach Road over taxis as the wind picks up. 'A knot or two,' agrees their man, 'judging by ground speed.' The playground of Asia, catering to Iranians, Germans, Indians, Frenchmen, Americans – pedophiles, packaged tourists, homosexuals, transvestites, honeymooners, sailors. 'All of us here for pleasure ...' It's a little like Alexandria in the war, where he'd even managed to enjoy himself. 'Listen, Molly, if you feel like spitting, don't care what the street signs say. Gob. We're nearly over the sea now.'

He swallows the last of his French toast and peers down in search of the caftaned Egyptian in a fez who prefers his ratty-haired Thai women to walk several feet to the rear; or the three-hundred-pound Arab, creased by fat and bathing trunks, eating dates from a cellophane pouch and joking with a prostitute who – *Whooooooooooosh* ... Guests wave from the compound of the Royal Cliff Hotel as they sail up and over its hill. Consider the toadstool grass canopies along the golden sand. Consider the double-decker cruise launches at anchor. Consider – consider how wonderful he feels with no more edges to his life, how boundaries lap over, flow into, are wide open to possibility and unrestricted by any need to persuade a colleague, say. No axe to grind, no view to put, no personal changes to undertake on pain of failure. Lately, so *many* flights beginning and ending with the smell of jet fuel, their entries and exits at airports, turning him into a voyeur with nothing but time on his hands, sand. So? Honorary visits to rural clinics? Will the real doctor please stand up! Is he the man on the left, the man in the middle, the man – Still, he no longer misses the news. Watching the news from Afghanistan – is it months ago now? – he was saying Kalashnikov at home. Had he heard the name right, Kalashnikov? Rebels were manufacturing Kalashnikov rifles. In border towns the Afghans were copying Kalashnikov rifles they had captured from the Russians. Saying aloud the tongue rollers on the news he'd felt informed. It was a feeling he'd mistaken for knowledge and having a place in the world. Kalashnikov. Tamil Tigers. SDI ... But lately he hasn't sensed any loss of place, though he's missed the news and something to get his mouth around. Ethical Mutual Funds. Tunagate ... He used to be away to the races when a new world popped up on the news. Interferon. Smack. Now, having travelled *this* far, he's begun to lose the focus he once thought mattered. Attila the Hen? Consider yesterday's glass-bottomed boat –

'I think Ted's too sarcastic for his own good,' she's saying, her coughing arrested for now. 'He can't go on with that chip on his shoulder. I think housesitting in the country will be good for him. A winter of frost in the fields is full of surprises.' Providing we reap what we sow. Too earnest a son breeds another one rolling in waves of distemper and no life jacket. Poor Ted, even Devin, both adrift, business schemes coming out of Devin's ears ... But so am I adrift, at my age still, in more knots of wind than I really care for, see, under the red, white, and blue? Colours of Thailand. And half a dozen other countries, including Heaven, you can bet. '... So anyway, when they get to the pearly gates, St. Peter salutes them, and one of them notices he's wearing only a single stripe ...' The three-arfers have that little something extra, an indefinable atmosphere you could say, the appetite brought to them – or maybe it's the way the cook times his plates. Who can say? A joky atmosphere for sure runs through little tragedies. Like these poor country clinics; even this Italian restaurant they've been going to, run by Thais ... very funny, actually, very nourishing. 'You folks enjoy your breakfasts?' inquires the mahout. What is it about the friendliness of Americans at breakfast, the highway waitresses, the – 'That there you're looking at is the USS *Something* helicoptor carrier – but if you don't mind, I'm gonna give us another burn, 'cause we shouldn't be drifting offshore. This wind has started to pick –' *Whooooosh* ...

But it makes little difference, the wind's got them revolving like a slow corkscrew now, aided and abetted by champagne, and gliding toward American naval power, the same pair of anchored ships they cruised past yesterday, among their fellow passengers a hedonist French couple, grooming each other's tanned skins like monkeys, waving mischievously at ship-marooned sailors, young woman's breasts bouncing like volley balls, the sailors hooting, the warship underneath them flexing muscle at Cambodia, where recent dry season offensives under way by Khmer guerrillas (according to *The Bangkok Post*) were drawing sharper than normal response from the Vietnamese. Was he starved after all for news? Molly thought so. Yet these ships made him feel like they were a lot closer *to* the news. Valour. They'd appeared overnight. Last night their sailors were already trickling ashore in civvies, headed for the Disco Duck, squashed inside little Toyota trucks that served as taxis. He and she had had to assure one suspicious boy Ted's age five baht was the going rate, so that would be ten for him and his girl. 'Yeah?' This sailor said he especially didn't trust the glass booths where you changed money in the open on the street. So the doctor asked his wife if the navy shouldn't invest in Michelin guides, and not just condoms, for its sailors. 'For heaven's sake,' she is saying to their own guide, 'we're heading for Coral Island. We were just there yesterday.' *Whoooooooooosh* ...

Fire, air. It turned out the gondola they'd all climbed into yesterday, as soon as their launch anchored in the cove, had floorboards that lifted to reveal a glass bottom when they raised their legs. The guide had cut the outboard engine and they'd drifted a while over brown coral, looking for tropical fish. They didn't see one. Didn't matter. Peering from one element into another they saw only water, finally, so they passed over that, once the guide got his putt-putt going, to the shed ashore. (This earth, or rather sand, underfoot – as they ate a fish lunch and flapped away at flies – was nothing as nice as Phuket Island, said the French couple.) Coral Island had been a jungly destination, forty-five minutes offshore ... Wait though. It's closer by balloon, even if the mahout refuses to look when they point it out to him. 'Don't worry, folks, these knots'll die down, we'll catch the next bus back.' *Whooooooooooooosh* ... Their gondolier, the fire fumbler. He rebuffs the big wind – or is trying to. Her coughing resumes. How her hourglass figure has filled in around the bottom, how this standing around's no good for the legs. She gets hold of her own throat and gives it a good throttle, because she wants to speak without choking. 'Aren't we overdue?' she wonders. 'I mean for the amount we paid – because by an hourly rate we've already been up in the air close to ... I mean we're floating to beat the band in the direction of Malaya, aren't we?' His life, his soul for fifty years, a billion times lovelier – What's one more flight in an unscheduled tailwind? 'For Godsake, Molly, let the man alone. Let's enjoy the experience.' But it's hard sightseeing on your pins all day, the veins in a tourist leg start to look like rivers draining into –

'Say,' he asks politely, 'I wonder if we *are* heading a bit off course?' *Whooooooooooooosh* ... Maybe drinking champagne in the tropical sun is their real problem, lightheadedness, two airheads in need of gravity? Time to pull a valve maybe. Maybe if they both sobered up they could encourage their man to make landfall on Coral Island, bring them down with a bump in the jungle, where they'd be in touch with earth again. If he keeps on mahouting around with this Bunsen burner he's going to miss the whole bloody island ... 'I mean we've already sailed downwind of the warships, Laurie ...' (Hard to tell exactly how fast you're drifting when the waves all look the same. Isn't that his name, Laurie?) 'Keep your hat on, Doc. Doing our best. See if there's any more champagne.' Cables pulsing, wicker in a tizzy, and her cough revving. Well, might as well lean back and enjoy this freedom from being in touch with any knowledge of how the world operates. The mastery of the thing! Listen, pretty soon they'll be throwing more than Kleenex overboard, just to keep up in the world! Magnum next, the icebucket once they all have a pee to lighten bladders, their cutlery, the plates, glasses, tray next, then the whole damn table ... Far harder for the rich ballast to pass into heaven, than the camel ... 'D'you hear the one,' asks the sandy-haired gondolier, 'about the sailor in the desert who thinks he sees an albatross drinking lion piss?' Coarse professionalism annoys the doctor – who decides this joker's going to get the best of him if he doesn't scratch memory for something just as cavalier to keep the orchestra playing ...

Scratching now, all he comes up with are cathedral tours in Europe when he and Molly never once commented to one another, nor, as far as he knew, to themselves, about religious experience occasioned by apses, holy stones, and little monk dolls for sale with moveable dongs. There wasn't any. Does this mean they aren't traditional? Father, Son, and Holy Ghost? Experience is what they were after, mild pleasure, a good enough time without being greedy. *Whooooooooooooooooooosh* ... They *have* given of themselves to their community and family, without regret, and never been, so far as they felt, excessive in their longings to get away; nor, during time away, wished to prolong their absence or indulge themselves without wishing they could be sharing all this with children and grandchildren. They were salt-of-the-earth folk when you got right down to the sniffy – Hey, Molly's started reading a magazine and looking quite calm in the middle of all this spinning. A frequent flyer by virtue of her stiff upper – Mind over matter. 'It says here,' she reads, '"champagne breakfast in the sky with an exciting balloon ride around the resort".' Glances up. 'By the look of it, we're getting our baht's worth. How much fuel's left in the tank?' Her pages whipping in the breeze. He asks to peruse them. She gives them over with a warning that reading makes you dizzy. *Whooooooo–* Ignoring yet another quick ascent (this hot air's brutish the way it rushes the vacuum) he asks what she'd like to do upon their return this afternoon. 'Mm,' she decides, 'a snooze?' And what about a restaurant this evening, the Italian place again, or try somewhere new? 'Oh, let's just have a quiet supper in the hotel and go up to bed early.'

He pokes calmly through *Explore Pattaya*, Vol. 1 No. 2. Since this is to be their last night in the resort, he tots up pleasures they've had insufficient time to taste. Not counting waterscootering, they've done no laser sailing or windsurfing, chartered no boat to go deep-sea fishing, ridden no hydrofoil, not played golf, or even gone for a demonstration by real working elephants at the Elephant Kraal near Pattaya's Orphanage (see map p. 16). They continue to sink like an elevator, but never mind, maybe they're saving fuel for a favourable updraft. '... We've also missed scuba diving, rollerskating, shooting at the indoor range at Tiffany's (.38 bullets are nine baht each, targets six baht), horseback riding, hill climbing, tennis, waterskiing, archery, parasailing, badminton – is that enough for you? – camping at the YMCA camp on Jomtien Beach, boxing (evidently there's a training camp seven kilometres from Pattaya, where we could've rented gloves, speed and body bags), bowling, and darts. We could've also worked out on weights at Frank's Gym, just below our hotel, for an hourly rate of one hundred baht, including sauna.' She's about to start hacking again. By the length of this, or any other holiday list, it's as if they've never partaken of the least of what life's party has to offer, so why bother travelling anyway? The clinics? He turns to the last page. 'Come to think of it, my chevalier, we haven't really eaten any Thai food ... Which does remind me of the Indian from Madras, who liked his curry hotter than an engine, so one day his daughter ...' *Whooooooooooosh* ... Cough's back, with a little nausea it appears, dizziness. Mucus penetrating her middle ear via the Eustachian tube. Up and down they go like a ride at Playland.

Their hearts in hiding, stirred for these years together, and they complain about catarrh and a little drift to the west? He can remember how sheer trudging kept them going in the thirties, that and the old rattletrap wedding gift to themselves, before their valley began earning enough to pay him, following his return from the medical corps overseas. When things seemed bleakest, they had put their faith in the future. Their son who amounted to the future, learned from them that renewal was ever possible. Trust to the future when things looked blue – like now, the sky above, the sea below. Up and down, pleasure and distress, they seem interchangeable when you get nicely humming on a morning air. 'I don't think we really need this table, do we folks, now that breakfast is over? It'd give us a nice lift if we chucked her, hey?' So over she goes with the last of breakfast. *Whooooooooooooooosh* ... Hard to say how close they're coming to water before these lofty reprieves. Waves slope longer to their troughs out here, they deceive the landing eye. But hang on, listen ... Two men and a young woman in a boat, nothing to eat for a month, the first fellow taps the second on the shoulder and whispers in his ear – Three men in a boat, no water for seven days, the third one turns to the first one and says – Is the real captain the man on the left, the man in the middle, or the man on the right? Will the real – So anyway, they'd been standing around in this basket it seemed since the sun came up. To the east the sky had burned like their legs were starting to now. And when he couldn't stand it any longer, the older gentleman turned to the young mahout of his soul and said ... 'I don't think my wife is up to this much longer. You can see, she's suffering from nausea. I'd advise you to put us down the first chance you get.' *Whooosh* ... The flame is getting shorter, the burns briefer. So anyway this older gentleman decided he'd just have to take matters into his own hands. Wh– he began to say. Blow! Wh– which of us is more valuable than the other if and wh– when it comes to sacrificing one of us for the sake of the rest?

What rest, he thinks, when we, ah my dear, fall ... You see this older gentleman figured the younger man was going to jettison the past, so he wanted to make sure he – *Whooo–* Not much gas left in the old bottle now. Better blow for all we're worth ... Wh– blow! So the old gentleman turns to his wife, you have to understand this, and he gives her one of those mouth-to-mouthers, deeper than the very ocean, with their tongues swimming around in there like bottom fish, tickling the grainy floor of the hemisphere itself, when – *Whoo– Who–* Flame's dead, hot air cooling fast ... love alone on its way back up, and nothing to bottle it with for the next journey, a no-arfer, no coming up for air, no ... Blow! Wh– Who is she, this mother? Wh– What elements conceive us? D'you hear what the doctor says to this svelte young thing comes into his office, Molly?... Arf, he says, sitting up like a puppy. *Wh– W–* So he blew out the party candles and turned to travel. But he got tired of travelling and decided to set about fishing with wh– what health of his remained in the narrowing craft of the world.

COMMENT: *Just before we went to press Keefer Ives passed away, aged seventy-three. His Comment below and perhaps also his story were written while he was quite ill with cancer. Keefer will be sadly missed. To the end, his was the fluent mind of a generous reader and an affectionate soul. Our reading club would like to commend his memory with a quotation from Samuel Butler – as suggested by his friend Jim Constance: 'A friend who cannot at a pinch remember a thing or two that never happened is as bad as one who does not know how to forget.' – P.M.*

Although I am not an autobiographical writer, *Memoir* is in part a thinly disguised account of a reunion my wife and I had with the place we met in many years ago. But it began with Blake and the annoyance of an implanted voicebox.

I especially enjoyed writing the bits describing the past as I remembered it – summer nights, Sinatra – though it wouldn't be fiction if I hadn't somewhat jazzed it up. My daughter for instance, a happy mother of three, is the least likely model for Alice. And my wife is not Della Morra. As a photographic equivalent of my feelings toward the woman I married, however, I would have to confess the story is pretty accurate.

I was reading Blake deep into a difficult night last November, when the translucent past suddenly placed on the empty sofa beside me a young man I recognized as myself. I felt he recognized me, too. Quite simply, the future and the past were at peace in me and I learned for the first time what it was to feel truly, marvelously, voiceless.

– K. I.

K. Ives

Memoir

HOTEL KISSING is more passionate, I decided, because a hotel takes
the individual kisser out of his or her own home. Or in case of a
couple, especially an older pair of guests, out of their own home.
Inhibitions fall away. Grudges and irritations vanish. This is the
pleasure of travel. Or rather of a hotel – since you don't have to
travel far to stay overnight at the Palace Hot Springs Hotel – the
way it is sure to improve canoodling between a man and a woman.
You have to remember, and this is the point. The best way for a
partner to seem exotic is for you to feel foreign too.

So get out of town, come to the mountains.

Some such come-on is what I wrote down in the summer of
1951, on a sheet of hotel stationery, to show to the manager who had
hired me at the Palace. Did I feel this was how the hospitality
industry should attract business? That I would make my mark as a
deskbound pimp? Of course, it was not then called the hospitality
industry, not until degrees in hotel management came into vogue
and made more sense than the kind of apprenticeship that once
yoked me. My apprenticeship didn't make sense even then, not to
the manager, who read over my proposal for an advertising blitz-
krieg of the Lower Mainland. '"Hot springs",' he remarked drily,
'will no doubt be taken in the lewd way you have in mind. But
"hotel kissing"? You make it sound like we're offering copulation
with the building itself.'

From the front office I rotated to the laundry room, where he
said I would receive notice of further rotations in keeping with the
terms of my apprenticeship. I waited.

When the hotel called the other day after thirty-five years, I felt
no desire to accept an invitation to come back for a centenary cele-
bration. I told the caller she must think I was a whipping post with a

short memory. What I actually said was I would have to get back to her on that one. 'But the dance,' she urged, 'the whole weekend's going to be wild.' Some such come-on. I recognized the hyperbole, which held out to me, and I suspect a million other past staffers and guests, festivities befitting the grand old girl who still availed herself of a garter belt. Or maybe she said a Walter Scott. Something dildoish, probably, in keeping with my young caller's idea of an old girl's wild time.

She went on. As for returning stolen property, she felt the memorabilia contest might interest someone of my 'vintage', who sounded like he 'got off' on history of a local nature. She was flirting with me. I had to admit it sounded wild, but I would have to get back to her on that one too. Hanging up, I supposed I could win first prize by bringing back under the guarantee of amnesty – not a bar of witch-hazel soap, or a tarnished sterling fork piked from the dining room, the usual tourist peccadillos – but a chambermaid. I had used and abused their purloined property for many years now, and it would go over very well, I thought, very humorously, Della got up in the black uniform she wore during the summer we met as lackeys in residence.

When I put it to Della over dessert that I had had a call inviting us to the centenary of our dirty laundry, she lowered her knife. 'What,' she said, 'are you talking about?' The scene of her jitterbugging, I commented, the place where she'd tramped the corridors in underwear and less. 'You remember, the palace of your first and, so far as I know, last passion for a future real estate tycoon?' She had heard this before. 'Oh, is there a reunion?' Not, I replied, as far as I was concerned. She surprised me with her riposte. 'Fiddley doo. Naturally, we're going. It'll be nice for us.'

And so we came.

* * *

It had been on the streetcars, under a raincoat, that I had learned to canoodle. This is what a wild time meant after the war, when privacy for highschoolers was a raincoat to hide under from naked bulbs and the drafts of folding doors. A wild time on a streetcar consisted of jerky stops, lurching corners, and spotty acceleration.

It is a wonder we learned anything, except how to control lip drift. Yet few places in life were so stimulating, except Happyland, beneath the timber girders of the Shoot-the-Chutes, where overhead the boats went down even faster than we, in hiding, could launch tongues down one another's throats. It is unnerving how history slips away. Happyland gives way to Playland, and rides like the Giant Dipper are torn down. Who even remembers the Giant Dipper – or its reputation as an abortionist for girls in trouble? The timber joints of most rides get dry rot and rickets, the same way links that move these rides up their tracks and over the top, grind away to rust. I can still hear the wash of boats hitting the water.

After my botched apprenticeship, Della and I came back to the city as a number, later returning to the valley where I set up office as a notary public in Carthage – but only after several years as a motorman on the interurban coaches, scrubbed from the valley in 1958, the year I returned to school, the same year our little Alice entered first grade. Aside from a hundred million depositions and affidavits taken since then, contracts authenticated, bills of exchange protested, this has been my life. I wish I could call these millions hyperbole. The fact is I have not had my oil changed in thirty years.

I like to pull in to the Shell station on the highway and listen to the girl who works there clean my windshield and check my tires. This is the way she talks, broadly hinting of other things without meaning any of them. Years ago, as part of a famous advertising gimmick, she would have been asking to put a tiger in my tank. Her dirty hands on my oilpan would be enough to convince me that our daughter is right about her father, and men in general.

Alice is a lounge singer in the city, friend of a thousand men and property of none. She has taken the vow of singlehood, and is not unvocal about it. It is her conviction that husbands kill their wives – dump on their scruples, treat their friends coolly, expect submission, dole out the silent treatment if we don't get it, and, offered the least encouragement, screw around. She says that as husbands we kill them. They do not know until we are gone they have been waiting all along for their lives.

Our daughter has been unhappy. She seldom visits, and when

she does will bring along tapes to pass the afternoon. She thinks it enough that she comes. I am sorry to say we bore her, the countryside bores her, she feels Perumbur needs a coke merchant. She misses the city, yet dreads Sundays alone in it. She's really an extrovert who looks to strangers for stimulus and approval. Caveat emptor. Through her I first heard the crooner Joe Cocker sing. The name alone was enough to make me think she was putting us on. I was recumbent on the davenport.

I say crooner, which is what you would expect from someone of my generation, whose favourite song dates from our summer at the Palace Hot Springs Hotel. Each night that I went to bed under the eaves there, listening to a crystal set grounded on my bedsprings, Sinatra was singing 'You're the One'. The song seeped into my brain. I was falling in love with Della Morra and learning, not so much the words, although I did learn those, but the control and phrasing in that rendition, to croon it to this girl. I did not want to sing it any other way than the way it lay in those grooves in my head.

Since last Easter, I have been listening over and over to the other song, on the tape Alice forgot to take home. The crooner in my time has undergone a change. He has lost his nerve. He repeats the same line with gaps and spasms. He twitches like a paint shaker in the hardware store. He sings falsetto. He screams at times and can't reach notes. He has a voice like our local gravel quarry, and I imagine, when he sings, the shape and firmness of his veins, resembling pumped-up peashooters. Yet it is his persistence in face of fear that makes his song sound true. When I hear the piano and listen to Joe Cocker sing 'You Are So Beautiful' – if I were a woman, I would believe him. I am moved myself. If I sang this song to the gas station girl she would, I venture, fall in love with me.

But I too have lost my nerve.

Lost it, that is, until I did what I did tonight at the centennial dance.

* * *

I did not know until we got here who was behind the centenary celebrations. Like me, Frank Stockton had been hired to learn the hotel business that same summer, and he too had given in his notice by fall. He was very smooth. It was with Frank's hand more or less up her dress, upon my arrival in the laundry room, that I first met Della. For the next two months the three of us were inseparable, not because Frank and I were friends, but because Della could not make up her mind between us. Frank, after removing it from up her dress – and in what I wanted to believe was vengeance against ground lost – had turned his hand to real estate. He now owns commercial properties the length and breadth of this valley. In the media his reputation for having a fiscal finger in every pie is legendary.

Which is why I suspected his motives right away in this enthusiastic commitment to history of a local nature. What was he doing here?

I asked Della.

'Pimping, probably. Look at the forests.'

Before dinner in the ballroom, she and I were strolling the lakeshore recalling a summer regatta, the nights we three soaked in the hot mineral water after curfew, the laundry chutes, the ticklish masseuse, our kitchen raids, the covert love-making of guests in bedrooms and stables. This hotel is not the original, which burned up in 1920, but a reincarnation, renovated further the year before our employment. We have our own bedroom tonight, our own bathroom, but it isn't the same sort of splashy room Della remembers servicing as a chambermaid. Today the building feels worn; history has worn away its grandeur.

For the sake of curious tourists, the manager would force Frank and me to recite how a few dirty miners had discovered the steaming springs on their way home from the gold fields in the last century, when sternwheelers plied the lake with prospectors heading into the interior by ox-cart and camel. The facts titillated those guests who pretended to care. By resurrecting a regatta in 1951, the village of Palace managed to entice speedboats from as far away as Washington and California.

That summer we had wild times like skiing barefoot and stealing horses. The blue stars threw down spears; we got qualmish stomachs from August pears. A pear rots from the inside out. I don't remember if it was the same with apples but the punch line in response to *them* apples was always, sure, but do you know how the worm gets in? It was a summer of remarkable wit.

* * *

The dance was earlier tonight. There were six or seven hundred of us, swinging the night away to the Freddy Simms Orchestra, reminiscing among ourselves in swirling figures and seated at tables set up around the ballroom's sprung floor. There were balloons and streamers. There were corsages and boutonnières. There was boogie-woogie. Della wore a blue chiffon semi-formal. We noticed Frank across the room, the centre of attention at a table for the manager of the Palace, two Japanese couples, assorted dignitaries who looked like boiled beets, and Freddy Simms himself, whenever the orchestra took a break and he came off stage for a drink of something in a yellow thermos. Della suggested it would only be polite of us to go over and say hello to Frank, and ask him how he was.

'Tight, probably. Like us.'

We underestimated his geniality. Not long before the home waltz Frank started gladhanding his way around the room, flush with the success he had helped to engineer. 'Look at his wife,' whispered Della.

I saw what she meant. Frank had killed his wife. I could tell by looking at her she was dead. I was surprised he had brought along the corpse. What I actually saw at his side was a dark, ravishing girl in a black gown, certainly – by the way she was holding his arm against her breasts like a polevaulter getting ready for a run – not his daughter. Her black hair flared aggressively.

'Let's dance,' I suggested to Della.

'My feet are gone.'

'I don't think I really want a chinwag with Frank,' I croaked. Her naked chair suggested an escape, had there been time to dress it in a skirt and waltz off.

To avoid him I walked away in the direction of the bandstand. I had been drinking a lot of Okanagan wine fermented from Napa Valley grapes. Not a blend I discovered sympathetic to prudence. The orchestra had just finished a popular number, near the end of the last set, so I climbed up and shook Freddy Simms' tanned,

California-spotted hand. I chinwagged a little with the musicians, remarking properly on their instruments. I walked over to the old-fashioned microphone and looked down across the floor.

Then, into this silver watermelon of a mike, I began to croon.

No one quite knew what to make of me. I did not know what to make of myself, crooning, but the song felt liberating. The feedback was barely audible. I was picked up by a few unbuttoned musicians with sentiment in their fingers. A hush fell when I finished. I came back down to Della, right across the dance floor, and kissed her.

* * *

The rest of course you know. As our host you went up on stage to thank Freddy Simms and his orchestra, whose big-band sound you said made it seem that they must have played here in another life because of the era they had so smoothly brought back to us at the Palace. You still have a silver tongue, Frank. You thanked everybody for supporting the centenary of the hotel, and reminded us, if we had not already entered something in the memorabilia contest, to get it in by breakfast, when you would be judging the entries and sharing them with us over pancakes.

'I notice we have a menu signed by Bob Hope, from 1948, the year of the big flood. So dig around in your luggage, ladies and gents, and find something old – you all brought a memento, didn't you, for old time's sake? Maybe the long lost chandelier?' Your audience laughed and glanced up at the gold ceiling, trying to remember what it had once been like. To think if it had even existed. Perhaps an earthquake had loosened and dislodged it.

The last thing you announced, too casually I thought, was the impending sale of the hotel to Japanese interests, who were planning major renovations reckoned to appeal to honeymooning couples from Kyoto and Osaka. 'I think we owe our Japanese friends here this evening a big round of applause for saving an institution. How 'bout it, folks?'

You did not disclose whether you owned a piece of the action, Frank, or whether you were merely the promoter, the salesman, the broker. I remember you once boasting to me you were a backdoor man. I thought you meant *re* your aspirations at the hotel, which you did mean, but not in the backroom way of getting ahead. You were always louche. This evening, did you want us to think you were returning something to the old girl, before dumping her to offshore interests? Your philanthropy made me think how those crooning machines I once heard young Japanese clubbies singing into – probably it was a filler on the news hour – made them sound very smooth.

Long after the dance, Della and I were sitting alone in the churning sulphur pool, when who should come in but a couple with a flashlight. 'I knew where to find these two burglars,' you said, shining the light in our eyes. 'Didn't I tell you we used to sneak down here after hours, back in the dark ages?'

'Hello, Frank,' we both said.

'This is Clark,' you said, relocating the beam. 'Clark, say hello to Bill Williams. Bill Bills, we called him. He's a prince. How are you, Della?'

And so there we were after thirty-five years, noticing how only one of us looked the way we used to, free of gravity and the rust of time. Your companion smiled, and slipped into the rotating water beside me in her black, one-piece suit. She is what, Frank, twenty-two? It is unlikely her wardrobe will acquire colour for at least another ten years.

'You old dog,' you said, coming down the steps wearing a diver's belt, which was really your girth. 'Who'd have thought you had the woof still in you?' But you were looking at Della, not me. 'What've you both been up to after half a lifetime? Where's home anyway?'

'I liked your song,' Clark said to me, floating closer with breasts like softballs. 'Wild.' I recognized her voice from the phone call. She put her hand on my knee, under the water where no one could see it, including me. Nothing heavy or unappealing. The movement of her nails had a trace of symmetry.

You and Della sat chatting – in the horizontal shadows cast by your flashlight lying on the pool's lip. You were looking at her the way you used to, Frank, peering at her underwater breasts for a better glimpse of the future, perhaps, moving your arm up against her thigh, she told me later, with your fingers sometimes threatening more foreign parts. Do you remember how you once charmed

Charlene Downing, the Regatta Queen, but felt Della was the one, because she was distant, more alluring? Catholic? You are still a tom, Frank, sitting your kittenish companion down beside me and watching us at a distance. Were you, for old time's sake, anticipating the wild time to come?

I know I was.

The rules have changed since our time, in that rules exist where there used to be none, and the first of these is not to soak while under the influence of alcohol, which made us all violators. The rules pretty well cover the waterfront now: No bathing with nerve or cardiovascular disorders, high or low blood pressure, diabetes. You still have a handsome face, Frank, but the hot water made it perspire as if you were due any minute for a seizure down there, owing to your driven life.

Do you remember as a young man how you left Della when resigning your service to the hotel? You told me she was now mine. You were leaving and did not expect to be back. Addio, signorina. You who had already told her to expect a surprise that evening, and to leave her door unlocked. I thought you were leaving because you were fed up, as I was, with apprenticeship. I knocked. Her room was dark. She did not know it was me and said, of course, to come in. I am still ashamed to say that when I entered at last, it was under false pretences.

'Was that my surprise?' she asked, turning over at the end to face me for the first time.

So we both betrayed her. But I was betrayed, too. Nothing to be bitter about, Frank, except you both knew what I did not, for some time, recognize. That Alice was your daughter, not mine, and how later when I tried to forget all this I sounded anxious. A foghorn in heat is how Della put it. I seemed doomed to repeat the same line over and over. How could I tell Della Morra that she didn't really love me? Because her Catholic past made her refuse a ride on the Giant Dipper?

Remembering, I still sound anxious. Much to our daughter's disappointment, I've long had trouble expressing love for my wife. This is my flaw, Frank, but I suppose a very common one when most of us are killers by consent?

***

I am sitting up here in our room, in the small hours this morning, writing out this affidavit. As a voyeur, Frank, you would find nothing exotic in this, and be wrong. For I have discovered what I believe you were hoping to find tonight, by trading me your young girl for my old one. That the flesh of an older woman is imperfection worthy of desire. Some such come-on. Not a revelation that pounces like danger you spy burning bright in the bamboo, Frank. But the prospect appealed to you. You must have dreamed how singularity can inflame lust. How the blemish of the little local vein can give rise to an unaccustomed passion. This is what makes Della and not your polevaulter – who you will admit can wear a little thin – exotic. Your idea of a wild time, Frank, is shagging softballs. You really cannot imagine what you missed out on there, when Della turned you down.

I will waken her before morning and see if she doesn't agree as she reads this through, that any memoir is an amnesty in its own right. 'You see,' I will whisper to her, caressing the knobs of her spine, unbuttoning them, 'I am writing this for Frank's memorabilia contest. He is reading it right now, even as we talk. Frank is watching us here in bed, Della, with our conniving. I feel like turning to him, don't you, right now and asking him over my shoulder. "You are, aren't you, Frank? Reading this for auld lang syne? What are its chances, do you feel? I mean, will you be reading these sheets of hotel stationery to your guests at breakfast, along with that menu signed by Bob Hope, and sharing the chandelier miraculously restored?" Della, my witness. My treasure. Here, let me lick this. My dear Della. You are so beautiful to me.'

You are   so beautiful   to me

COMMENT: After Keefer Ives read his story in February, I decided to scrap the one I was planning to offer about a purser with incipient torticollis, which wasn't something I knew about anyway. Keefer seemed to be asking us how memory is kept alive in a community like ours. As it always has been, I was thinking, through juicy gossip. (Hasn't memory since the Greeks depended on oral recapitulation, till it seems *worth* repeating?)

I'm scribbling this on the bus to Richmond, where I work as a flight attendant. My mother is in a nursing home, her own memory leaking away. I often need to repeat things for her to grasp and remember them. I recall a San Francisco doctor, flying back from Hong Kong, telling me memory loss is a menopausal thing, noticed less by lesbian women than straight ones. Quack or not she went on to say that Mother, way past menopause, sounded like she depended on me to *give* her a memory.

For instance, she'll remember (wrongly) I belong to a phone tree that calls in bomb threats to Lower Mainland abortion clinics. But not remember who I fly. She's proud of the language she bequeathed me, and remembers there's a connection. Or else Edward the Fifth will be on her mind. Did his wife die and then he follow her – inconsolable – or was it the other way round? She wants to remember.

Cathay Pacific, I repeat gently, hanging up when she drifts off.

I dedicate this to Keefer's memory. And to Mother's.

– *R. H.*

Robin How

Foster Story

MR FILBERT DIED, no one guessed why, till we found out it was through grief at the death of his wife. No one knew that he'd ever been married. Until one afternoon, not long before dusk, an ageing woman paid us a visit. Our children were playing upstairs in Mr Filbert's old bedroom. It was raining outside and growing dark.

'The bit I don't get,' persisted Gwen, 'is why she bothered coming here to tell us this.'

'To set the record straight?' wondered Adele Fonyo.

'D'you hear that, Mary? As secretary we elected you to tie up the loose ends.'

'... I think she just *told* us why. To get us thinking about grief.'

'Grief?'

We pondered destiny.

'You know, the sincerity of his grief. Filbert's.'

'He was cruel, obviously.'

'Yeah, obviously.'

'Not totally. Wasn't he using her money to help his orphans?'

'More like to do her in ... By the sound of it.'

'Don't forget, she refused to have kids.'

'Okay, but do we *know* how he treated her in the sack?'

We wondered. We were young ourselves then. Someone removed Mr Filbert's doubtful snapshot from a file and we reexamined it, giving him a big benefit of the doubt.

'The fact remains, doesn't it, she refused him.'

'Patty, it's only Miss Franklin's word.'

'That's right. If you ask me,' said Norine, 'I wouldn't be surprised if she was Mrs Filbert herself.'

An appreciative *hm* went up at this brazen twist.

'Listen, there wasn't any Mrs Filbert. That was a made-up name.'

'But just suppose Miss Franklin was Mrs Filbert under another name. She'd have had to plot her own death.'

'But why?'

We were ready to say why. Let us say, heroically.

– ii –

When we found him, his house was crawling with insects: inside his sofa, in an oven he seemed never to have used, inside open pill bottles, a narrow bed, polished and now lustreless shoes waiting to be worn. Insects had squeezed out eggs into the breadbox, strung up hammocks in cupboard corners, pushed far into the drawers of his desk on colonizing expeditions, and preyed as big populations do on one another everywhere – web over wing, a misfortune of the world.

The web-and-wing theory didn't hold. Upstairs in Mr Filbert's bedroom we found a budgie flying room to room with primitive habits and a full crop. We never discovered its cage. The house itself was a mew. Alone except for his bird, Mr Filbert had been taken over on the floor and laid out like a new subdivision with roads, sewer lines and long lots. Urban blight had moved in. Ants, spiders, moths, beetles had inhabited his clothes and settled his body. Not a clock ticked on. Downstairs, the fridge shivered and then it wheezed; coughed twice like a hibernating bear, before resuming its snooze. Sealed by old paint, the window in his room invited our husbands to take shoes and break it for the country air outside. The stench put a rush on the ozone.

What surprised us were snapshots of children all over his walls. Fresh and faded, pinned to the wallpaper as if kidnapped and slipped inside, Mr Filbert's hidden life. His bedroom resembled a gallery for obsession when the heart has dried up. That's what Amy Nowens said. Even when the truth of his heart was established by our investigation of his drawers and the papers they held, along with silverfish, Q-tips and a cracked pearl fountain pen, the source of his income remained a mystery. The secret of his wife was not yet out, or even imagined.

The source of Mr Filbert's income had pined among Perumbur's less important mysteries during his lifetime, but in death when his swarm of children became known, and their poverty revealed, this secret ripened and no one cared to say above a whisper what she thought of the latest story spun of thread no stouter than a spider's.

'It's quite a romance,' said Alina Belansky, caught up in the flimsiest gossip. Alina was our sardonic one. 'O God, make us unbelievers,' said she with the busiest tongue and a taste for decay. But this was later, when the meatiest morsels were getting high.

At first the story was that his children were a restitution for self-indulgence and sin. We could easily imagine what his lapses might have been – gluttony, self-abuse, loitering around hens. Didn't matter what. Because in the end, or rather beginning, we could not abandon his orphans anyway. Their deprivation made us rethink the bratty fabrications of our own kids, who would fake starvation to get attention and a Popsicle. Mr Filbert's children had names like Pedro, Nianseye, Renuka ... each with a code name imparted for his own reasons by Mr Filbert ... Crowbar, Little Monkey, Licorice Stick. Lots of these, we discovered, had written letters down the years to thank him for becoming their dad.

Every year, as the eldest came of age and dropped away, he had quietly ordered fresh ones, extending his family by mailing out bigger and bigger cheques as the cost of its support grew with each new decade's inflation. His files bulged. His ambition showed. At his death, payments to this 'International Foster Plan' were coming up for renewal weekly, but his bank account was empty. He died intestate. A memorial society, of which Mr Filbert was a recent and prophetic member, took care of the burial.

Free publicity served to advertise our bingos. A Vancouver news crew arrived to poke around between cards, and the next evening we watched Norine Wakely itemize our war chest, such as it was, gifts like mitts and canned peaches sent to one Abdullah Aziz, for example, in the Atlas mountains. 'Can you picture the need?' she asked five hundred thousand viewers. None of them, as Amy put it later, kicked in with mud.

We required three committees, one to organize fundraising, another to collect and package gifts, a third to write letters and enclose snaps of our own brats to share with the children abroad – who didn't necessarily lack parents of their own, only the means to avoid hunger. And nakedness, probably, and the runs from pestilential water. Renewing their subscriptions we wrote to every child in turn that Mr Filbert had passed away and that the bunch of us were carrying on in his name. Mr Filbert's name. Patty Sweet was puzzled by a photograph misguidedly returned by an Egyptian family ... unless his was really a slimmer and handsomer figure than *she* remembered, Mr Filbert was also a confidence man. She showed us. The inscription on the back read: 'All the best, dear Adl, Morgan Filbert.' We said little at the time, and put it down to a latent desire of his for self-improvement.

Of his secret predilection for cash gifts, beyond an annual payment for each child, our treasurer, Nancy Lowe, just laughed. 'Having to raise fifteen thou a year for bare necessities doesn't leave a princely surplus for gifts.' Somebody else asked why we didn't assemble a collection of homemade remedies, say, to sell in stores. 'Like rubbing garlic on your eczema?' asked Nancy. She thought this one and the one about rummage sales were old-lady notions, worthy of Mrs Kabush.

– iv –

Mr Filbert died, no one guessed why, till we found out it was through grief at the death of his wife.

'But there wasn't any Mrs Filbert. That was a madeup name.'

'But just suppose Miss Franklin was Mrs Filbert under another name. She would've had to plot her own death.'

'But why?'

We were ready to say why. Let us say, heroically.

'She ran out of money like she said!'

'She resented him throwing these kids in her face!'

'He used her!'

'He was always raining on her parade!'

'He didn't appreciate her as a person!'

'She was sick and tired of making sacrifices for these kids and playing second fid!'

Norine concluded, 'The old girl had nothing left to live for. She already had dowager's hump.'

'I still don't understand,' said Gwen. 'Are we just supposed to dump these kids on a doorstep because Mr Filbert was a prick? What's her line?'

'*If* ...' cautioned Lucy, 'he was a prick. Nothing's been proved in court.' She was sucking a tender hangnail and hooked up to her Walkman like a terminal case of ennui.

'No, but it's natural to like the version you like. It's like having your favourite kid. You're not supposed to, but you do.'

Nancy said, 'Listen, though. If we only look at the facts – you know, the true facts – then the fact remains Mr Filbert, or whoever he was, died of natural causes with too damn many adopted kids and no money in the bank to support them. We've seen all this for ourselves ...' She allowed her intensity to percolate among us. 'The other facts we've been told.'

'Okay,' responded Patty. 'But aren't we always hearing about the whole world secondhand? From the boob tube? Doesn't mean it's not true.'

'I can buy that,' said Norine. 'We even have to tell ourselves a whole lot we don't really believe.'

'Like what?' asked Nancy, studying her.

'Like what?' mimicked Norine. 'Well ... Like being a mother is better than being myself. *Is* it better? I've always wondered in my worm's eye view of the Homo sapiens heart just how true that was.'

'If that's the fucking case,' said Jenny Saddlemauer, who was new that year, 'we all may as well close the book on Filbert's floozies.'

Then Alina Belansky said too much talk started to be like what happens to elastic on underpants. 'It gets loose and frays.' According to her, of all people, we had ended up with a bunch of gossip about a man named after a nut. 'Where's our prospectus?'

'By which I think,' Lucy said politely, removing her headphones, 'you mean perspective?'

In time we received fresh snaps of this child and that, from 'miserable' Mali and 'icky' Ecuador (alliterative codifiers courtesy of Jenny), adding them to the wall in Mr Filbert's room, since it was his mouldering house we got permission to squat in when the government, beneficiary of his estate, caved in and turned it over as a philanthropic shelter. Our real proposal, as we had no long-term intention of keeping on a mob of orphans – not with families of our own to tend, houses, husbands, and unspecified yearnings to do with regeneration and out-of-body experiences, provided we got to classes – was for the government to sell his acreage and create a fund for Mr Filbert's family.

But the proposal fell on deaf heads. And because we could not abandon his dependents, we voted to hang on for an entire year. We began to feel worldly. The municipal council had forgiven taxes to match the government's loan of the house. Our suspicious spouses had contributed a new roof. We continued to pay for the light. Gwen Shumka divvied up the neglected chickens among those who didn't mind bedraggled necks. 'They'll lay like nobody's business, with a little coaxing.' We exterminated the insects and caged Mr Filbert's bird, introducing it to seed and cuttle bone.

And we began bringing our own children to the shelter. We brought them to meetings, knitting bees, letter write-ins. We introduced them to their brothers and sisters standing shoeless outside hovels. Our children earned their first pen pals, by writing lavish tales of slippery skateboards and fast ponies, by sketching houses, mountain bikes, dumptrucks. We vetted their letters for racial slurs picked up from sulking fathers.

Into a second year we barged ahead with a blueberry festival, the monthly bingos, and a letter-writing campaign to encourage donations to Mr Filbert's Foster Children's Legacy. This was long after we were a forgotten story in the media. This was when some of us were already giving secret thought to mutiny – 'of dropping the whole show and splitting', as Mary Buskim put it in her slangy, self-willed way. 'Keeping ends and family together is beginning to give me Mrs Jellyby-cramp.' Mary, having no small obsession with the angularities of gossip, was a college girl who'd married down.

— vi —

Mr Filbert died, no one guessed why, till we found out it was through grief at the death of his wife. No one knew he'd ever been married. Until one afternoon, not long before dusk, an ageing woman paid us a visit.

She arrived from Lincoln, a town of five thousand, famed for harness races and car demolition derbies, beloved by our husbands since they were teenagers. Trish Sandilands answered the door, startled. We never would've guessed Lincoln was home for a caller of such fastidious appearance. Navy linen suit, white doeskin gloves, an aspirin for a hat. With accustomed dignity she accepted a straightback kitchen chair, like an endangered falcon a commanding perch. She rested a while, her considerable hazel eyes lingering on us each in turn as she pretended not to hear our rambunctious children upstairs. Removing her gloves she introduced herself as Miss Franklin.

'Loretta Franklin. Spinster. I prefer to be forthright around mothers.'

And then she plunged. She wanted us to know the truth about Morgan Filbert. She thought he was getting a little too close to canonization when in truth he didn't deserve the sendoff of a deceased tomcat. He had had a wife in Lincoln. And it was Miss Franklin, an old friend of his wife's, who was entitled to let us know he had walked out on her years ago, because she'd either refused or was unable to bear him children. 'Poor Lily,' she said. 'She shouldn't have let him get to her, but she did ...' The sad truth was she'd accepted without rancour his right to leave her. And agreed to pay whatever costs he might incur for the rest of his life, so long as he never divorced her. These were the facts. His wife had evidently been a comfortable woman with a family name to shelter.

'... And she was as good as her word,' continued Miss Franklin. 'Long-suffering, too, because when he started charging up his foreign children after the war, plus the cost of his farm, she began a long and frightening decline.'

'What do you mean?' asked Mary.

'I mean,' replied this regal woman, 'his story was a vindictive one. Filbert spent the rest of his life getting revenge for the father-hood she'd denied him – one really didn't know why – when they were young and in love. Filbert wasn't even his name.' His name, by the way, she pronounced with the ding dong of a slow church bell. Phil Burt. Giving it a disdainful and broken ring.

According to Miss Franklin, Mr Filbert's compulsion for black children owed more to vengeful desires than to wanting offspring of his own. This scoundrel, she called him, inflicted more and more urchins upon his wife, by bringing pictures to her every month of his latest procurements and reading aloud their stories in a tender voice. She felt his malevolence, keenly. And at every visit dipped deeper into her capital to cover his costs. She'd aged noticeably. 'He must have relished the decline,' said Miss Franklin, 'transforming her body.

'... Beginning in her eyes –' playing over us with her own – 'the flirty sparks went out of them. Pretty soon veins in her feet bulged to the surface like worms after a big rain. You know what rains we get. And even though Lily never went into the sun, her chin with-ered and pocked. Her skin wasn't pretty skin any more. Her elbows wrinkled up like the mouths on dead frogs. Ropy tendons grew down those long arms and she forgot, you might say, how to float. Her nose hooked so she could touch it with her tongue. Ugly we all thought. Hands shrunk ... face went cheesy ... her throat creased, you know, in skin necklaces. All before her time, you realize.'

We realized our guest was enjoying the sound of her own voice. But so were we, leaning closer to the table. Her own skin was immac-ulately preserved, as if with injections of estrogen or mayonnaise.

She went on: 'Lily's earlobes stretched and her eyelids drooped. About a hundred wrinkles hooped over each knee like croquet wickets. She got a bow in her spine from, I guess, this premature brittleness of the bones we're all hearing about now.'

We sat back, straighter now. We knew how to eulogize as well as she. How to build a child's volcano out of tinfoil – lava out of baking soda, vinegar, detergent. When to put ammonia on a hangnail.

Then she said: 'You young women can't imagine what it is to lose

your memory. You have yet to go through the change. It's a shell
game, trying to imagine why you hit blank spots and have to repeat
yourself. *She* was like that. Empathetic though. Too empathetic for
her own tooting good.'

Our spinster concluded, placing hands lightly on the table. 'Filbert drained her slowly dry. Don't forget, when the trust fund
dwindled, Lily had to leave her own family home for smaller and
smaller rooms. I suppose he couldn't help himself, but he must have
known when the money ran out there'd be nothing left to support
his … the sins of the father being visited on the children.'

Miss Franklin paused. The budgie had distracted her, raking its
gravel over befouled newsprint.

'… He went on buying these children, knowing full well every
child, instead of brightening her life, aged her more cruelly. And
then she died. On welfare, it turned out, because she'd lied to the
government by way of mattressing her capital for the likes of him.'

A child's inky doodles on the oilcloth suddenly resembled the
whorls of a periwinkle.

'Why are you telling us all this?' asked Gwen Shumka.

'It's interesting,' conceded Lucy Chisholm, who was president
that year, 'but I don't see how this account has anything really to do
with us.'

We felt custodial of the legacy. Flies on the wall, ears at the keyhole.

Then Miss Franklin said, as if challenging us: 'The reason Mr
Filbert died was through grief at the death of his wife … chagrin,'
she added, 'for the loss of her income.' Telling us this she sounded
quite pleased. She smiled, either clemently or vindictively.

Curiosity had already made her take in his old-fashioned stove,
its sawdust hopper and warming oven, before deciding it was time
to arise, sprinkle her goodbyes, and proceed erectly out through his
windowless door.

'A very august bit of business,' observed Mary. 'That getaway of
hers deserves an Emmy.'

The old bird had driven herself to the farm in an ancient Hill-
man with yellow flags in the doorposts. She now flapped one as she
turned from the lane of Mr Filbert's farm back onto the road.

'With wings that dinky,' commented Gwen, 'she'll never get off the ground.'

'Look,' said Lucy. 'Guess what she forgot.'

— vii —

Mr Filbert died, no one guessed why, till we found out it was through grief at the death of his wife. Our children were playing upstairs in Mr Filbert's old bedroom. It was raining outside and growing dark. We weren't about to forget one detail of the saga that had yet to be told in full.

'The bit I don't get,' persisted Gwen, 'is why she bothered coming here to tell us this.'

'To set the record straight?' wondered Adele Fonyo.

'D'you hear that, Mary? As secretary we elected you to tie up the loose ends.'

'... I think she just *told* us why. To get us thinking about grief.'

'Grief?'

We pondered destiny.

In the following weeks we recounted both their deaths, Mr Filbert's and his wife's — his alleged wife's. We discussed them both at his table, in his pantry, over enamel cups sipping tea, or applying a straw broom to his floor. For a while the most popular saga, introduced by Norine Wakely, was that Miss Franklin, his real wife, had staged her own death when the trust fund was eventually depleted — or looked like it soon would be (by *him*) if she didn't get a wiggle on. We even passed around her white doeskin gloves to sniff for fresh kill. She had done what Norine herself would have done, in the same predicament. And now she was free! She had what we ourselves — well, some of us — wished to have. No more husbands, children, obligations stopping us from sailing the world, if we wanted, on a love boat.

'Come again?' said Mary.

Yet she was old, argued Gwen Shumka. Miss Franklin was wrinkled and decrepit. Would we have to wait till her age to be out of the kitchen? Widowed and wrinkled? Snotty and grey? Our crowning glory a flight in a boxy little car?

'As old as Mrs Kabush,' said Amy Nowens. She didn't want to support Norine's story any longer either.

Mary Buskim had a new one. Listen: quote: Old Miss Franklin was the queen of a rival philanthropic group who resented our success and wanted to disillusion us by turning the man behind our throne into a rotten apple. 'Did you notice how cleverly she looked us right in the eye? No respect let alone grief for the daisy-pushers. She had the air of a do-gooder.'

Adele Fonyo, of course, wondered. 'A do-badder, though … That's pressing it.'

'Well, rot comes into it somehow. I can smell it.' She tossed down a glove.

Another story making the rounds was one about –

'But listen,' interrupted Patty Sweet, laughing. 'How do we even know, you know, for an absolute fact that Miss Franklin wasn't, you know …'

'As far as that cookie crumbles,' said Lucy, 'how do we know Miss Franklin *was even a woman?*' She sounded smirky, whispering. *'What's actually been proved?'*

Gwen's voice then dropped to a mirthful whisper too. *'You mean, just suppose …?'*

Clearly, ways to succumb to truth were many, sands on the sea shore in multitude. Mary Buskim wrote them down. Were all such gambits any different in kind? Trish claimed the smell of a rubber band could bring back the sea, sinking into salt on a summer tire.

'Whupdeedo,' said Jenny. 'Barbecues.'

'What exactly do you mean by "succumb", Mary?'

Prior to this dissolution we'd become quite deft at respinning Miss Franklin's designs, Mr Filbert's goals. Now our imaginations flagged and came up barren.

'Cheer up, Mary.'

Time, yes, to bury the past. To bend to our children with renewed engagement, or none at all. To teach them to remember others, that kicking your way into the heart of a thicket, for the plumpest blackberries, was just a beginning. Wasn't truth dependent on time … a child the father of illusion? Gradually we let the tales about Miss Franklin and Mr Filbert go.

At times after that we might hear a bird knock against the window, cut short in its migration south. The *clump* of a fat man's soul. We argued for our favourite seasons. We brewed orange herbal tea and spooned in honey for resilience.

Then one winter evening, in the kitchen over correspondence, Alina Belansky decided to announce what she'd discovered. 'You're not going to believe this ... I decided to do some sniffing around? Yesterday, I was looking through his desk again – you'll never guess what I found.'

She was smiling at us cattily.

'This yellowing obituary on the winciest cutout scrap of paper ... at the back of his drawer ... I've got it here in my purse ...' She was making a mess of her bag trying to put her fingers on it. 'This obituary ... whose do you think name it has?' She was flushed, excited. 'I can't remember how it goes exactly ... something like, *"FILBERT"*, in capital letters ... I'm quoting from memory ... *"Lucille Clara, passed away August 21, aged 66 years, long time resident of Lincoln and late resident of Palace Hot Springs, predeceased by her husband Morgan, and survived by sons Larry and Colin. No service by request of the deceased ..."* You can believe me or not. I swear it's true. I've got it stashed in my purse here, somewhere ...'

A lively silence ensued from all present at this fresh turn of events. In our hands the snapshots of children faded. Headbands tightened. We looked at one another across the old oilcloth, ready to start picking.

Then Jenny congratulated Alina. 'That's a good one, Alina. That sounded very convincing.'

The rest of the committee wasn't so certain. She might have been telling the truth. In which case, remarked Adele, the truth might never be unravelled. We were a scrap of paper away from putting all the old gossip to rest and starting over. Ours would not be the old story of the good Samaritan or the prodigal son. Ours would be the true one of grief and deprivation. Oh yes. We were on our way to wisdom. 'Listen, Alina ...' and we sidled up. This new turn of hers was going to recast the legacy of which we were the mothers and inheritors. We were a scrap of paper away from putting all the old gossip to rest and starting over. Mrs Filbert died, no one guessed why, till we found out it was through grief at the death of her husband, a stranger.

COMMENT: I grew up in Surrey so I'm fascinated by self-defence. It's really vanity, still dabbling at my age in the martial arts when the kids are asking to be driven to hockey and harp.

I have the sort of botanical knowledge you would expect from a ship channeller. Very little. But I *have* been in court. I hate dirty fighters who think getting in the first kick is cool. Could be, but it's not art. More like fashion masquerading as history. A good storyteller is like a good defence lawyer, shaping facts aggressively to suit her client's interest. Paid by the defendant to perform on his behalf – fearlessly, without malice, and fashion doesn't come into it. Though deception might.

Here I let the defendant speak, but I let his lawyer speak more. They seem convinced truth is the one you make up, since the prosecutor is out to make up his. Getting in the last word, rather than the first kick, is what I think fiction is about. The reader must judge which kind of history is going to last.

– S. P.

Stevie Platzer

My Honour, Your Honour

Quite clearly the accused, a very educated man, has a remarkable memory when he thinks recalling an event is to his advantage. Otherwise he is prepared to lie, or not remember or not recall an event or document that prejudices his case.

— DEFENDANT —

Your Honour, with respect. I did not expect to be liked but had hoped to be forgiven for not remembering if I ticked 'yes' instead of 'no' on a piece of paper thirty years ago.

I do recall my family and me visiting Perumbur a month after immigration. It was fate bringing us to visit a Dutch farmer who knew my father before emigrating after the war to help supervise better dike-building. By the time we located his farm I was feeling something strange. My heart?

His daughter greeted us with a squawk at the door. Rock 'n' roll boomed, unroomed, unhoused. My own daughters, a little younger, smiled shyly at her saddle shoes. Her squat father welcomed us in Dutch, which only I understood, Anna my wife being German. Below his rolled-up shirt sleeves Mr Geersing's forearms appeared to ripple with tendons.

It was a November afternoon and fog lay in his pasture and over the river, beyond. After our long drive from the city I would have dismissed the place as fake lowlands, except for my funny *feeling*. This feeling had spread to the diaphragm where I was breathing deeply, serenely, as if in through my navel and out through the soul. Perumbur reminded one of Holland in the thirties, near Roden, but it did not depress me. Why? The mountains, soaring?

We had tea with a string attached to a bag Mrs Geersing fished from her pot. Mr Geersing named other Dutch immigrants in the polder and around the valley. He suggested I come to Perumbur with its alluvial soil, purchase a cheap acreage to settle on. He thought I could resume my farming life from the Chaco – the dike would 'protect' us from 'anything unexpected'. My wife looked at me. I looked at my hands. I explained I was a teacher by profession. We did not talk about the war.

I then had my Damascus, your honour, on departing that afternoon from Mr Geersing. The sun had broken through and the fog was lifting up volcanic mountains in the distance. I had not seen such a pelt of rainforest since childhood. There was a sweet *mortal* smell of burning leaves. Towering poplar trees lined fallow fields like freshly rinsed paint brushes. I noticed Geersing's unharvested leeks (*Allium perrum*) lying flat and stringy in his wife's damp garden.

This soil looked rich enough for any of my cherished herbal remedies to grow in – such a new, untried country. I could grow an emmenagogue for my daughters, any number of plants for digestive and endocrine systems, and so deepen my understanding of botany. I certainly needed to deepen my understanding of science. I stared up at the sunlight against a million conifers and, touching her elbow, softly reminded Anna of my dream to be a botanist. So it came about that I was reborn into paradise.

Your honour, watching myself on television, as I arrived for that last court appearance and suddenly stumbled to my knees, I was struck by the wide-combed hair still in place on my crown. My still-young hair looking dignified in its unplastered way. It was satisfying to see it had not thinned greatly during these four years of torment inside your overheated city courthouse. For I had taken to calming myself daily by flavouring a little white wine with tincture of valerian root and the butterbur leaf. I sincerely wish I had some now, travelling backwards into dawn.

My Mountie has slumped to sleep as I tap. I worry that the past as I audit it is no deeper these days than Air Canada's profit margin. The cabin is dark except for my battery-powered screen crowding up with words. To raise the plastic blind, now, I would probably see a scarlet thread in a pitch sky heralding Europe, but this would only bring back the 'blood squad' one bitter woman accused me of leading. I fear this is all my children and their children will remember, your honour, her saying I 'slapped' her. Did she have any idea how treacherous this was, regardless of her 'belief' it was me? I was *never* inside her house. Nor was I ever in Assen Jail, where she said the Germans imprisoned her in February, 1945.

My honour, your honour, is the price paid for my Jobish suffering. If I *had* done as she alleges I would certainly, before God and you, confess it. I have nothing to hide – these years have stripped me of pride and shame, both. I wish I could remember the simple Chaco word for 'succour'.

I will be flashbulbed again as I disembark at Schiphol Airport. I am to be rushed off and cast like Eichmann into a Groningen jail cell, while my new Dutch solicitor demands a royal pardon. The Dutch have freed even the worst old Germans, so it is preposterous for an alleged small-fish *fout* of Dutch extraction to be held long in jail, when these life-sentenced Nazis are free to hobble home. Groningen had better be warmer than Camp Westerbork was, where November skies used to fall like sheets off the North Sea and make me shudder, dying.

My last solicitor, I think even the press agreed, was not a woman to inspire the court. A *European* education is required to argue European cases one feels. I should have defended myself, your honour. Legal fees have drained my pension funds, I am in a poor state of health, the court heard too little to persuade you to allow me to stay in Canada. The bare facts have another, fuller side, and had this side emerged, with nuances no less courted than deserved, I might not have begrudged my counsel her inflated, mafiosa-like fees. No, indeed.

I am therefore wondering if I might respectfully request a favour, your honour? I do *not* expect you to agree that injustice in my case has happened, except insofar as years of delays have robbed me of dignity, resources, a devoted life among family. A not insubstantial cost. Is it therefore possible you could redeem the system, if not me, by authenticating the spirit if not letter of the following summation, and passing it on to one of the more lucrative Canadian newspapers?

A covering note with your letterhead would suffice.

I will courier this disk by return flight along with necessary elaborations. That my solicitor was particularly ineffective in court does not prevent my offering the following, contracted remarks as her own. Of course, should this diptych prove unexpectedly popular I would not be unwilling to open up more fully on my past, and to collaborate without prejudice on a larger memoir in book form. I do not mind sharing the past. What else is left me?

— COUNSEL —

Your honour, with respect. The man before you didn't expect to be liked but *he did hope* to be forgiven for not remembering if he ticked 'yes' instead of 'no' on a piece of paper thirty years ago. This was like those cartoons the prosecution asked him to remember peddling, or the supposed slap given to some woman's cheek, or a Christmas-eve visit to the house of the father of one Dirk Kok. You will recall, your honour, how I objected at this reliance by the prosecution on memory. *And was overruled.*

I think we might've forgiven the defendant had he let go and *laughed* at the so-called case against him. And he is composed by nature. He smiled, yes, through more than one of his hearings in these years since proceedings against him began. But this was not contempt, your honour. Closer to detachment.

For him it was like hearing someone else's life retold by witnesses trying to out-mock themselves. My client isn't bitter, just disappointed in their eye-for-a-fault world. Should your honour decide to deport the accused, and I trust you will not, he will have no choice but to resign himself to hearing a Dutch street organ again after forty-five years, trying to imagine how that music is no longer pulled around Groningen on horse wagons. He's a man of peace, not vengeance. A genuine and modest man of Christ.

But *is* he to be deported from his own country? Where he has conducted himself as a model citizen, devoted father, and professor to the young for thirty years?

On his way 'home' the first time this person before you had nothing at all to remember of the Netherlands. He had never been there. He was 'returning' with his parents via Suez. Along the way his family took him to visit Antwerp Cathedral, where he saw the Peter Paul Rubens altarpiece of Christ's Crucifixion. A revelation, your honour. The boy discovered the master couldn't paint a single limb or loincloth without rippling it with muscle. The paint rippled. The dog fur in the foreground rippled. This straining pyramid of flesh spoke to my client of *power*. Alas. Averting his eyes he grappled with the background foliage of this canvas in the cathedral's poor light of 1932. The leaves belonged to a tree unfamiliar to the boy, arriving as he just had from the Dutch East Indies.

Taken aback his unbelieving father scolded him, 'Jaap, it is an oak tree!' His powerful father ...

— DEFENDANT —

Its leaves were the only things unrippling in the picture, your honour. Some looked blown, but in queer directions, one clump straight up like waving hands in a classroom of closet lavatory smokers. This flora was no more believable than the grotesque fauna, including the Johnny Weissmuller Jesus, rippling in what the arthritic old guide told our family had been a Baroque craze of an earlier period. The guide noticed my smirk. 'You should not be too hindsightful,' he warned.

I was not then a convert to religion and it would be some years before I found the use of it.

— COUNSEL —

Your honour, the defendant hadn't thought of this painting again until these deportation hearings began. To shut out the bitterness of *other people's hindsight* he'd begun to wonder what the effect on him had been of growing up in the Indies after his birth there seventy-three years ago. We've heard from the prosecutor how Buitenzorg was a colonial paradise full of tropical vegetation, where the defendant's father was a *vet* and a 'telling' influence on his son. But *did we ever learn* how happy the boy had been pressing leaves between wax paper of a scrapbook inscribed 'Jacob's Plant Album' – or how much more taken he was by flora than cattle? Seldom in the business of advocacy is truth what it appears.

With so much noise from the other side in this circumstantial case, perhaps I ought to have objected more vigorously to *hearsay*. My client has testified how his whole life now seems like a film he sees through God's eyes. He knows he hasn't lived a blameless life, but is quite willing to put the past behind and start over with His help. Indeed, he did this years ago, upon entering Canada.

'Have you ever been convicted of a criminal offence?'

The accused swore he knew of no conviction whatever, regardless of what his sister is alleged to have 'told' him in Paraguay, after the war. He was concealing nothing when he entered Canada and is saddened how small misunderstandings have compounded into this current travesty, your honour. The defendant is not nor has he ever been *dishonest*.

In light of these threats to strip his citizenship, to deport him, is it very surprising he answered the Justice lawyer as *carefully* as he could? That man's harsh summation alerted the defence too late to the possibility of my client being sentenced like a foreign criminal for allegations he can't accept.

Be this as it may, your honour, the man before you holds no grudges as to the nature of circumstantial evidence used to disgrace him – not when he knows Christ has forgiven him though Canada hasn't. He has tried to maintain, at increasing cost to his self-esteem, a *pleasant* expression throughout this farrago of defamation. It was wrong of the court to mistake his benign demeanour for contempt, as I mentioned.

In the Netherlands, upon his arrival, my client felt homesick because his family's return had uprooted him from the Indies' jungle and transplanted them all to a treeless polder, weedy with dairy farms. This boy tried to close out the ferly *emptiness* like some desert nomad focused on tea-brewing. Instead of embers, however, my client found himself coaxing the 'nether' soil of a new flower garden. Imagine his look of adolescent absorption, tending to white squill in that soulless landscape, his medicinal herb of minute starry flowers and swollen bulbs, recommended he knew as an emmenagogue.

Emmenagogue?

Your honour, at that age he didn't understand the effects of *all* his herbal remedies, let alone what menstrual bleeding could've been. He'd skirted his father's interest in mammals by deliberate choice. He did know red squill had come to be used as rat poison. He had red squill, and bluebell squill too. He had a whole world he was trying to replant at his father's Roden villa, to replace the jungle fecundity lost in returning to the family's barren seat. The Suez desert had shaken him like a great divulgation and now Holland seemed almost as unpromising.

He was an obedient son *who wanted to please his father*, if only his father had shared a passion for plants.

I feel, your honour, the baggy testimony given at these hearings has denied the tale of his particular passion *interrupted*. Could no one understand his pain? The elderly man before you has lately confessed to me how he remembers his father entering his youthful garden one morning and stopping at the betony (classified *Stachys officinalis* on the boy's printed marker), a delicate plant the ancient Greeks once sold their clothes for, and saying to his son, 'Jaap, it is a weed! A cow would not manure it!'

— DEFENDANT —

My father was pumped up for a speech against bank managers and Jews, your honour, before a political rally in Peize of guilderless milkmen and sour pig farmers. By now he had his cherished plan for National Socialism by 'heart', from many public meetings and impromptu palavers in smelly barns. I remember him sucking the Bayer aspirin he usually fancied for his health. He had stooped over to cup my pink flower in a rump-plumbing fist.

Cow rumps, your honour.

— COUNSEL —

The son needed plants for his homesickness, and recognized betony might've helped his father too. For my client knew that underneath his father's stooping hand those oblong leaves with serrate teeth could be used, and the bigger ones with crenate teeth, as poultices for the old man's varicose ulcers. The boy said nothing *for fear of betraying his sightings of the naked father* in their large tile bathroom, lathering at the mirror.

— DEFENDANT —

My father would conduct Schubert lieder in here with his razor, your honour, his voice carrying the assurance of an edified man among peasants. I suspected, but did not mention, betony could also be used to cure insomnia and pains in the head.

Following his derision of my betony, I had gone and reread *Herbal of Apuleius*, for what our ancestors knew of it: 'It is good whether for man's soul or for his body; it shields him against visions and dreams.' I felt that my father, as the self-elected seer in our district, would not have appreciated this knowledge.

— Young man, are you taunting your father?	*— No, father, only offering a sedative.*

— COUNSEL —

Your honour can see how my client's preoccupation with herbal remedies came from hoping *to cure a longing* for his birthplace in the Indies. *Was* there a cure for it? He was an adolescent looking for himself in the flat landscape of Roden. He'd lost his direction without trees. He'd lost his happiness outside paradise. There was no jungle to surround him with bright sun-stropping leaves, unfurling like angel wings. How could he regrow heaven in a desert overcast by the grey Waddenzee sky?

'Jaap, try harder to please your family. You brood. You say nothing. Do you speak to those ugly plants?'

His father was speaking round the countryside to poor farmers on their moral choice between Communism and salvation. This did not seem so *unusual* for the time. Chaos threatened Europe. To tame it the father wanted his son to study law at the university in Groningen. The defendant himself preferred botanical studies, yet dutifully entered law to keep the family peace.

— DEFENDANT —

If I may interject again: your honour will have a much finer appreciation of the difference between law and botany than a pensioned-off
scientist like me. As courtroom conductor, madam, you enjoy
greater insight into right and wrong than a person ungraduated in
the litigious distinctions of human deportment. I trust the law
implicitly to sort out the choices before it in an even-handed way.
Something my father thought he knew how to do but, in the end,
did not achieve.

— COUNSEL —

The defendant tried to please his father by harvesting leeks, and ran
into a wall. 'I wonder,' his father would comment sourly over soup
prepared by the mother, 'if neighbouring Leek was the originating
town for Jaap's treat.' History for the father was like an ice-skate
across a painted pond by Breughel. A slippery man knew what he
liked. He didn't like vegetables, and prohibited garlic no matter
what its reputed value as a digestive. To *his* mind eating garlic was
only a swallow below onion-chewing, and farmers could keep these
cuddish secrets to their pantries. He was willing to discuss with
farmers public affairs and bovine matters only. The bad influence of
a father cannot be overestimated.

Your honour, allow me an example. A year or two before the
Germans invaded, in 1940, and before the accused entered into law
school, I've learned his father proudly told him a story of the party
leader he'd admired and esteemed in their colonial community. One
day, six years earlier, Anton Mussert had questioned my client's
father for advice about some tropical cattle tick in Buitenzorg.
Then stood back while the father gave an answer. The father gave a
dispassionate answer, systematic and thorough, very pleased to be
asked. Mussert then 'repeated' what the defendant's father had told
him, word for word, including the Latin terminology, *tickus bur-
rowinnus*, or whatever it was.

'I thought he was making certain he had understood me, Jaap,
yes? Then I saw him begin to smile while repeating the explanation

in my own voice, Jaap. He was speaking in quite a *flat* voice and smiling. He is mocking me I thought.'

My client's father was shocked a little by this man he'd worshipped. 'Yes, I admired his brilliant memory for regurgitation off his cuff, but why had he been cruel to me? I had not to worry long. "You must learn to be a leader, Pieter," Herr Mussert now told me. "Speak from here!" and he gave his stomach a sound smack. "Be simple and forceful. Make your cattle tick sound like a burrowing Jew!" He shook my hand most warmly before walking off to join his entourage waiting that year in our monsoon mud.'

My client noticed how his father liked to be *worshipped* in Roden, just as the man's mentor Mussert was worshipped in the Indies. In Holland he was nearer the big-city proletariat he hated and the plutocrats he also hated. He wanted his son to be a leader too.

Later, when the invading Germans asked students like the unfairly accused defendant to take a loyalty oath, your honour, only a tenth of them agreed and the Germans shut down the university in Groningen. The defendant went home and pushed paper for Weer-Afdeling and the Landwacht. He wished to do his duty as he saw it, or rather as his father saw it, and his uniform pleased the father every morning when his son came out of the bathroom neatly combed and respectful.

The man before you believed he was fighting for the little farmer, squeezed to destitution by Communists to the east and banking capital to the west. The landscape between these factions was a lowland he was doing his best to defend *without admiring it.*

So treeless was Holland that he felt he knew why the soul had gone out of it. He never thought a threat from outside so bad it couldn't be accommodated – but a threat from within seemed a disease. His homesickness seemed a disease. Civil war seemed a disease. He treated it to the best of his ability by searching cinemas for layabouts, by rounding up resisters for a return to their own homeland, by writing reports on singers of unpatriotic folk songs. The defendant, your honour, felt his duty was to *assist* the 'Landwachters' who would resist destruction of patria from within.

— DEFENDANT —

I was never a violent man, your honour. Like my sister, who joined the German Red Cross, I made myself useful to the good as I understood it of the poor and underspoken. In their own ways the poor farmers that I was helping were also homesick for the promise of a time before the oak trees disappeared from their country. And for a time, though it still lay in the future – a time I am to witness soon for myself – before Dutch elm disease ravaged its way across Europe.

— COUNSEL —

This business of trees, your honour, would soon possess the defendant from South America to British Columbia. Trees, the crowning plants in his lost paradise, he missed them as he missed childhood, more than ever and with all his soul – I nearly said 'soil'. It was a simple love, his love of botanical glory, turning him into a *nomad*.

Of death and deserts, does the bench remember John 19:5? *So Jesus came out, wearing the crown of thorns and the purple robe. Pilate said to them, 'Behold the man!'* Let me submit to the court Pilate's not very distinguished remark as a recommendation for the necessity of law-school training, your honour.

Irony and ridicule have *no* place in court, as your honour knows, but as the inartistic prosecutor did not, in my client's case, appreciate. Allow me to mention that the defence's interest in John's unforgiving scene is in the *plant* used sarcastically by Roman soldiers as a *crown*.

I am informed *Ziziphus spina christi* grows up to ten metres tall with an ovate, noticeably nerved and dentate leaf, sporting a pair of spiny stipules, alternately straight and hooked. The sandy soil of Samaria and southern Israel has produced this plant since deserts began, your honour. My client once glimpsed the Christ thorn near Port Said where his family disembarked briefly on their last leg from the Indies to Marseilles. This thorn tree was as foreign to him as the oak tree, when he arrived in northern Europe a week later, and experienced stained light for the first time in his life.

Today, your honour, *the desert came back to him again* while thinking of Christ's sham trial as an antidote to this one. Forgive me, your honour. But you will remember him testifying that after Canadian soldiers liberated Holland, he went with his mother to a modest church in Roden where the pastor wouldn't shake his hand nor would others. *He couldn't understand.* He was persona non grata because of his political views. 'Fouts,' he heard them muttering like grumpy camels.

— DEFENDANT —

'Collaborators', your honour, is not a precise translation of 'faulties'. I believe it is a more forgiving word in Dutch, though you would never know this from your Dutch testifiers. It was quite unbearable in church for my mother to hear and feel the odium toward her family. She refused to believe Christians could *hate* other Christians when Christ Himself taught that many are called and all their views valued.

— COUNSEL —

The defendant couldn't understand this sniping, about his role in WA or Landwacht, and if the court looks again at his photo as a young man, published so often it has benefited the prosecution many times over, you will see a nonviolent, tulip-skinned boy who happens to be in uniform. (Yes, of course, *wrongly it would seem now.*) Consider the trusting eyes and respectful haircut, the sensitive mouth waiting to agree with his family. When I tried to introduce that boy in court, your honour rejected his photograph as irrelevant.

I would never claim the accused's Landwacht face is hard evidence, yet it *is* at least as scientific as 'facts' entered in evidence by those who thought they could 'remember' what my client *is supposed to have said and done half a century ago.* One feels the trial should've allowed for forgiveness in light of human fallibility. And not just *this* man's fallibility.

Look at Matthew (27: 27-9), your honour, and note how the

colour of the robe at Christ's trial is scarlet, *not purple* as in John's account. Sloppy translation? You would probably overrule my observation as a minor impertinence. Minor, possibly, but not impertinent if it shows how errors creep in over time and how the power of suggestion takes precedent. A photograph in the hands of a judge like yourself doesn't lie. You were trained to ...

I almost said 'eros' there, as if to prove my point! 'Errors' to 'eros' – almost – as I was translating my thoughts rapidly in open court.

The bench will therefore appreciate what havoc is committed when we attempt to bring up the past. From Hebrew to Greek – and Latin to English – we require *such faith*, your honour, to believe even *Jesus's* told and retold story. So then what, I humbly submit, in the case of my client's story, from German to Dutch to Spanish to English?

Did the prosecution's so-called witnesses all understand German as well as this man is apparently supposed to, and did they draw the same conclusions about his conversations with the oppressive invaders when he interpreted for them at roadblocks during the last year of the war? How did they know what he was saying? Did they – did your honour – appreciate the distinction between *translating and interpreting*?

We aren't even talking here of my client's years in Paraguay, the addition of which I submit *compounds* the difficulty of understanding this case in any other terms but allusive. Mythical, your honour.

Matthew talks of the soldiers stripping Jesus, before dressing him in that scarlet *and/or* purple robe, crowning him with thorns, and mocking him from their knees – 'Hail, King of the Jews!' So much humiliating business seems to come back to the Jews. Why, your honour? It isn't *their* fault if they failed to see the jungle for the trees when Christ was among them, and I mean no disrespect.

But can the man before you be blamed for alleged slights? He really had no idea what the Jews had endured at German hands until he spent *fifteen months* after the war in the Allies' prison, Camp Westerbork, and saw for himself the horrible conditions to be borne in transit. He personally endured sickness and diarrhoea and thought he would perish before escaping through a fence and making his way to a Mennonite camp in East Prussia.

It's simply untrue he didn't pay the penalty for his wartime views. My understanding is he turned *himself* over to the Canadian allies, just to avoid retaliation at the hands of 'Christians' who thought he deserved punishment for his minority belief in patriotism.

Those who suffer homesickness are a cursed minority, your honour, and possibly they deserve to wander endlessly, I do not judge. The only forgiveness my client ever received for his months of anguish in Westerbork was a sentence in absentia, in 1948. He was living by then in the 'green hell' of the Chaco, settled by Mennonites from the Canadian prairie who were baptizing the Indians.

— DEFENDANT —

I was grateful to be back in the jungle. But it was scrub jungle, your honour, not the rainforest I remembered from childhood in the Dutch East Indies. The trees grew as they might in a Flemish canvas, by a minor member of the Rubens workshop.

I did seem condemned to remain unhappy. I had endured threats from my countrymen and been held in that prison camp with no recourse for having exercised my views as a Dutch citizen during Nazi occupation. Now, my only comfort was Christ – Christ and plants, for I had begun a second garden after my long absence from earth. I mean soil, your honour, forgive us our translations.

— COUNSEL —

My client and his new wife excused themselves from the German co-op at Fernheim to join the Canadian Menno colony near Loma Plata. Here, happily, he experimented with oleander and foxglove, while Menno's followers were turning millions of acres into farm land. Razing trees, your honour, something the defendant would never collaborate in, these prairie people having very different values from those born in paradise as he'd been. They were like the Dutch, he discovered, these settlers from Canada.

Is it so surprising, then, the man before you was *still* looking for a homeland?

I haven't yet mentioned his history teaching. In the Chaco he came to believe trees could be used as historical models. Shittim, your honour, was his pedagogical guide, the common acacia tree of the Bible, its wood used to build frames for the Holy Tabernacle and, I would hazard, the Holy Cross. I understand the acacia tree is the defendant's *favourite* caducous tree, its glabrous leaves lifting to a canopy common to desert and rainforest both. I beg the bench's patience. He *also* began to believe most textbooks of history retained witnesses *who were never there*. He soon decided we have an obligation to be our *own* witnesses, your honour. His interest in botany had uncovered dendrochronology.

False rings, your honour, and true ones. Please hear me out, as my client's fate hangs in the balance.

He taught his young pupils that a 'dendrochronologist' can use our oldest living links with the past to date precisely historical events, assuming he knows *which* trees grow multiple rings in a single year and are therefore *not* to be relied on. The juniper is such a tree – a 'scrub shrub' my client would teach. It was the *scientific method* that interested him, learning from nature instead of cutting it down. Nature rather than human nature *still* seems to my client the most reliable witness, if we learn to treat her with respect.

His pupils learned they could cross-date timbers in an uncovered site, for example, by using the surrounding trees to set up chronologies farther and farther back, matching ring patterns in reliable timbers of overlapping periods. The possibilities of such precise knowledge have since *comforted* this wrongly accused man. Botany remains the *only* way he knows to understand the baroque confusions of the past. I have noticed, your honour, false witness is usually borne by those who think they can picture what they've never actually seen.

— DEFENDANT —

This is why I respect protesters from Greenpeace, your honour. They resist the destruction of trees as far away as Brazil, and as near as our own watershed in Perumbur. I discovered the rainforests of B.C. to be magnificent – the way they spread like lava down mountainsides to the polder, where I and my family found *home* at last in the temperate, startling fusion of Buitenzorg and Roden. Over thirty years ago, your honour, I cured my homesickness by coming to Canada. I think my recent sympathy for the guerrilla tactics of protesting Canadians shows I was not against radicals as a young man either.

— COUNSEL —

He was an opponent of false rings like Communism and the Banks. And haven't we *since* seen how right his side in the Dutch civil war was to *oppose* Communism, which has now collapsed from its own rottenness? I'm not arguing my client deserves an apology, your honour, but why has forgiveness become an anachronism?

I'll be brief. Some twelve years after qualifying as a botany instructor, and twenty years after landing in Vancouver, the defendant was accosted in the spotless corridor of his university department by a friendly Dutchman who asked for a word in his office. It was he, a journalist from *Asscher En Drentsche Courant*, who told the defendant of his sentence in absentia. My client felt bemused.

He never dreamt anyone could still be interested in prosecuting a petty 'fout' after forty years. Those young students flirting in the quadrangle below, your honour, what did *they* care if an old fart was a fout or a fruitcake, or a good father, so long as he taught them about plants with humility? He was a Canadian citizen now. A deacon in his church, where he taught Bible classes. The defendant made his own case very well. He wanted this Amsterdam journalist to see he had *nothing to hide*, including the name on his office door.

'Ach,' the journalist then said in German, smiling, 'wie glücklich sind die Toden,' and withdrew with a polite bow.

— DEFENDANT —

The day after that visit I attended a Campus Crusade for Christ, where our handsome premier was guest speaker. You will remember, your honour, how *he* grew up in Holland during the war, eating garlic-garnished tulips and wearing wooden shoes. *He* was not afraid to stand up for what he believed, either. 'Real politics,' said this man, 'means responding to the true will of the people. False politics is where the will of the people is falsely influenced by the lack of a code, weak leadership, and biased media.'

When I was in Paraguay, people had accused the Mennonites of collaborating to keep a 'dictator' in power, your honour, but these settlers were not political. Alfredo Stroessner could have been Mr Walt Disney for all we cared, and many of us thought he was. Our pacifist attitude was always to get along and not influence politics, a bedevilled business fraught with fathers and fatherlands, and I think this gives your honour the reason for my supposed 'getting along' with overbearing Germans in Holland during the war.

— COUNSEL —

Your honour, my client little imagined this Dutch journalist would soon uproot his life. The report syndicated in our local Dutch newspaper, *Windmill Herald*, was all about finding the man before you living abroad. The biased media couldn't get it right, of course. The defendant was now living *at home*, in his own country, as a citizen of Canada. He was a different person, willing to talk about the past and the man he used to be.

I wonder if the court will recall the prosecutor making the accused look at a newspaper he is supposed to have peddled for the Dutch National Socialist Party in the summer of 1941? A cartoon showing a man wearing the star of David and carrying a suitcase? *What will happen*, it said underneath in Dutch, and the prosecutor asked if the accused agreed it illustrated the deportation of Jews from the Netherlands.

My client thought it depicted Jews *returning to their homeland* and said so. Who in that early year of the war could've guessed the existence of concentration camps, your honour? Or the exterminating *horror* of them in a later year? The 'war years' are always lumped together like a single year – *pourquoi?* – creating a false past against people like the defendant. The court's reconstructions from false rings are therefore based on a *misleading* tree of events. Its wood, if I may say so, *should never even have been admitted into proceedings.*

My client had an operation three years ago to replace his hip. He suffers from angina now. You can *see* how his sapwood has shrunk in ratio to his heartwood. Ironically, your honour, the dead heartwood of a tree is valued *more* highly because of its density and resistance to disease. Its cells are impregnated with resin. Heartwood supports the trunk. My client's heartwood supports his spirit.

'How happy are the dead' as that destructive Dutch journalist observed. Caricatured, the dead seem destined to rise above themselves. *This suffering defendant among them.* He has no desire to throw himself on the mercy of the court when his case is such a sound one. When it is, your honour, dead right.

For the record, finally, allow me to relate to the court a dream my client had after the worst day of his trial, a cartoon dream depicting the art of justice, your honour. In it a businessman is holding out to a sidewalk beggar the shirt off his back. The businessman's suspenders dangle in a silly way and his tie, around his now collarless neck, dangles too. He clutches his briefcase under one arm. The beggar has glanced down at the offered shirt, but is still plainly dissatisfied. He says to his benefactor: 'Any chance of making it "a home where the buffalo roam"?'

In summary, your honour, I would submit this Canadian expression is precisely the way the man before you feels about the court's beggarly witnesses, *having already offered them the shirt off his back.* They weren't happy with stripping him of dignity – they wanted to divest him of home and country too. Your honour, don't allow the man before you to be deported from his native country of rainforest and truth. The court should show mercy. He has tithed his dues many, many times over. I rest my case in confidence of an acquittal.

— DEFENDANT —

That is what I wish my counsel had told the court, your honour. All of the foregoing.

It *is* true I tripped the other day outside your courtroom, and that newspaper photos appeared with my daughter helping me up. But, your honour, *I tripped on purpose.* You will kindly forgive me for insisting on this like my learned counsel. It gave me pleasure to fool the 'noose' cameras – not once but twice, I confess, hoping to fool you too. For I also tripped *inside* your courtroom, where cameras were banned but from where the press reported it and of course mixed up my second fall and my first fall until both became one.

I think this supports my discredited defence, since the truth of a matter is seldom what is reported by eyewitnesses, who in *my* case were little more than drama critics waiting to report false steps, or waiting to comment on how 'convincingly' I played the role in little 'razzias' on suspected hiding places, *or* with what authority I seemed to speak in my Landwacht uniform to some credulous child on Christmas Eve. I could have been Santa Claus or Falstaff, your honour, depending on my assignment. *I was acting a role.*

To have deported me for rave reviews seems to have missed the point of that staged war in the confused little theatre of northern Europe. My critics were responding to something that never really happened except in an *artistic* way. They were juniperous to condemn me for mouthing things in someone else's play. I was homesick for a self I had costumed like some immature braggart hiding his pain. I never fired a shot.

Your honour, this afternoon in the failing light, as I was kissing Anna goodbye, and before immigration officials arrived, my daughter's flash camera discharged twice, three times, and I suddenly had the title for the defence I never received.

Outside, at the end of our country lane, the media were huddled in wait for their own parting shots of me inside the warm white van. I had recalled, sadly, how one of your misled witnesses mentioned everybody being scared of me – how 'at one time' I was known as 'de schrik van Roden'. Might such a moniker begin to repay me for all my unwanted infamy? Why be aloof from exaggeration in the marketplace? *De Schrik van Roden?* This title, this allusion to me in the interrogative, might offer a suitable straw-man target for the true aim of my life as sketched in counsel's remarks above. It would remind one of Christ's ordeal – and I, for one, would bear my own cross gladly in company with the atavistic past.

> – *The Scourge of Roden.*   – *I am another man now.*
> *Can you believe it, Jaap?*   *Listen, is that a street organ?*

Your honour, kindly take into consideration how long since I last slept, the altitude and thin air up here, and this noxious Mountie peering at my laptop screen across the empty middle seat where his chrome handcuffs lie like Malaccan earrings under my raincoat.

COMMENT: The restaurant in this story is loosely related to one my handsome cousin owned, not an upscale fish restaurant in Mission City, but a plain side-of-the-road diner in Agassiz. When business fell off he just packed up his bags to 'go fishing' and never came back. His wife, when she learned of his rivery adventures through a mutual friend near Hope, petitioned for divorce. There was already an encumbrance against their shingle-sided bungalow, with balding tires I remember in the yard. She decided to sell it under-valued through a spotty real estate agent and slip off to Oregon. But the bank caught up with her, via fast post, demanding to be paid the restaurant's mortgage arrears. The bank felt because she had worked in the diner herself she *must* have been in partnership, which, legally speaking, she was not.

Waitressing and cashiering she'd once gone after my cousin for back wages, if you can believe it, household expenses, with a meat cleaver or else his ivory-sided banjo. I suppose *he* felt there was nothing else he could've done to escape this unpretty domestic mess except to 'go fishing'. I think my story grew from the idea of excess in the lives of two attractive but mismatched people. I knew I had something useable when I began feeling like some pissed-off Nemesis, stalking my cousin. The boy I remember was a farm kid who spurned girls.

– M. T.

Mavis Terwiel

Sturgeon

SHE WANTED CLOSURE but the vendor decided hold on, he couldn't accept, wouldn't sell. Having lied to her about his willingness to come down, he now seemed moored to a self-important dock he called his conscience. So a wasted evening, driving all this way with an offer for his 'bosky getaway': five hemlocked acres with a tear-down and spring-fed stream, off a dirt road cul-de-sacing in an oil-drum cache two miles from Steelhead. A marginal listing at best.

Something had given her a vile dream last night, not about his refusal to sell out, but a smelly little mirage about waifs in the Philippines. Maybe the vendor was mistreating his sons. They looked forsaken when she left, motherless. Three mustard-lipped children she was unlikely to see again, given the man's impromptu paranoia. She should've refused his shack two months ago when he told her more or less weirdly she had bad hair.

**

Driving home she calls her brother. They talk cellular, he in his fourteen-foot Lund in the middle of the Fraser, somewhere east of Mission. '... I hear they've parked a vehicle on the tracks and dinged the tires' – meaning the aboriginal people have, a purloined school bus, with rifle shots. With history on their side they could be weeks, Bryce says, charming the media. He knows several of them, nice enough toughs, buys their bootleg coho for his restaurant.

Their nation is blockading the Canadian Pacific tracks near Ruskin. In the dark he wants to know if she can spot any campfires near the Stave River Bridge. Where *is* she, again? Her brother blames the blockade on Oka and counsels her not to waste 'Narciss's' money on advertising any more upriver property till the Mounties reopen the line. He doesn't mind counselling his sister on selling property. 'Stick to the high-growth areas and, for fuck sake, don't keep not buying pepper spray. OK?'

A year ago, attacked in an empty Open House on a quiet street in Lacey, she suffered a concussion trying to talk off a parolee with a crowbar. Colleagues agreed she was lucky to escape with her brain unscrambled. She wondered at the time, had she been killed in the line of duty, would they have come from far and wide like policemen or firemen to march behind her coffin in a long pastel line? Unlikely, all were on commission. One of them sponged off the tiles in the ensuite bath and sold her MLS listing two days later to a volleyball manufacturer and his Taiwanese family, without mentioning the crowbar caller. Agents she'd never met sent flowers, better suited to a mortuary than her hospital.

A real fire, this one a glowing beehive burner making sparks and fouling the night air with invisible smoke, has seeped into her air-conditioning, its smell of cremated butt-ends and sawdust from old-growth watersheds responsible for the same shakes, she thinks, exported into the high-end roofing market in L.A.

Bryce mentions he can see, horny on the hill above him, the abbey's Spanish bell tower luminous in moonlight. An erotic sight. His rudeness gladdens her. She can hear his throbbing outboard turning slowly over, keeping him stationary in the current as he mooches. Or whatever they call threading a lump of salmon roe over a hook the size of a baby's coathanger and letting it sink to the dirty bottom of the river while he waits brainlessly for a bite.

He took her sturgeon fishing last summer and they spent the afternoon trying to persuade an anchor with retractable wing-things to catch hold like a vulture in the riverbed. It kept hopping off the bottom as she measured their velocity downstream without a bite or sunscreen. Her brother, like some sunstruck monk, had started abbey-chanting then, as if fish-mongering in Steveston. '*Rotten roe, rotten roe ...*' Bites, his gauge of spiritual transcendence, had left him burned and depressed. There weren't any bites. Skunked, they'd motored back.

Some miles downstream, and driving the winding highway in light traffic away from him tonight, she can see his glittering river through trees, their connection immaculate. Giggling – two distinct *hee hee*'s – he sounds high from an illegal substance. Probably the sturgeon flesh he's poaching, high on the crime itself, though possibly weed, sweetly perfuming the humid air over dimpled eddies around him like saucers in the moonlight. She tries picturing his restaurant's now darkened decor, till she can see cobalt-blue walls past flickering candle bowls and mitred napkins, warning her eerily away.

Won't ask him if he's lit up to port and starboard, remembering his deckless boat has no place for running lights. Ill-equipped to follow rules, anyway not while its skipper poaches, Bryce's dented hull resembles his recent life, bruised from idling among a backlog of patients awaiting radiation therapy, bumping round in a pool of shadowy x-rays. His life lets his restaurant take the hits. A sudden rise in the number of men with prostate cancer has given him the perfect excuse to fish while he waits – to goof off, she feels, from liability. He's told her he can't afford the quicker treatment in the States that would get him back into the kitchen sooner.

Would it?

She hasn't ever mentioned that an older acquaintance of hers, diagnosed like Bryce via a digital rectal exam, had gone regularly to Bellingham from Sardis and discovered visits to America hadn't solved his own slipping business. Just as prognosticated, after six months of cross-border shopping, the valley's top developer (nauseous) died.

'... *Rotten roe* ...'

He seems determined these nights to make peace with himself. She has never heard him blaspheme the Benedictines' bell tower with the same affection before. Never heard him blaspheme it at all. The wound-up cheeriness of his tone reminds her of how he talked at her house last Easter to Wayne and Kellie over his preparation of Peking duck. The same floating whine of dissatisfaction. *Spooky* how a guy, who no longer loves his wife, seems to expect continuing adoration from her children.

He is bedding down these nights where he can. Will admit no more. She imagines him living unhappily with a native weaver who smokes little cigars in her handyman's special off Highway 7 somewhere near Hatzic. One is vague, he is vague, on everything but his cell number. He says he takes calls on his boat, brick patio, and the toilet. 'I have trouble *going* to the toilet ...'

And complains that sometimes when he tries to pee standing up in his Lund it takes him so long – and its stream is too thin to detect – riverbank fishermen feel he's flashing them like some groin-grabbing Michael Jackson after The Fall. This was two weeks ago, after dusk. Tonight she hopes the full moon will turn his pee into a sparkling tributary discernible from, attentive to, respectable distance.

He enjoys the June river because uprooted alders and jetsam from shingle mills float quickly past him in the broad current, leaving a surface smooth of all but wrinkled eddies. The snowfields of the coast range, he'll report, are on their last squeeze.

* * *

'Hold the phone, have to untangle my Walkman ...'

She guesses his cord in the downrigger could tug him neck first, overboard. 'Are you safe?'

'As in communicable disease?'

'Fish, idiot.'

Recalling now what he's told her about angling for the white sturgeon: men rumoured to be drowned by these monsters were disappointingly *few* this century, since most of them (fish, not fishers) had vanished through overfishing and toxic dioxins. His chemicals had sounded like a redundant rock group, that day together on the river.

'There,' he blurts. 'Be able to tune in the riverbed now.' Adding, 'Still need a fish finder, though.'

She'd encouraged him to share his new sturgeon lore as a way to buoy up self-esteem when his marriage was foundering and Crab-cakes wasn't attracting the early numbers they'd projected. She learned sturgeon can live for hours out of water, so poachers will wrap them in wet newspapers to deliver live, unbelievably fresh, to restaurants. His restaurant.

That had been Bryce's introduction to sturgeon, buying them from blackmarketeers for his kitchen and serving the elusive dinosaur as a Jurassic Park dinner special. He was reborn a sturgeon fan in the course of an evening's shady transaction with local aboriginals. Longevity hadn't toughened the scaleless flesh, which could be cut into lean steaks and broiled till it flaked delicately if you cooked it longer than normal fish using lemon butter and thyme, after chopping through the barbed scutes.

'... Canneries round here were awash in roe, ninety years ago. You had caviar piled up on scows way down to –'

She had listened to him, wondering at such hoary hearts, slow-pumping organs that let these creatures live outside water, and in it, suspended, along slough bottoms and in river caves for a century plus.

He now sounds like a native poacher, with his slant on how many fish a local boy should be allowed to take and when. He respects the sturgeon, hates government, and believes in family – even after dumping on his own (family) by quitting a superintendent's job with B.C. Packers to open a restaurant, just because he thought he was the best gourmet cook in the Valley. Possibly, he was.

Almost a joke between them, that she couldn't coddle an egg, but had agreed to underwrite a fish restaurant in a city that liked pork goulash.

Then, about six months ago, she began noticing serious gaps in the food chain at Crabcakes, concluding that his overhead, managerial incompetence, or cancer had begun to plunge him into crisis, cutting off simple supplies like broccoli and bread rolls. Politely, whenever she happened to be listing property near Mission, she stopped dropping by.

Bryce never mentions her absences. And seems to tolerate his own absences from Crabcakes without feeling the need to mention these, either. Except he will, by telling her his 'second chef' Sarah is 'covering' for him while he fishes. He'll tell her this without a quaver, though the phone in his restaurant goes unanswered, though she knows he's lying. His (like the natives') is a 'food fishery'. And he insists, 'Got a kitchen to supply,' when there's no question his place is *dark* – darker than his rectum.

Since childhood, and maybe before that, in shared amniotic fluid, her built-in mooching antenna has allowed her intuitions of a brother's unseen twitchiness. And his of hers, though he never says, knowing they don't have to talk about the twin thing to justify the business bit. Which makes dishonesty between them puzzling, knowing as she does his position at Crabcakes is hopeless whether he dies or doesn't. Death will not absolve his debts.

His second chef told *her* last week Crabcakes had closed down two months ago 'for good'. Sarah is worried now, unable to afford college in the fall for her graduating daughter who wants to study 'Crim'.

Bryce owes his underwriter an explanation.

But finds it difficult to admit failure, unless it slips out the way his cancer did, bad news masquerading as good when it helps to rationalize his over-the-top poaching expeditions after dark when he should still be at his stove. 'I can always pull myself together with a bite.' It sounds so masochistic, she longs to ask if this biting doesn't *hurt* him.

* * *

'You still got that widow's tire-farm listing?' Having de-downrigged himself, presumably by removing fishy-fingered earphones from around his neck, he is wondering again if –

She keeps quiet. Maybe he'll forget about 'tying up' this widow's property with a deposit – in order to flip it to somebody he says he knows with recycling interests in Clearbrook, before having to surface with final payment himself. Bryce couldn't afford the first mortgage on a gum machine, the *deposit* on a gum machine, even if it were being sold by a thief willing to take a rye mickey for the entire rig and throw in the gumballs.

'Sarah was asking me yesterday at lunch if there wasn't some way we could jump our cash flow and live another winter.' He's telling her this? With *her* house on the line as collateral, he's telling her Crabcakes is still serving meals and its mortgage payments aren't in shit default? How can she even believe he has cancer?

She now suspects her trying to cover both their assets accounts for her recent poor judgement, like agreeing to potentially commissionless listings such as a widow's tire-farm nightmare or a handyman's shack.

'Just forget it, Bryce. I won't deal in bad faith with Mrs Sauvage. Full stop.'

She accelerates, speeds on in silence. Has he got the message? As unethical to sell to a member of her own family as for her in her old Nancy Sinatra boots to walk right over a ... Sto:lo native in supine protest on the rails.

Sto:lo. If you were going to tease your name, the colon seemed a boffo piece to do it with, très post-mod: like studs in your nostril or gas rings in the kitchen.

She smiles and slows down. Loosens her cellular grip. Resolves to reprint her 'Narciss' card at the earliest opportunity:

> Bi:anca T:se / NRS
> Med!allion Clu'b
> Go:Go Boots for Hu*s*le Plus
> (Play:mate, Auˆgust 1973)

then braid her hair in a pigtail and hand out this card with green tea sachets and a copy of their great-grandfather's head tax paid in full. Stylish as cold pressed, extra virgin olive oil.

'You're amused,' says Bryce. 'If you're worried I'm soft-shoeing you on the commitment in Clearbrook, Bi, I'll give you his number to check out.'

Whining again.

She flashes her high beams at an oncoming car. It flashes back to show she's blind and bullets past. Now finds herself in the dark having accidentally killed her lights. The green glow of the control panel has vanished, silkily, forcing her eyes to adjust like ears to a *hush*.

Moonlight beckons, reflecting off her hood, off a leather dash, pouring through open sun roof onto ebony seats and rugs, creamy on her arms. Light enough to drive by the moon and stars without electrical assistance to either port or starboard. And so she allows herself to speed on a hundred, two hundred metres in this manner without navigational accompaniment.

Wh:ee!

Temporarily empty in both directions the road like the river is carrying her west ... won't stop as it meanders ...

Liberated by darkness she floats right up through her roof for a picnic on the moon. Caviar in all this moonshine has the effect of making her think Bryce probably *longed* for his restaurant to fail, if it meant having highs like this every night when he should be serving up halibut off a hot range. Hence his desire to make a quick killing off worn-out tires. Off the used-up momentum of millions like his sister who drive carefully, responsibly, and never catch a white sturgeon in hay-scented moonlight, hell no, under a silver campanile looking like an abbot's bell-rung co:ck.

Lowers her arm with the thin instrument in lotioned palm, listening for imaginary bells. For a vintage 78-rpm crooner in love with Ramona, or in the new CD version with herself. What she really hears is her last lover, humming idiotically, refusing conversation for 'security' reasons, although she'd bought herself a scrambler. A cabinet minister who used to enjoy surprises, peering down on her fast car and calling her up from his ultralight.

'We're all in the gutter, Ms Tse, but some of us are looking at the stars.'

She wondered, when the tire-farm widow said this to her, if the unfortunate woman knew more about real estate and its connivance with the truth than she was letting on. The listing had been between her and a Re/Max guy and she got it by overvaluing this dump and promising its vendor the moon.

All right, stars.

Gutter too culpable? She –

'How many kids have Hef and Kim got now, Bi?'

* * *

His voice brings her back down to the disappearing road. 'What?' Reaching for lights to save herself from a head-on collision at the bend.

When the road is white like this, shining, death by darkness seems impossible to believe in. Surely his own illusion is induced by grass-smoking on the river.

At times, when he wants to skirt the truth, he'll ask for domestic news of the Mansion, his expectation in no way diminished by his twin sister's now twenty-one-year-old lost place in paradise as a Bunny. Something has since happened to the hutch – earthquakes and fires, drought and mudslides – to give it wrinkles, faults, broken veins. California, that is, the dream. The Mansion seems immune. As far as ex-Bunnies know from the tabloid grapevine, Hef is going strong again after a minor stroke, his young wife and family the fuzz on his peach.

She says nothing.

Her fling with fame had lasted five months, from eight weeks before she was to appear as the Miss August centrefold, to the time she hopped away from the last of Hef's pals in pre-Kim pursuit through games room, zoo, and waterfall grottoes where virgins appeared and disappeared in his underlit pool. She was nineteen, looked seventeen, and had come to L.A. on an unexpected invitation from the Mansion, soon after emerging from the magazine's Canadian files as a potential Playmate. Spinoff from her title faded fast, after Hef lost interest in her chances of making it in Hollywood with small Oriental boobs.

To fill dead air he returns to the Sto:lo, repeating himself. 'Seeing any fires?' Rushing in then to speculate on motives, whether his fellow fishers aren't hot to trot with power gone to their feathers – the road closure now *de rigueur* for any self-respecting nation – or whether they might not be genuinely aggrieved at historical mistreatment and shoving it to the CPR as a foursquare corporate target. No shutting him up. '... We're all in the same boat, I reckon, with the multi –'

She drops his voice into the adjoining bucket seat to take better control of her wheel, when a Greyhound bus, heading east, sends a block of air cycloning across the line. Navigating clear of disaster, along a friendly shoulder, she pushes in a James Keelaghan tape and rescues her brother's voice.

'... used to fish sturgeon, in the dark ages.'

'The reason I'm calling, Bryce ... is to ask if you know anything behind these reports of Virgin sightings on Doreen Kynock's family's farm. Remember Doreen Kynock?'

No response, no muffled motor burping in the background. His background. 'Bryce?' She turns down the tape. Her scrambler accidentally disconnect them?

Then his dirge, growing louder, *'Rotten roe ... ROTTEN roe ...'* Mocking her tape perhaps.

Anyway, amused. 'Doreen?' he asks.

'Was she in our class, or the one behind?'

'She *flunked*, Bi.' *Dor?* she hears him thinking.

Croatian Catholics from Bosnia-Herzegovina, staying with Doreen's ageing parents, have recently spotted the Blessed Virgin Mary in a pear tree. Irradiating the fruit like spray, making these pears questionable eating come August, since something toxic has killed off the rusty juniper virus speckling their leaves.

She reports to Bryce what she's read of this local happening, without mentioning her listing up Polder Road from the Kynocks'. The Virgin is now appearing every Tuesday afternoon at 1:30 and they (the Croats) have promised her (Doreen) if she (the Virgin) will only cooperate, they could go for the longest serial sighting in the history of BVM appearances.

'What Vatican Guinness book keeps those kind of records?' crackles Bryce's voice, through interference.

She mentions it is really only one of the Croats, a Ms Meike Dragicivic, who sees the Virgin. 'Can you hear me ...?' Secrets or at least heavy messages in Croatian, rumours of which have spread faster than herpes in a hot tub. The Kynock farm is suddenly attracting hundreds of weekly pilgrims, clogging the road with Caravans and Cherokees.

'So?' His voice clear again. Uninterested.

'... I was just wondering, big brother, have *you* had any recent contact with Doreen yourself?'

He could be forgiven for wondering if this is her version of his Hef-and-Kim question, to keep the conversation rolling by diversion.

It is, in a way. She's hoping to divert a few of the devout on spec, those with stars still in their eyes, to Tuesday Open Houses at Mrs Sauvage's nearby tire farm. Who knows where the Virgin might decide to appear next, perhaps stage-managed by a complicit Doreen Kynock, spreading spiritual values in her role as Ma:ry, while upping property values in the surrounding polder?

'She's a sexpot,' remarks Bryce.

Still? But she knows what he means.

Doreen would never have been invited to pose for *Playboy*. You'd never have had to see Doreen Kynock nude to know what she looked like without clothes. Always wore them too suggestively. Never realized you needed to dress tastefully, especially as a sex object, to be sexy. The hint of mystery was a required fiction, if fiction was required, as in Doreen's case it wasn't. Dor was clueless. She dressed like a harlequin in heat.

What would she be wearing to welcome the Virgin?

'Not much,' suggests Bryce. 'I've run into her at the Wild Goose Inn.' Giving it the rude name, where guys his age meet for stags, annulments, uncontested divorces. 'She's a table dancer, decades past prime.'

So, he's socializing. Or else drinking by himself to avoid people, hoarding his scorecard like a skating judge.

'She's one grinder you don't really *care* to watch.'

Even though Doreen had once adored him, unrequitedly, in a cotton T-shirt with 'Hip' over the left tit, 'Hop' the other.

'... I doubt it's Doreen seeing the Virgin,' his voice staticky again. 'For one thing, she wouldn't be living with her parents. Unless she's between marriages. Heard her husband –'

'Bryce?'

'... tried to knife her.'

'Bryce, listen.' They could dance around all night like this.

'She ought to see a counsellor, not Mother Mary.'

'Tell me the truth, Bryce.'

'What I heard.'

'I ran into Sarah the other day, chaperoning.'

'She's no friend of Doreen's, that I know of ... *Chaperoning?*' His wireless voice, ironic in its weed-easy inflections, despite the air's electrical resistance.

'For fuck sake,' she tells him straight, unwilling not to say what's distressing her. 'I *know*.'

* * *

She listens closely, waiting for Bryce to come clean over what has befouled things between them. The collapse of Crabcakes. She wonders if her run-in this evening with the backwoods vendor hasn't unsettled her. Her eyelid twitches. She can't wear a *watch* any more without sooner or later spoiling its time. Hair and accessories marred by vibes she picks up like some assailable tart.

The vendor, dressed in a lumberjack shirt, was showing skin where his stomach tugged buttons in directions they didn't want to go, a pitch-black navel chug-a-lugging the light. Something immense about him, smothering, had disturbed her. She could never trust a balding man with lank yellow hair not to pass gas in her face. Not one living in the rustic equivalent of a welfare tenement, probably hiding sons from their mother.

The little hotdog eaters had listened, unsurprised. Three unwashed boys, shaded by poverty and second-growth rainforest infested with alder, burping quietly. It was getting dark.

Was it her Mercedes SL in his yard, where jet ski engines lay around in clumpish parts, that made him glad to announce he couldn't, 'now I had the chance to sleep on it,' come down from his asking price? Matters must have soured overnight, after his acceptance of her telephoned offer from a Hong Kong propeller merchant.

When she responded that it seemed unrealistic to expect to get *everything* he was asking, he just flipped.

Mall sprawl was now killing this greedy effing valley. The once natural world had become golf courses for rich dicks. In fact, natural was now unnatural. Or hadn't she noticed the Indians being goaded into unnatural blockade tactics as a result of excesses threatening their survival? *Their* tactics had made him rethink his priorities. Selling out, sweetheart, was off.

She said she would try calling him again in the morning.

'Hang up on you, then.'

Where had she seen him before?

Biking to the lake this afternoon, across flat farm land, she'd glanced aloft for ultralights. No, that was yesterday afternoon. Today she'd driven home to change into clothes more suitable for her resort listing. Her secretary had discouraged slacks, judging Mr Douglas's mood likely to be 'jeanish'.

'Thanks, Holly.'

Still-bright American pennies, the lucky ones in her loafers, had then conjured up these same kids and last night's nightmare, just as she was setting out: underchinned men on a charter flight to the Philippines, where impoverished boys from eight to eleven were available in a Club Meddish setting of swimming pools and treats, sybaritic meals and Riesling wines ... Pink-fleshed men, buckling up doeskin belts and rearranging their desert boots, as a chartered house prepared to lift off its foundation after the lumbering fashion of a Boeing-747.

Chartered house?

As if in *punishment*, this nightmare. Who knew why? Perhaps for selling some heritage turkey she can't remember to developers she knew would doze it.

She still describes as 'peeling' the motel room she lived in after returning from L.A., age twenty. She describes it graphically to realtor seminars from Semiamhoo to Chilliwack, spinning Coffeemate like detergent into her Styrofoam cup with a plastic paddle. Getting *into* real estate had allowed her to sell this stinky motel for its disgruntled owner, invest in personalized notepads instead of breast implants, and eventually to move into her own manor, where she could recharge a cell phone and pasture a horse. To *lose* her property, now, would betray the legacy of a pioneering great-grandfather, her (his) driven nature responsible for sweeping her to the top within six months.

Old Tse, unlike the Sto:lo, resembled Doreen Kynock. He too had hoped to go all the way, but with style. A Chinese who panned for gold and thought We:st.

Gre:ed, Mr Douglas would call it, in his snorting screed against development.

Her ancestor had tried to buy into the national dream, shouldering baskets of it and dumping rocks into Hell's Gate, helping lay the CPR railbed, refusing against odds to give up on the dream. Taking in dirty laundry and not dying till after she was born.

Bryce might die this fall, before he turns forty. Twelve minutes after she does.

* * *

'By the way,' he says, ignoring her obscene remark about *knowing*. 'What're you doing up this way tonight. Agenting?'

The dishonesty between them is naked now. He can't not know she knows he's lying.

The mystery is why he bothers, except to make his dream more dangerous. Crabcakes is his dream. He's lying it still exists ... that he's part of it, for Godsake, the gourmet chef still dreaming up his own risky revue.

She isn't indifferent. Can't *afford* to be and survive herself. He should come out and tell her the truth. That his dream is gone, along with ripe old age, his kids' kids touting him as a way better cook than their grandma. So what's putting him on air tonight, hearing nothing he doesn't *want* to hear – the grass prescribed to cancer patients?

Or, she wonders, is the weed bootlegged too. The poacher's rush making danger the drug of choice for him, like lying. She thinks he could now walk from boat to shore.

'You still there?' he asks.

She says, 'To answer your question ...' And mentions frankly her aborted sale. Of white-trash property taken on for the sake of Crabcakes and how its cabin smelled of a backed-up drain. 'Worse than sour,' she says, 'other side of sewer.'

Pause. Him thinking.

Her ready to say goodbye.

She wonders whether to speed up or to let herself be passed by fast-closing headlights. Her desire is to avoid moving over.

'If your restaurant's gone under, Bryce, like Sarah told me, I'm going to need commissions from even scumbags to bail out your mortgage.'

'*Sarah* told you that?'

Fuck. 'I *know*, Bryce.'

But her echo, like his moonlit reflection in the river, carries no bad news for a poacher. He just ignores it.

Could he be telling her the truth?

Odds are against truth. As if among the illicit acts giving him a rush his biggest thrill is self-deception. As if trying to deceive his twin is an unaccountable act.

'Said you were chaperoning?' he asks. 'Where?'

Guiding conversation the way it doesn't want to go.

'High school grad. Keeping my profile high by doing community service. Dishing out my card, if asked. Being friendly and available.'

Silence. No more *hee hee*'s. Reception again crackly.

'I can't believe Sarah told you that,' he says after a spell of motor revving to reposition himself in the current – probably letting out more line to judge by the *whiz* of his reel.

The headlights crowding her rearview pull out to swoop by, music detonating inside a painted van with bubble windows. She checks her hair for frizz.

'She quit, Bi. I swear. I'm still wide open. Hosting the public and being a creative Chinese cook ...'

Adding, their clear contact suddenly restored, 'Except for one evening a week ... tonight, when I fish for supplies. My customers crave a fresh menu.'

His voice brazen in her ear. 'You think I'm *fibbing*? I think you should drill Sarah about her agenda.'

'Meaning what, Bryce?'

'Wants to marry me, little sis. Fact one. Can't get me out of her mind, *she* says, fact two. In short, a misguided woman ...'

This twist confounds her. Indifference to Sarah supposedly prompting his spurned admirer to avenge herself. Sarah as liar, not him. *No way him.*

'You asked about chaperoning? I was chaperoning the high school grad. Keeping my profile high by doing community service. Dishing out my card, if asked. Being friendly and available.'

'You said that.'

She said that.

'What's the matter?'

'I believed what Sarah told me.'

'Come and have supper, Bi. Any evening you like. Tomorrow if you like.'

Maybe he's planning to drown tonight, so she won't catch him out at his darkened door.

'The restaurant's usually full for supper, not like lunch. So your host *may* have to neglect you ... Anyhow, you'll eat good. I'm about to catch a nice sturgeon for your dining pleasure.'

She isn't sure how a two-hundred-year-old fish might taste, having led its life on the muddy bottom of Nicomen Slough, already a mature fish when old Tse arrived here as a young man from Shanghai to wash other men's tailings for gold.

More reel-whizzing in her ear. Then his voice, unexcitedly: 'Got a bite.' Is he just telling her this? About the big one soon to get away, his fading life reduced to the predictableness of an effing fish story?

Last Christmas, snorkelling through Hawaiian trigger fish, she had tried to imagine him poaching sturgeon on cold nights, as if his obsession were as natural as riding reindeer across a roof.

She imagines Douglas, the backwoods vendor, telling her excessive fishing is what brings these long-lived sturgeon to the surface now as monsters. 'Common as salmon once, now as unnatural as goddam monsters.' His rubbery lips gobbling wieners, telling her how poaching among Sto:lo used to be known as fishing. How dairy farming had become an unnatural act of dumping tires.

Trying to brain her with the tree-hugger's equivalent of a crowbar.

As Bryce would like to (he's huffing now), all of a sudden scrambling her head with stuff about comas, fish or no fish on his hook.

Sturgeon dive. Rise at. Motionless. As death.

She thinks he must *enjoy* fishing in little grunts. Limits? Upstream. One. Yearly. Downstream. *Daily.*

He's definitely fighting *something*. 'Rod bends. I come alive.' He sounds alive.

Tonight, east of the bridge, he is over his limit by about six months. 'Of course,' adding lightly, 'if Fisheries shows up. I'll just drift. Till I'm west of the bridge.'

But the forbidden is more fun. Even believable, he hopes. And since he's pretty sure of an imminent and indefinite sturgeon closure all along the river, poaching will finally be assured, *everywhere*. This same river their ancestor worked, panning it, her brother now regards as his personal pond. Mourning himself in it like a heart throb.

Telling her how dead sturgeon washed up by the dozen last year. Sturgeon living on the bottom for aeons, eating garbage like spent oolichans. Then curtains. Creatures so long-lived, he whispers, the females don't bother spawning till age twenty.

All this by way of deflecting the truth.

Maybe she ought to take his lying as an offering, given what a stick-in-the-mud she used to seem to him as a little girl.

Has she missed the joke of his vain audacity?

His reel's not whizzing any more. He seems to have lost his bite.

Maybe she should just show up at Crabcakes and be surprised, not by the absence of diners, but by a beatific dinner prepared specially for her, sturgeon done in a traditional Bosnia-Herzegovina sauce, its high-grade protein an antidote to disease and extinction. At this dinner her brother might finally come clean, over a fresh flower in the exact centre of his tablecloth, surrounded by his empty parquet floor.

'You'll be open? Tomorrow evening?'

No answer. Silence now. 'Bryce?'

'Yep. At your service, madam.'

She challenges him to back *down* … 'You know, Bryce, I just might come.' Warning him against mendacity.

'Make sure you do.' He is unwilling to give her any power over him, over his life, by dissemblance. 'Seven-thirty?'

'Make sure I do,' she echoes.

'Over and out, then.'

Gone, like that.

'Yes,' she replies. And not even this last word is hers. 'Goodbye, Bryce.'

She puts down her phone on the bucket seat opposite, and glances left, long and fervently to the white river.

She can see his ghost crossing it, leaning over his boat for a last look in the moonlight below.

She will not go. She will go.

The moon is a flower on the river. Her German engine purrs. She makes a mental note to buy pepper spray.

She knows his face like her own face, down to the deviated septum they share, one nostril slightly smaller than the other, this single blemish on their beauty like the blockage in an artery.

Having listened now to the deeper edition of her own voice, she wonders. Could she look over the transom and see his bewhiskered face reflected back at her in the star-salted river, would she see it was her face too? Who are you? Who, if not yo:u, is your brother's keeper?

COMMENT: My tale was inspired by Geoff Denton's C & W cousin. This girl was on my mind for seven months, before I started. Maybe, snobbishly, I wanted us to evolve musically from the adolescence of that rural story to a reflective urban adulthood. I don't exactly remember. I was just trying to tell a story.

As a set & lighting designer, looking for my name in a recent *Pearl Fishers* programme, I had discovered the following advice to Bizet from his former teacher, Gounod: '... Envision several pieces before writing one to assure unity and variety ... don't pay attention to known successes – be very much yourself, which means being alone today but in demand tomorrow ... and have faith in your own emotion.'

Unfortunately, the young Bizet was unable to follow through on Gounod's advice to enjoy his later fame. After struggling for twenty years he died miserably, aged thirty-six. I may have been thinking of Bizet when dreaming up my narrator, since a singer has no such illusion as Gounod's. Singing (like lighting sets) is mainly doomed to the present.

I remember when the gorgeous Gilly Pond sang *Carmen* several years ago, how I swore to give up smoking to hear her rehearse more often. It torments me still she lives only a few miles down the highway, that we occasionally work on the same production, and don't know one another from Eve.

– P.M.

Patricia Melmouth

Telling My Love Lies

— AN ELEGY —

'OUR FRAMES OF REFERENCE have changed,' she told me the week I was home. 'What your father and I have in common these days is what I say we have.'

I felt for this man. My mother had to remind me again at break-fast, after he came in from the barn, that if his memory cells were vanishing like petals in a windstorm his brainstorming cells still had a good tread. My father agreed through a mouthful of waffle, right, he was managing okay in the opinion department.

For example, watching me drive him down along the river later that May morning in 1980, to visit the federal penitentiary, he delivered this:

No matter where you live in Canada the pop music is imported, family cars are foreign, the highways long. According to him, driv-ing in our own country had become an international event. Throw in the French kiss, even one banana, a backseat copy of *Time*, and you had rewritten our national I.D. at the level of asphalt.

This level was fine by him, of course, a specialist in bald tires. Tires kept us together. Wasn't Canadian Tire a brilliant name for a company and the tire a more patriotic emblem than the beaver? 'In my opinion, that name says it all.' Even if most of our rubber like the national debt came from other countries it was rubber that kept us together.

'Count on rubber products,' was his behest to me.

He hadn't forgotten his behest to me, stippled into his memory like a tattoo. *Rubber Products. Valour and Country.* You could forget the bloody beaver.

He interrupted himself to stare appreciatively out the pickup's windshield at a glinting current of steady traffic rolling the other way. Our front wheel was whupping from the accident caused by his seizure. So I kept us under the speed limit. 'Be a big believer,' he entreated me, counting vehicles. Chances were good that scalps of some of those wheels would end up in TIRE MEADOWS.

He was the equivalent of a colonial plantation owner, tapping rubber trees for the white goo that became black profit, advising his offspring how my future should carry on his past. So far it hadn't, he knew, and wasn't going to. I did not know if opera singing was the exact opposite of tire-farming, but it must have come as close as the well-known duet of chalk and cheese, in Puccini's beloved opera *Olio e Acqua*.

'I take it you're being humorous.'

'Witty, yeah.'

My teenage friends used to narrow their eyes at his rubber fields, unzipping to leak on his B.F. Goodrich inventory in our poplar-lined drive. I was mortified to be the son of a man who'd turned his dairy farm into a tire dump. I was ashamed of having had such a blackish youth amid once emerald fields.

'I take it you're being witty.'

'Humorous, yeah.'

Stretching the point now, I can see how his obsession with rubber might be viewed as prophetic back then – if not in the way he expected. He didn't live long enough to see condoms take off in the marketplace, not long enough to see the latex condom become a kind of international flag of operation, blowing like a windsock from every airport's control tower where sex is a commodity for disembarking young singers like me, and every other kind of tourist scrambling for a place in the sun.

— 2 —

At the time of our penitentiary visit my father had two years left to live. He would die in a mystifying traffic accident. His affliction, about as rare as AIDS then was in 1980, seemed partly responsible for his death. Unhelpful to call it marble-loss, although this is what it amounted to with epileptic overtones. The neurologist had no idea what had caused his brain seizure, leading to his recent physical collapse.

And I thought they could trace the serial number on these failures.

Earlier that morning, my first in a week home from California, I'd learned from my mother the extent of his affliction before the neurologist put him on an anticonvulsant to stop his auras. The auras had been washing over him agreeably, or so she reported my father telling her, for two or three years before this, each one amounting to a mini-seizure, a little stroke in the brain he didn't know he was having except to remark to her on its gratifying premonition of a pleasant b.m. – beginning in his intestines, but then, changing direction, and pushing up through his trunk and flooding down his arms. She said he claimed to think a lot about death at such times. Quite pleasantly, in fact.

'Erotic.'

Erotic? I tried, but could only picture a mini-seizure as resembling a match scratching on brain putty and never quite catching fire inside the humid temporal lobe where his trouble was located. She mapped the geography of his affliction enthusiastically on the oilcloth, before breakfast, with a red lacquered nail.

'It isn't the occipital lobe, if that's what you're thinking.'

'No.'

She tapped her map. 'It's the lateral lobe.'

'The lateral lobe.'

Her swirlish nails had always surprised peeing callers at TIRE MEADOWS, used to farm moms who deplored such honed razor blades. This was several years before punk came in – otherwise they might've viewed her grandness with less suspicion. She liked to think she was not an unfashionable woman, given the workglove milieu she was forced to endure. Only dresses by Omar the Tentmaker spoiled her grand design.

'He was enjoying himself, mon cher, in a manner of speaking.' Still on auras. Evidently my father hadn't made the connection between his premonitions of death in the last three years and his growing forgetfulness of events over this same period.

The failing memory had become her chief concern. He'd

completely forgotten a weekend plane trip taken together last year to visit her sister in Calgary sick with kidney stones; and, worse, couldn't recall it when she tried filling him in on the 'dreary' tower restaurant where they ate pepper steaks, not to mention that her sister's haggish cat had been 'ill' in the lap of his new hound's tooth slacks. 'I might as well have been talking to the cows,' she told me before breakfast. By October he'd even forgotten their visit to the PNE in Vancouver, for the Holstein heifer competition, followed by a Giant Truck scrunching in the Agrodome of half a dozen worn-out Renaults.

'... Goes without saying he was riveted to tires big enough to drive up and over a whole car. Now he can't remember the tires *or* the heifers. I've never heard louder engines, anywhere.'

My father had evidently mentioned his fickle memory to Perumbur's G.P., joking about his Alzheimer's at a prostate checkup, the agreeable sensations he was having in an out-of-body kind of way complete with pleasantly unpleasant premonitions of death. But the doctor hadn't recognized what turned out to be his petit mal symptoms.

'You remember how casual Hopkins can be. When he retires the great man wants to tootle around Asia.'

Not until my father had a grand mal seizure, and my mother rushed him back for another appointment, did the light in the physician's brain finally switch on.

Driving them in for groceries, my father had suffered a shuddering paralysis and collapsed in his pickup. Rigid, gagging, right out of it. Luckily, he ran into the gatepost, wrecking his suspension but stopping them dead before reaching the paved road where sloughs on either side were skindiver-deep with winter runoff.

The violent jolt bloodied his teeth against the steering wheel. By now he'd lost consciousness. Gone purple, choking on his tongue: before my mother, listening to the sound he was making, 'like keening at an Ibo wake', felt she should stick in her fingers before he suffocated. Prying open his mouth she broke her nails.

'Have you read *The Idiot*?' Dr Hopkins asked him.

'It sounded insulting,' said my mother. 'But then you have to remember Hopkins is as sideways as a skate.' Trying to get a straight

answer from Hopkins, I could recall, was like consulting a high
school counsellor for a hunting licence. No comprenez, no dice.

He suspected my father's earliest fullblown seizures might have
started some time before this first daylight seizure. During the
night he meant, sleeping. He knew this was difficult to document.

'If you had a seizure in your sleep, Bill, Jane wouldn't have
noticed it unless she happened to be awake. Even then, how likely a
witness in the dark? She might've heard something, of course. Did
you, Jane?'

She volunteered that some mornings her husband had complained of aches clear through his body, like he'd been run over by
an eighteen-wheeler. She put this down to arthritis, the dairyman's
disease, from decades of stooping and lifting, squeezing and pouring. Her information only bolstered Hopkins' theory of nighttime
comas.

He sent them straight to a neurologist at the Royal Columbian,
for tests like standing on one foot and trying to remember unmate-
able words – fudge, horn lessons, Buick; numbers: 58, 17, 143 – and
this specialist hospitalized my father for a week to monitor his cells
and blood pressure, and to gauge his reaction to anticonvulsants.

Then they waited for a turn at the twenty-first century. To have
his brain imaged by a CAT scan my father had to inform hospital
staff he had no cerebral aneurysm clip, middle ear implant, or any
stimulatory device like a pacemaker. He had to put aside his loose
change and credit cards. His good health was supposed to be worth
it.

Since March, two scans – both tests placing his head like an egg
inside a wind tunnel, and my mother's nerves on eggshells, from
driving him back and forth on the Trans-Canada – had turned up
no tumour, or even scar tissue from a possibly traumatic birth. The
neurologist, studying the inner brain routes, must have wondered at
the all-clear results. 'He was very polite,' decided my mother, 'très
cosmopolitan. European Semite.'

The results, while compounding the mystery of my father, were
a relief to them both. If the seizures' source remained unresolved, at
least the pills had stopped them, provided he stayed on anticonvulsants the rest of his life. He was also on Elavil for depression, and

Tums Extra Strength to counteract the bone-sapping side effects of a drug binge.

My mother had rattled an amber-coloured plastic tube next to his placemat at the breakfast table and set it down again like a salt shaker. I picked it up and tapped out one of the pretty yellow capsules, engraved MSD 45. In my palm it resembled a premature jellybean.

He was no longer allowed to drive. And he had to expect a 'diminishment of libido', as this nurse, charged with the responsibility of keeping their bed on an even keel, confided.

According to her he'd never felt better in his life. Alert, nice to be around, sans hangups d'any sort. My mother isn't one to deploy a simple compliment when a fancy phrase might better complicate her effect.

My father came in from milking, pleased to hear us popping off in French.

— 3 —

Because the lot was full I parked the pickup on the street. That week the B.C. Pen was shutting down after 102 years, with an Open House for the public to cruise inside its castle-like walls before letting them fall to crooks who built condos. Inmates had relocated to a new facility in Agassiz.

My father wanted a glimpse of his family's criminal past, which constituted one of his earliest and lasting memories. He had decided to test himself today, to see if he could remember what he'd never actually seen, a revolver, said to be on display.

He recalled his mother's stories about the famous inmate who once owned it. She knew him as a young girl when, to her awful delight, he had unpocketed it. His secret weapon was always the highlight of her recollections, that and his piggybacks.

So my father's memory was really, in this case, my grandmother's. His recollection was *her* recollection of what had happened in her brief acquaintance with a train robber. This piece of family history, received as gospel, was no more forgettable to him than the parable of the prodigal son.

He seemed unsurprised that his childhood memory should remain entirely untouched by recent seizures, though perhaps his deterioration had begun by spreading backward in time with earliest recollections still his most vivid.

His mother and her older sister had met the be-weaponed 'Mr Edwards' while herding their stubborn cow across CPR tracks in Silverdale, some miles upvalley from Perumbur, and even more miles upriver from the prison where this holdup artist would eventually land when it was still a new institution.

'Need some help, girls? Uppity cow gotcha mad?'

An old southern gentleman, slender, soft-spoken. My grandmother remembered a tattoo of a dancing girl on his right forearm when he flashed them his pistol. Aunt Betty corroborated the pistol, but disagreed over the existence of any tattoo. Neither girl had suspected an iota of 'Mr Edwards'' criminal past – nor of his future in which their farm indirectly figured. My grandmother was five or six, not too old to be piggybacked but still too young to be suspicious of a stranger. He loved children. A feeling reciprocated. He'd shown up day after day, evidently reconnoitring their land for an escape route, reminding them playfully not to betray his secret.

His was the first train robbery in Canada.

Not until the wanted poster appeared did the old man's true identity become known to my forebears.

'It was like a revelation to them,' my father reported. 'Instead of hating him, they stood up for the guy. He'd told them stories and flaunted his gun. Helped them gate the cow every afternoon. They loved this masher more than ever. Probably owing to their father's religiosity and such ...'

I knew he was remembering accurately what more or less happened. I'd heard my grandmother tell her version of this same romance at Easter and Christmas dinners.

Our prison tour began in hot sunshine and a long line, snaking through a little oak door in the large Fantasyland gate. We climbed stairs to Admitting and Discharge, my father hobbling some from his arthritis, into a large room where each newcomer had had a military haircut in the chrome barber chair, followed by a disinfectant bath. My father approved both measures.

'Sent up the river,' he joked, his once baritone voice now fraying into a higher register. 'You can bet a guy was pumping his paddle to get outta this load of grief.'

This may have reminded him of his own predicament, because after a while he said:

'I never said it to your mother, but those turns I was taking? Before I got put on medication? Bliss. I think you know what kind of bliss I mean if I say bunk bliss. Shacked-up bliss. I miss my auras.'

He was peering into one of the monkish cells in Block B7, left as it had been for the tourists before its last resident vacated. Grey white-striped blanket, a wall-mounted TV, gravity-defying centre-folds on the ceiling with sprouting nipples.

'... Happiness of being and body you can't imagine. All I remember of my big fit is this joy, before I blacked out. And then when I woke up – for some reason, guilt. For cheating my body out of the death experience? Some weird crime like that.'

Concluding, a little sadly, 'Taking the pills has stopped the bliss business.'

Of all the cells we saw later, in the Hole and in the north and east wings, he would remember liking best these few with the river view, staring down at log booms and lazy sawmill smoke threading the cage of the Patullo Bridge. I never got an opportunity before he died to see how long he'd remember our visit. Longer, maybe, than I knew. For during my week home I would soon discover the reliability of his unreliability open to question.

We found an exhibition of prisoners' paintings for sale in The Hub. *Treed Hills. Screw in a Tuxedo. Doodles Like Graffiti. River Scow with Woodchips.* 'Con jobs,' joked my father.

He was quite taken with them, really – I think because he could see through them, how they'd come about in response to some flimsy Art Rehab agenda. He pinpointed this as the explanation for an otherwise useless waste of time. The prisoners' paintings were all about 'lying their way outta here. Kinda glamorous.'

His opinion caused me to conjure one of my own. To me none of these 'Stop-Points of Interest' seemed as exotic as the flimsiest jail set of a *Tosca* production in some school lunchroom. I said opera, with its emotional sort of truth, you saw through right away. I was trying to reinforce his own opinion. This made it glamorous, I suggested, the total commitment to two-dimensional cardboard and passion.

'Interesting,' he remarked.

And looked over to see if I was mocking him.

At last, the gym. Menacing objects confiscated from inmates lined a few portable shelves, including carved wooden pistols alongside Bibles opened up to pages gouged out in the shape of these fake weapons once concealed in the hands of putative penitents.

'Is that not clever?' said my father, admiring their industriousness. 'Artistic.'

The family pistol, a real pistol, was mounted by the trigger guard on two nails inside a glass case. The card said it was the weapon Bill Miner had used to hold up the CPR express on September 10, 1904.

I glanced at my father to see if it was the weapon he remembered, as it were, the same pistol his mother had seen in the flesh. A pearl-handled, black Colt .38, with an obscene prick of a trigger, a dorsal-fin hammer, and a plumpish cylinder with six little tunnels.

'That's the one,' he said.

And insisted his mother could still remember the night the Express was held up, a few yards from her farm, associating the sound of her gate opening after dark with 'this oddity' of a train stopping where it had never stopped before.

The squealing brakes woke her up.

He was clearly moved by our adventure into his family's past. 'And *this weapon*,' he said grimly, 'was centre stage.' It was his certainty of the fact, his arthritic grip on reality, that seemed to reassure him.

The more he studied the pistol the more he recognized its details. Clearly, guilt by association improved his memory.

If short-term memory was a problem, he was still flawless on the prenatal stuff.

He examined the wanted poster pinned up beside the stark family heirloom, a picture from which his mother and aunt would have recognized their gentleman friend: jug-eared, white-mustachioed; above a printed description of his colouring, and his inspired escape from these same walls.

My father was calculating something on his fingers. 'Hey,' he said. 'I'm exactly the same age as this guy, sixty-five, when he Houdinied outta here in nineteen-seven for the States.'

'Dad,' I said. 'Aren't you fifty-eight this year?'

'Me?' He suddenly looked sheepish. He thought over the possibility of seven lost years. Then sighed, a little pissed off for having misplaced his future if what I told him could be confirmed in an independent audit by my mother.

'Lately, I seem to be throwing away the odd half-decade.'

Another Miner poster – issued by the Pinkerton Detective Agency in 1903 – for a train robbery in Corbett, Oregon, exactly one year before the CPR holdup, showed a much younger man than the one posted in 1907. I glanced through the fine print.

The family felon had been 'liberated' from San Quentin in June, 1901, where he'd served twenty-five years for 'stage robbery, less good time allowance.' Under 'Peculiarities and Marks' the description concluded: '... Mole on breast near point of right shoulder. Walks erect. Is said to be a sodomist and may have a boy with him.'

So what was his dancing-girl tattoo, a decoy?

– 4 –

I had been born on this same day, in 1957. At precisely three-thirty that afternoon, as my father and I drove whupping home, I turned twenty-three. Back at the farm we found my mother making a birthday supper, and she wasn't surprised to learn her husband had come home seven years older. 'He's like a fox terrier, if you let him loose. He counts in dog years.'

Was it that? I felt older than my age too. Baritones do, I believe. Growing up I sometimes wondered if our worn-out tires gave me the world-weary sense my friends found comic. It took the horizons out of adolescence. It made me passive-aggressive. I hated TIRE MEADOWS for its contradiction in terms.

I was staring out the kitchen window as my father departed to milk his six last cows. The driveway was rutted from transport trucks still arriving twice a week to dump tires. Our once green fields were heaped up into black ridges. In between lay pockets of pasture, kept clear by the bulldozer he hired monthly in a losing range war to maintain his cows and preserve the tax status of a farmer. A mile away they were removing part of a mountain for gravel. The light we'd lost here to tires was beginning to show up there.

'You're right,' I said. 'It really has some gaps.'

'What does?' asked my mother.

'His memory. It's not like he forgets something called fish and chips then remembers. The idea of fish and chips is totally foreign to him.'

I had treated him to a late lunch downriver at King Neptune, baffled to find this swiftest of fast foods a surprise to his taste buds. 'I could get to like fish and chips,' he said. I didn't think he was joking. He poked at our exotic order. Cod rolled in a tawny crust, potatoes cut into oblong fingers. The whole cliché meal swamped in tartar sauce.

'Fish and chips is a new one,' said my mother, dumping pasta with a swishy flourish into boiling water. 'Usually it's some event with him, like he can't remember it ever *happening*.'

She smiled through the steam. 'Have to envy him his virgin tongue.' For such a confirmed farm widow her nails still looked seditious. 'Maybe dying is all about discovering your taste buds.' Comically, she smacked her lips.

'*Is* he dying?'

'You mean, at a faster rate than us?'

She said this with the aplomb of a soprano trailing her exit line. 'Voilà. Where's my colander?'

She was preparing my favourite childhood meal, chicken thighs and rigatoni. A meal I could take or leave now, accustomed lately to hauter cuisine. My mother thought at worst I'd find her home cooking droll.

'They prevent constipation,' she said.

'Pardonnez-moi?'

'The bay leaves.' Little petals were mottling her tinned-soup-

and-sour-cream sauce. 'And you know what your father always used to say about going to the bathroom.'

By now the three of us were sitting at the dining-room table, after my mother had changed into a new azure dress and adjusted the dimmer switch.

'What was it I always used to say?' he asked, grateful to be noticed.

'Well,' she warned, 'it wasn't the prettiest thing you ever said.'

'No,' he agreed. 'Bet it wasn't.' He winked at me.

The mood elevators had had a noticeable effect on his humour since my last visit home, between graduation in Vancouver and post-grad coaching in San Francisco. My mother had been giving *in* at the time to his growing depression and absent-mindedness. His life had been controlling hers, in an increasingly resentful way to them both.

She turned to me and in her grand manner repeated what he always used to say, but which I certainly did not remember him saying:

' "A crap in the bowl is worth two in the bowel." '

The laugh I was then polishing at opera school, the room-hugging *Ha-ha* that I'd eventually need as a bon vivant baritone beloved of after-performance green-roomers and, I was sure, media interviewers, went off. It was as phony as a three-dollar bill (a two-dollar bill in the country where I was newly resident). Its boom could blow the awning off a lawn party.

I call it my Shotgun. It serves the same purpose as the soprano's Hoot or the mezzo's Chortle. Pulling the trigger clears heavy air. Flirts outrageously, whether or not there's anybody to flirt with, anybody to impress. Its only danger is wounding by accidental ridicule. The tenor, incidentally, Whinnies. Very sincere. Always gets the girl by Whinnying in his oats.

(Not always. *I* ended up with her once, as Strephon the Arcadian Shepherd, in a college production of *Iolanthe*. Phyllis is the girl, Ward of Court. Sung beautifully, I remember, by fellow student Roberta Pardy. What's happened to Roberta in these fourteen years since? Or Marshall van Neer, for that matter. He was wonderful as Charles Tolloller, MP. Where are you, Marshall?)

'*I* don't remember him saying that!' I boomed cheerily, about my father's depressing toilet-bowl proverb.

'Thank your lucky stars,' whispered my mother, jouncing her silver bracelets as she hid coyly behind a billowing diaphanous sleeve. 'C'est incroyable!'

My father looked wounded.

At least he did until wrinkling his brow upward, saucering his eyes in a look of mock astonishment at her amazing disclosure of a confidence. I remember he used to do this if I happened to overhear words pass between them as a child I wasn't meant to overhear. This would tip me off not to take them seriously. Wanting me to know they knew *I* knew.

'Not pretty, she's right. Surprises me that. I was quite a philosopher.'

I laughed again. (Is it a French sage who says the man who exhibits a tits-and-haemorrhoid sense of humour deserves the laughter he gets?)

A laugh to belie my years. In auditions a baritone, unlike a tenor, must give an impression of ripeness and maturity. Corruption is all. I still didn't know then if I would amount to a professional singer of any distinction. Twenty-three is very young to know how corrupt you can be. If, at eighteen, I knew how to lie in public, I was still trying to understand why it seemed necessary to keep it up in private.

'*I* don't remember him saying that,' I repeated.

My mother now said, a little pompously, 'I suppose you don't remember us coming down to visit you in San Francisco either, last October. You're as bad as he is.'

She turned to my father. 'One memory going is bad enough, William. Two looks like a family trait. I hope his isn't going the way of all flesh, like yours seems.'

My father turned sheepish again, as he had that afternoon at the Bastille. He looked down at his plate and poked the orange lump of chicken with his fork tines. Fingernails rimmed with muck.

'Did we take a trip to San Francisco last October?'

You could tell exactly from his tone how shame arising from loss of memory should sound. At the time I made a mental note of it, and have since called it up in the role of Sharpless.

'Don't you remember Chinatown?' My mother sounded like she was scolding him for forgetting some bargain they'd got on half a kilo of ginseng.

He looked up, puzzled. 'I don't, no.'

She sighed. 'Or the restaurant, where Fin was one of the singing waiters?'

'Him?' The idea of a singing waiter seemed to tickle him. He chuckled. 'Did I have fun?' It sounded like a private joke they'd shared more than once. His teeth, where he'd smashed them three months ago against the steering wheel, had gone dark. 'Did I have fun?'

'We had a grand old time. Fin, what was the name of that restuarant again?'

'Max's Opera Café.'

'That's it, yes.' She smiled, remembering my performance serving them and then, as a special request she said, serenading their anniversary in front of the whole restaurant. 'I remember you sang us a funny aria.'

It was true I sang a funny Figaro in English, 'Now your days of philandering are over ...', even a tragicomic impersonation of Elvis Costello doing Rigoletto's 'La donna è mobile'. I usually finished up an evening with a heartfelt Marcello, 'Our love is still alive ...'

But they hadn't heard me sing any of these arias, and I wondered if I shouldn't stand up now and knock one off, to compensate for depriving them of the wonderful talent they'd helped nourish since adolescence.

'Excuse me, will you?' said my father.

Our merriment on top of his medication was pushing on his bladder. He got up slowly and hobbled out to the toilet.

When I heard the door close I turned to my mother.

'What're you saying? He never used to talk about his bowels, did he?'

'No, but it pleased him.'

I paused to digest this. 'Well, okay. But –'

She started being coy again with her sleeve.

I said, 'Aren't you worried he might remember?'

'What would he remember?'

'For one thing, the truth. That you and he have never been to San Francisco. At least, not to see me. What's with the BS?'

She dropped her arm, abandoning veil and flaps, squaring her padded shoulders to give me an imperious look in the candlelight, a look that over a finer meal I might have mistaken for majestic. She then picked up her knife. 'I'm telling my love lies.'

I couldn't help it, I laughed.

'Lies? Why?'

'Why?' She sounded like I ought to know why, given her account this morning of his affliction. 'Wouldn't you want a little filler in your life, if you'd had your memory neutered?'

I had no idea, if I would or not. Filler? Not quite mercy killing, more like mercy feeding. Fish and chips for the experientially famished.

'Our frames of reference have changed. What your father and I have in common these days is what I say we have.'

She put down her knife and picked it up again. 'He has a right to the same little pleasures you and I take for granted. His memories just need stimulating, is all.'

She speared a mushroom with her fork and put its sleek skin to her lips. She smiled. 'I crack a big whip. Pour le bon motif.'

It was as if she, too, were snacking on Elavil. Heartiness was in the air.

The ideal husband returned chuckling to the table. After tucking in his shirt he resumed pecking at his pasta and poulet, wanting to know if there was garlic in the sauce. My mother assured him there wasn't. 'Cherry head,' she called him.

Or garlic in the birthday cake? 'I hate birthday cake with garlic,' he joked. 'Anyways, I remember Fin prefers onions in his cake.'

I'd never heard them together so playful before. If this is what it was. She reached across and pinched a bay leaf from his plate. I poured us some more wine from a bottle of Sonoma Valley Chardonnay.

My father wasn't supposed to drink more than a glassful, but he didn't object to a refill. 'Mud in your eye,' he said.

'Mud in yours,' I said.

'You got plans for the rest of your stay?' he asked. 'Make free with the pickup. Needs a wheel realignment, as you know. But it'll get you wherever.'

Before I blew out my candles he sang me 'Happy Birthday' with good diction and a flawless memory for the lyrics.

Forgetting to make a wish, but pinching the wicks, I said I might borrow his truck to visit the lake tomorrow.

'Uh huh.'

I also mentioned needing to rehearse one or two roles during my stay. I'd try not to get in their hair.

'Not in our hair,' said my mother, patting hers.

'No sir,' said my father, keeping his hand on his glass.

After my third piece of cake I opened their gift wrapped in pillowy tissue paper and a yellow ribbon the width of a shoelace. A pretty cashmere scarf.

'I know how you opera stars are always being careful not to catch colds,' said my mother. 'Isn't your fog down there hard on the vocals? We thought you could wear blue in the sunshine without looking like an Eskimo.'

My father was grinning into his Chardonnay.

Nearer bedtime she confided she hoped dinner had tasted exactly as I remembered it growing up, or better, because she'd slipped in three garlic cloves. She sounded whimsical and a bit tipsy. The garlic was supposed to be for my father's own good. But I think she wanted me to know she wasn't unfamiliar with the kind of nouvelle ingredients I was helping serve at Max's Opera Café.

I wondered if it was true. I hadn't tasted any garlic.

Later that night I was returning from the bathroom when her low voice stopped me outside their bedroom door. She was talking to my father. The voice was muffled in the darkness, but distinct enough to follow from the hallway.

'... me either. You wouldn't let me sleep two winks last night.'

'What was I after?'

'You know what you were after. Tonight, you just better give me a little peace.'

'What if I don't?' My father sounded quite interested in the consequences.

So was I.

Something garbled from my mother here. By the sound of the gurgling and sloshing, she was adjusting her six-foot frame to get comfortable on their waterbed.

Then she spoke again. 'The first time I ever saw you, Bill, you were standing with sweat trickling down the gully in your bare back. Remember, haying? I almost had a bird. I wanted to come over and prick one of those drops, in the bushy hair over your neck before it started ... '

'Do it. Put your hands up.'

Silence. Followed by a fainter voice, hers. 'If I don't ...?'

I swear, on one of those hollowed-out Bibles in the pen, I heard him drawl sotto voce:

'Then I might have to pistol-whip you.'

I did wonder, returning to my room, whether I was overhearing a therapy session or a honeymoon. Things had got operatic since my last visit home. My old bedroom had new bordello wallpaper, sheers, and a Carnegie Hall poster of Sherrill Milnes.

The window was open, its curtains the same diaphanous material as my mother's dress, billowing like a tent in a sandstorm.

A dog or a fox barked at the hen run. A cowbell clanked once among the tire piles, some cow desperate for a bit of pasture in the wending valleys between tasteless, lickless rubber. On occasion, searching for a salt block, a cow could go missing overnight, necklaced and locked by its own horns inside a Dunlop.

I tried to fall asleep, counting tires.

It was like trying to doze in a clearcut, with the rings of every stump sprung loose, twisted and jumbled up like hula hoops until they obliterated the landscape a million times for every year of my father's greed.

(Given a choice, I think any son coming of age in similar circumstances would've preferred Sartre's idea of hell to Walt Disney's.)

To try out the cashmere scarf, I flossed it under my balls for an agreeable two minutes, before crisscrossing the tasselled ends around my consequent erection, arching my back like a catamite and knotting these tightly above my ass.

Then I jerked off into the night air.

Being home had stimulated my own memory in the manner of a bad joke. The *smells* of the place ganged up on my brain cells to smother them with trivial associations. I went back to counting tires. Soon found it was tires I was trying to forget.

I tried jumping sheep through them. The Arcadian past closed down on my face like a coffin lid. I could smell the tired air and decided this was getting silly. I might have to get out of bed to close the window.

By my late adolescence we'd become secure without ever being comfortable. And so it remained. My mother called this farm our cash cow, sardonically, as milk sales had declined in the twenty years since my father had begun replacing cattle with tires, from a total of seventy-five Holsteins and the daily equivalent of a sea of milk, to the present hobby total of six cows and a few gallons to sell as calf-mash mix.

Our dependence on milk had shrunk with the swelling revenue from tires. The rubber fields, as they hilled up over the pasture, had begun to overwhelm the landscape like coal tailings in the British Midlands. In winter, if the puddles froze, ice-skating between the crevasses felt claustrophobic, dark.

The dump grew, though so gradually the tires never seemed, at least in my memory of them, to be anything but *here*. They never really grew. Yet they must have been growing. When I awoke on the morning after my birthday, May 5, 1980, they'd spread up to the house overnight. They were rubbing against the windowsill.

I woke up dreaming. Closed the window and went back to bed.

I couldn't remember a time when tires didn't make me wish the fetid rainwater trapped year by year inside all of them, breeding mosquitoes, irrigating rodents, couldn't be siphoned out to fill my father's bath and waterbed for the rest of his living days.

Yet weren't we doing our share to keep the highways safe from accidents and the rest of the country pollution-free?

My father's opinion of the tire business had undergone a change since he first got into it. In more recent years he'd actually begun to dream of returning his farm to the green space it once was. This in response to the environmental movement, just then beginning to gather steam, but really in answer to his new idea for profit.

To wit:

These rubber fields would continue to rise in his belief that someday he'd be able to augment the tire-bounty fees he charged to tire-stores and auto wreckers, by turning over for a recycling profit the very tires he'd accepted for profit, thereby defeating all laws of capitalism by having people give him money for taking in their junk, and then having somebody else give him money for carting it away.

Ergo the equivalent of hanging *on* to our cash cow – yet not only *not* having to clean up after her, but being paid to let someone else do the mucking out.

No wonder neighbouring dairymen looked down on him: as well as a polluter he was an arrogant s.o.b.

My father really believed the future would see his farm become a win-win, profit-profit kind of operation – a kind of half-way house for tires without ruining the neighbourhood. And profitable for the whole chain of entrepreneurs up the ladder, who were soon going to possess the technology and ingenuity to recycle bald tires back into new ones, reselling them to wholesalers and retailers, until their products once again rolled through our farm on their balding ways to four-ply reincarnation.

'Believe in rubber products.'

With growing confidence he'd repeat his belief that recycling was going to make him a millionaire in the eighties. Even then – in the seventies, his memory still good – he was ahead of himself, having launched his business in the sixties when dreamboat whitewalls were still the fashion but growing skinnier by the year. (I remember as a child when they vanished entirely along with inner tubes from loads arriving at the farm, so he could no longer scribble figures on these funguses with his saliva and a grease pencil.)

Over the past year my mother had been writing dutifully to me of his green dream, on heavy bond paper of creamy hue, with an embossed crest of TIRE MEADOWS printed like BRIDGESTONE around the upper rim of a laurel-leafed tire. (*Residence of William and J. Francesca Speranza Sauvage ...*) The crest might as well have said OCEAN VIEW or FOREST LAWN, the euphemism made us sound like a graveyard.

Except nothing got buried here (or else everything did) and any hoped-for decomposition was imperceptible. Tires these days lasted forever because of tougher manufacturing standards: steel belt radials, indelibly efficient treads, fibreglass compounds in the rubber itself. They were now impossible to get rid of.

'A rubber tire is a tough nut to break down,' complained my father, still hopeful.

My mother had been ending her letters to me, mockingly, 'Believe in rubber products.' Though remembering to add, out of loyalty to her husband, 'Even if they *enterrent* the farm, they still help keep you IN VOICE. Speaking of *in*voices ...' You took her playfulness at face value and chucked the letter.

My father, knowing how much I spurned his idea of a family company, continued to hope I was the future he envisioned. My mother on the other hand expected me to succeed in the opera world and was willing to keep sending money till I did.

She felt I'd paid my dues as a teenager with a très drôle nature (her nature) in aiding and abetting le père's double-profit fantasy for recycling the common tire.

Example, tire slashers, a farm for juvenile toughs to come out from the city on day trips to carve away to their hearts' content. I urged us to dish out knives and collect them at the gate when they left. Make a killing from the Corrections Services, then sell the shredded rubber like excelsior to packagers of French-Canadian crockery.

'I take it you're being humorous.'

Tire chairs? For the haemorrhoidal?

'Witty,' he said.

My mother enrolled me in singing lessons, to help spike the sarcasm. She was still whisking me off to choir practice and piano lessons. Stuff to get me away from the depressing influence of the local crop. Stuff to stop me calling it *stuff*, for heaven's sake, at a time when I was still more interested in athletes than artists.

My only chance to help my father's recycling dream, and to put a dent in his inventory, happened the summer I got a job at Perumbur

Lake. The floats needed new tires and I loaded two dozen into the pickup and donated them.

It was like trying to lower the level of the lake with a teacup.

'How much you soak 'em for the tires?' asked my father.

'I take it you're being witty.'

'Humorous, yeah.'

Even he was struck with the growing evidence of his ambition, for all who passed to see. While farms around us were growing in value, ours had declined because the land itself had disappeared. Given the dramatic rise in property values, I think he now wished the price we got for accepting tires was enough to prevent him from wishing he'd never started.

How to relive the past. Rubber baby bumpers, said a million times, equals the present and so constitutes an absurd family of headaches. Sartre? Then some other French swot, babies on the brain.

When he saw his fields begin to fill up my father knew he'd need a dozer to push his inventory into higher and higher piles to give him more dumpage space per square acre for our product.

'You snicker when I mention "product",' he told me, 'but that's what it is. Instead of haying I bulldoze. I build up our return. Every pile represents dollars in accounts received. This is a very visual-type crop, Fin. Even pays for your cup and garter. Your mother won't tell me how much the Bauers cost. Without tires, though, you wouldn't be playing the national game. Not in summer hockey camps. Too frigging expensive for a dairyman.'

In the kitchen at breakfast my mother was standing by her stove.

'Did we keep you awake last night?'

'No. Why?'

'Him. He gets insomnia from his medication. I thought I heard you.'

'Visiting the john, probably.'

'Waffles or crèpes?'

'Crèpes sound good.'

'He hates crèpes.'

'Waffles then.'

'I've made crab and mushroom crèpes. Avec garlic.'

My father was still in the barn. I thanked her for the poster in my bedroom. Where had she got it?

'Milnes' people sent it when I wrote him a fan letter in New York. One day your people will be doing the same, for fans like me.'

I was warming up at the piano. I always recall Beverly Sills saying in an interview she never knew in what voice she was going to awake each morning. That morning was like coming up for air. I had the bends. It took me a while to catch the rhythm of breathing from the diaphragm.

Hay fever on a grassless farm seemed a contradiction in terms. When had my asthma begun?

My mother looked on from the kitchen, bemused by my vocal foragings. I was relearning the role of Rocco in *Fidelio*, since a university degree in Vocal Performance had foisted upon me bad habits – in Act One's F major trio, for instance, starting 'Gut, Söhnchen, gut …' To attack this phrase without forcing it was a small yet critical detail when coached at a persnickety level of hypersensitive ears. My mother's ears were more attuned to gossip.

'Why don't you phone up Holly Harker for an assignation?' she suggested. 'I hear she's home again. Things didn't work out with what's-his-name.'

'Kupe?'

'Rupert. Yes. The dairyman.' She pronounced his occupation as though her own husband had always been above cows.

Holly Harker was Seth Harker's younger sister. Five years ago she'd agreed to go along with me to my high school grad when I needed a date who wouldn't get embarrassed by my belting out O Canada to the assembly like one of these gallic Quebecois on 'Hockey Night in Canada', before seguing into an elegy for our friend Michael who'd drowned, a song he'd liked, 'Yesterday'.

'You might ask her up to the lake. I could pack you a picnic.'

'She used to claim to like quince,' I said. 'We got any quince?'

Eat well is one of John Goldsmith's guidelines for singers, as it should be for teenagers. Laugh a lot, avoid places with foul air, treat your body like a valued instrument, and pee pale.

As a teenager your whole life can go bad from the start.

After breakfast I drove up to the lake. Five years ago that week Michael had drowned. I passed a slim woman in stretch gear pumping a racing machine across the flood plain. At the boat launch I noticed tires I'd hammered to floats seven years ago still in good flexible shape. Which was why my father especially disliked Firestones. They'd probably outlast the floats. Might even outlast the lake. Flank Narrows was where the lake ended and the tidal river began. The last smells of sea gave way to a light wind tasting of snowfields.

Mr Douglas lived part-time in the houseboat tied up to a pile of four rotting logs. He was away, though you couldn't be sure, looking at his weed-hulled, dirty-curtained scow, if he wasn't just hiding. I knocked. The muscly man, inseparable from his T-shirt, didn't appear. A 200 Johnson outboard, bolted to his stern, would need mechanical labour in excess of its value before it would ever restart. I don't know where he'd got money to pay me in high school, unless misappropriated from the Forest Service. The Forest Service had erected two fibreglass outhouses for users of the lake. Recreation came cheap here.

So had I.

In season Douglas would supervise the boat ramp with its muddy trailer slip. To birders he rented out kayaks and canoes. When the season began, my job had been to bail out the canoes and keep things afloat for the duration of summer. Teenagers would drive up and launch ski-boats, throw each other off the floats, hang out at the aluminum trailer that advertised Joe's Disappearing Tattoos at one end and an Eats and Pop counter at the other.

The scene hadn't changed. Discarded safes and candy wrappers, rusted outboard gas tanks lying without hoses in a ditch of purple loosestrife. Only the carpark seemed unlittered: no vans or boat trailers, dirt bikes or hot carbs. The heat of summer just beginning to burn.

I could see smoke rising from a solitary cabin across the narrows. Downstream, at the end of a thirteen-mile meander, the Fraser swept away this slow current to the gulf. The lake itself disappeared

PATRICIA MELMOUTH

in the other direction, twenty miles north into wilderness.

On the marsh's boundary a flock of starlings suddenly wheeled and dove to sanctuary. Two recent watchtowers had cropped up on the dike's gated gravel road. Birders must've climbed these to spy on nesting sandhill cranes. No end to their petty peeping from day to day, as I once told Mr D. He liked the youth he hired to amuse and keep him happy.

The woman on the ten-speed had arrived and was resting sveltely, watching from shore. Without her helmet, with her dark hair loose and luxurious, she looked Chinese.

I found a bucket hooked above the cat mattress and carried it ashore, where I waded in to the submerged canoes. Douglas felt sinking his fleet discouraged borrowers and deterred the thievish. I hauled up an aluminum bow and bailed.

From the pickup I fetched my mother's picnic basket, nestling under a velvet blanket like Red Riding Hood's cape got up to resemble the curtain at Covent Garden.

'Nice day,' called the cyclist.

Waving warmly I slipped out past the L-shaped floats, paddling for Mallard Slough. Snow-tipped peaks pinched in under a weatherless sky. Geese, nesting in cattails, jiggled their heads like street trade, hissing when I laughed.

I could still reverse myself and head into the lake, a place of happier memories, away from woolgrass and bog. Michael and I, Seth Harker and his sister used to powerboat six or seven miles uplake with Rupert Kupe, to visit shorelines where the mountains dropped three thousand feet into clear water. Glacial falls, deserted lumber camps. We'd climb ashore to clang stones off a rusting steam donkey. Or waterski near Goose Island, watching Seth slalom, as Rupert drove and I listened to Michael over the engine's whine.

'That Pen Island!'

'That Goose Island!' I corrected him.

'Not according my father!'

'How come I've never heard of Pen Island?'

'You choirboy! Your voice change late! You get a pimple!'

Michael was Chinese. He sounded coltish when he laughed and I wondered about his pot calling my kettle black.

Holly Harker would listen from the bow, eyes closed, face sun-burned. In a bikini. When the boat stopped for her brother, she might tell Michael he was right, by disclosing some fact to which only she was privy. Convicts had once quarried rock on Goose Island, to help build the federal penitentiary. She would open her eyes and smile mischievously, at me.

'Hear?' said Michael, laughing harder.

We picnicked on a sandy beach and drank cheap B.C. blush. From that same summer, at the end of grade eleven, I recall Seth christening Rupert's new Sea Ray with an empty wine bottle he refilled with his own rich pee.

Broken glass wasn't all we left behind.

Michael, with his sinuous draughtmanship and a box of oils, contributed the now famous pictographs: eyes and mouths by an apparent faux-naif on a rockface. Photos of them would appear that October in a local newspaper as proof of non-European presence long before explorers arrived. 'Right on,' said Michael, his small teeth flashing. The accompanying article would locate his picto-graphs and propose the Forest Service declare them a sacred aborig-inal burial site. An elder of the Sto:lo nation would concur, wonder-ing about compensation for their historical neglect.

Michael was hoping to persuade his parents to finance his atten-dance at Emily Carr College. He envied me a mother who actively encouraged artistic talent. Forced to be devious, Michael wanted to pursue a career in wildlife oils, but his parents, strict Baptists, had no idea he was harbouring any secret desire let alone practising his art already. Empathizing with his sneakiness, I invited him along the following spring, up Mallard Slough, to sketch the birdlife. I thought he might teach me hatching.

I was celebrating my birthday. Steering clear of goslings we canoed through widgeons and golden-eyes. Michael stopped pad-dling to draw a long-legged bird, a great blue heron with the wing-span of a bridge, his pencil gliding across the page. After this we hiked up to tiny Mallard Lake, where I tried a pair of green-winged teals. An osprey, sailing on a thermal, wore out my eraser.

Hindsight is easy. Had we known what would follow lower

down, we could've camped here and saved ourselves the return hike and ruin.

'No hunter allowed,' said Michael, back at the slough. He was feeding crumbs to the mallards. The sky had clouded over and the air inside our tent had grown muggy.

Sketching me at the fry pan, he decided he wanted to be fed a sausage, half cooked, a risk we would both come to regret after evening settled in.

In the morning, canoeless, I didn't know a search party was out till a Sea King helicoptor circled at noon. Half an hour later the RCMP arrived in a pair of Mr Douglas's canoes, the creek too shallow for the rescue boat they sometimes deployed in the lake. 'Oh, good,' they called. 'You're okay. No injury to report?'

I now paddled up on the beach to the site where we'd camped five years ago. I removed my mother's lunch, then clothes, and sat down on the stones.

I ate steadily through her picnic basket, bananas for quince, before lying back to digest in the sun. I felt my skin for any burning or rash. When I opened my eyes an ultralight was circling at a thousand feet, but it flew away when I guyed it with my mother's ridiculous velvet blanket.

– 7 –

Back from the lake I found my father in his barn, silent beside the milking machine. He seemed in mourning for seventy empty stalls. Maybe he'd forgotten to take his mood elevator at breakfast. The light was muted, the air close with ammonia and hay dust. It made my throat itch. I prodded the blue-veined, whiskery udder he was preparing to slip into cups. The pulsator glugged dully, waiting to suck. I took the washcloth from him and wiped down the swollen hooters. I recalled their spongy, sometimes freckled flesh from my years as a dairyman's son. I checked for signs of mastitis, as he'd taught me. I stripped away a bead of leaking milk.

When he attached the cups, each making a straw's slurp at the bottom of a milkshake glass, I raised my eyes to his green Brunswick hanging under the hayloft.

It looked full of hay and probably unused since the night Michael capsized it.

'Dad,' I said, listening to the piston-like squeezings now under way, my palm lying in cow hollow, as smooth as tent canvas between hip and ribs. '... Remember the time you helped Michael and me carry that canoe outside, to go camping at the lake?'

He didn't seem to hear me.

'You trusted us not to screw up, Dad.'

After a moment he straightened stiffly from the other side of Lucille and turned, following my gaze. 'Yeah?'

Then bent over again to check on his machine's rhythm.

'You packed us a lunch, too.'

'I did?' He lifted his face to mine, as if expecting to hear what kind of sandwiches he'd made.

'Don't you remember, Nôtre Dame was away visiting her sister in Calgary. You were sweet about it, asking Michael if he liked chicken thighs. Michael enjoyed you.'

My father now smiled. 'What's Michael up to these days? Haven't seen him in ages.'

I managed to look surprised. 'He's dead, Dad.'

'Dead.' He frowned, distracted by a loose cup.

'Drowned.'

'Jesus. In the canoe?'

'No, fooling around. Cracked his head open in a swimming pool.'

'Christ.' He looked relieved.

He now checked to make sure the milk was running unimpeded through the plastic tubing to his bucket.

'Was trying to remember,' he said, upright again, 'why I'd hung that yacht up like some museum piece.' He was trying to remember, like any normal person, why the past had temporarily escaped him. I envied him.

I also felt pity, because like my mother I'd now figured out how easy it would be to have my way with him, to rewrite his experience on the tabula rasa of his affliction. She was right about new frames of reference.

'I should probably thank you,' I said, 'for straightening me out.'

'When was that?'

'When I turned eighteen? You jumped down my throat for getting lost in the wilderness. On that camping trip, do you remember? The ruckus over Michael and me?'

I thought he looked slightly pleased. He clearly didn't remember, any trip or ruckus, but was happy to be reminded of rehabs among sons still possible in the world.

I could now tell him anything about the past and he'd be unable to refute or correct it. It gave me an odd feeling of authority. A control teenage sons dream of having over time and fathers, especially when asked when they got in the night before.

His last cows were waiting to have their teats sucked and diddled on the machine. He used to have three machines and we would work them the length of the barn. I was seven or eight. Sixty flatulent cows eating hay, grinding teeth, collared by scritchy stanchions: the sort of pastoral fugue I associated with incarceration.

I mentioned Holly Harker. 'Her dad was home when I called by. Remember, Wallace Harker? Seth's dad?'

My father stared at me.

Had he forgotten his old friend, Wallace?

Dad had swindled him ten years earlier, on a tire-dumping contract Harker was keen to get for his own land and which my father promised he wouldn't bid on himself, telling Harker there was enough rubber to go around the world fifty times to breakfast. 'We'll all be in clover.'

With his knack for misfiguring the future, he'd probably begun to compare his utopia with Wallace's and decided his neighbour didn't deserve what my father had built up for himself. His neighbour was a deadbeat and a socialist.

Wallace was furious when he heard and swore revenge. A cold war between the two men, neither of them ever speaking to the other again, made it difficult for Seth and me. Our friendship suffered in the mutual hostility of two feuding farts. I don't think my father ever stopped worrying that Harker's acreage, a natural dumping ground because of poor land, would prove more convenient for trucks having to wind past the gravel quarry to reach our place on Polder Road.

'... Yes, I was reminiscing with Holly about that little episode with her old man.'

'Right,' said my father, bending over to check the action on Lucille. When he reappeared a thread of spittle was hanging from his mouth, and I thought the blood pushing to his head might have caused him another aura.

'What little episode, exactly?' Turning away and stepping heavily over the manure trough.

'Well, she happened to mention her dad's often said he was sorry the two of you never made it up.'

My father thought this over. 'Yeah?' I was watching his butt. A baritone is either wide in the chest or broad in the beam. Weight somewhere is required. I have my father's beam and overalls only make us beamier.

'I guess he could've had you in jail, Dad.'

I think I wanted to shock him, by revealing as if for the first time the greed of his tire-farming past. Of his collusion with tire jockeys and exclusive, no-cut contracts.

'He had it coming to him,' he replied.

'Pardon?'

'Getting outmanoeuvred.'

'... Then you remember?' My voice lifting an octave.

He turned to face me with a defiant expression. A kind of fierce calm. 'Why d'you think I still keep the Remington loaded in the house?'

The sharpness of this response startled me. The bitterness of his memory seemed undiminished.

'Don't let your mother fool you.'

I began stroking Lucille's rump. 'Fool me, how?'

'I recall more than I let on to her.'

Staring stubbornly at me now, like a lobster at its tormentor. 'For a lot of things, Fingal, my memory is still pretty good.'

Shame made me feel like a teenager again. I lifted my hand and it smelled of rubber.

'She just wants to juice things up, give herself a new interest in life.'

I was waiting for him to wrinkle his brow and make saucers of his eyes. 'I find it kinda glamorous,' he went on in the same unglamorous tone. 'Seeing how her brain works when she thinks mine's skipped. Disappointing, too, when I know she's fibbing.'

Holding himself stiffly now, as if aching from every joint, he sounded rueful. 'Instead of going snake, I listen to her. Gives me some control. She thinks she's the one in the driver's seat. So we're both operators. It's all a big pretend.'

I was embarrassed. His tabula rasa now resembled a secret sketchbook on betrayal by wife and son both. It could've been all the forlorn empty stalls, causing him to sound disappointed at the way farming life had turned out for a man who believed he cared deeply about tradition. But I sensed it was the way he felt his son was still bullshitting him.

Over supper my mother asked how Holly had liked her lunch. She was fishing for more than compliments. She wanted to know if I was on the right track with ma vie sensuelle.

'Loved it. We had a grand old time. Paddled the canoe up Mallard Slough.'

'Oh?' She looked pleased, despite her best effort to show concern. 'Where the Wing boy drowned?'

'No,' my father said, looking at me. 'He drowned in a swimming pool.' Sounding a little sarcastic, as if the lobster and his tormentor had switched roles.

My mother looked at me. My father looked at my mother. I changed the subject, to the blue scarf.

This reminded my father. He suddenly said, 'What month is this?'

Seems he'd recently found a bill for about a hundred yards of dress silk, and a few pairs of pumps, and been unable to figure out if payment for the circus was overdue.

That night I did wonder about the nature of families and if any philosopher, French or otherwise, had ever composed an elegy to shame without first experiencing imprisonment.

In the years since this week home I've come to hear how the overture to *Don Pasquale* resembles a blissful seduction, full of passion and joy, with moments of tenderness and sometimes sadness. Its conclusion seems comically rambunctious in the way copulation is.

Singing the role of Dr Malatesta, I now wait for the curtain, thinking how this overture sounds like a tragedy.

— 8 —

I recently turned thirty-three. Not yet a household name in the opera firmament, if that isn't a contradiction in terms. I sing in regional theatres across North America, do summer stock, contract for roles like a utility infielder and maintain my base in San Francisco. For Dallas Opera I've sung a replacement Sharpless in *Madama Butterfly*, performed *Masked Ball's* Renato for Calgary Opera, Ping in *Turandot* for Indianapolis, a Malatesta in Baltimore, and Escamillo in *Carmen* for Sarasota. Lately, I made my debut at Santa Fe as Silvio in *I Pagliacci*. These days I am preparing Rodrigue in *Don Carlo* for Opera Theatre of St. Louis.

This last was what put me in mind again of the penitentiary and my visit to it with my father.

That spring had been the spring Terry Fox started hopping across Canada, from St. John's to Victoria, to raise money for medical research after losing his right leg to bone cancer. He was planning to run the length of the Trans-Canada Highway, but, four months after my visit home, had got only as far as Thunder Bay when they discovered cancer in his lungs and he was forced to abandon his 'Marathon of Hope'. He'd run over two thousand miles, without crossing half the country. He vowed to complete the run.

Canada, according to my father who should have known, now took the faith of a cripple.

My mother sent newspaper clippings to San Francisco. L'héros was one year younger than I, but already famous. He came from a small town a few miles down the highway, and was travelling with his girlfriend who followed him in their camper truck at a turtle's pace. 'She cooks for him,' P.S.ed my mother, making sure I knew what the gossip of a Canadian hero consisted of, 'and changes his leg.'

My father quipped in a P.P.S. that their camper's tires would never wear out at a measly twenty-four miles a day.

My athletic compatriot turned out to be the hare and turtle

rolled into one. He won the big race by losing it.

He died at the Royal Columbian the next year, where my father died a year later. His death came as a shock, because it came in the wrong way. I went home for the funeral, but left before the inquest. I think my mother would've liked me to sing 'O My Papa' at the service, lilting like Eddie Fisher on Elavil. Instead I sang Verdi.

My grandmother attended in a lavender coat and Aunt Betty, now eighty-seven, in a walking frame. My father's family was long-lived and no more susceptible to memory loss than normally governed by old age. The past tried, but could not consume them. Both remembered Bill Miner's pistol in detail but argued at the reception following internment over the tattoo on his forearm. My grandmother remembered a tattoo, but her sister remembered none at all. How each could be so certain seemed a wonderful example of how death is cheated by detail. Neither seemed so alive that wet October afternoon, sunk heavily into my father's sofa, as when they bickered over the tattoo of a dancing girl on the forearm of a robber.

I refused to chip in with any documentary evidence from a poster I remembered, because nothing could have erased the conviction of opinion on either side. After almost eighty years their youthful memories had taken on the indelibility of dream. The consensus of my family's oral history confirmed the hand-held pistol in detail and this seemed as far up the arm as they could get without dissolving into disagreement. It was something.

By now I'd finished at the San Francisco Vocal Arts Studio, with the renowned coach Ricardo Tibaldi, and was wondering if I had a future in opera or not. There were a hundred baritones of my generation. Roles were plentiful, opportunities few. Tibaldi with his Gray Flannel perfume advised me to carry an adrenaline pump for my asthma and a small grip for the overhead luggage racks. 'Forget the carousels when you're in a hurry. Fly first-class and require a limo.' He was a good-natured womanizer, whom I still visit for help with demanding roles.

I quit my job at Max's Opera Café and concentrated on serving a career instead of food. A debut with the SFO seemed years, if ever, away. I needed work with the Pocket Opera or else Opera in the Schools to keep up my confidence and bank balance. I thought of going back to live in Canada. What did it matter as an Italian baritone where I was based, Alberta or Alaska, singing Puccini's Sheriff Rance in *The Girl of the Golden West* for Edmonton or San Diego? Have Pipes, Will Travel. Ditto Laugh.

My mother had no idea now what she was going to do with TIRE MEADOWS. Sell out, if she could, but who wanted a dairy farm full of tires? Who wanted a tire dump with no space left to dump in? Who wanted a tire farm with nowhere to recycle the product? The profit in the place had run out. The land had long ago disappeared.

She sold the remaining cows to Rupert Kupe and stopped any more dumptrucks from arriving after my father's death.

Perhaps his death had been an accident, as the inquest concluded. Maybe his mind *had* drifted to the centre line, causing him to walk into the path of Wallace Harker's car. What was he doing on the road anyway, walking alone with his back unguarded? My mother testified he'd gone out that afternoon to milk. Had the way to the barn finally slipped his mind, like the last line from a zeppelin?

She phoned to tell me Harker was suspected of manslaughter but wouldn't be charged. Tire marks had allowed the RCMP to trace the hit-and-run car to Mrs Harker. Wallace said he left the scene of the accident because people still remembered bad blood between him and his neighbour and he was scared of them jumping to conclusions. Homicide was not his idea of order.

'Poor man had no idea William wouldn't have remembered him, even if he'd stopped the car and offered him the tires.'

I avoided the inquest, remembering how an earlier one, into Michael Wing's death, had caused my hay fever to worsen. Also I had no desire to deal with my father's estate. If some legacies never changed, mine had. I made up my mind to stay abroad and make a home there.

Here.

Where, headed into my mid-thirties, I now find every fermata counts increasingly against the past.

A decade since his death my mother still lives in growing despair of her dwindling capital. Lately, she has decided her only hope of resuscitating it is through her husband's dream of recycling their tires. God help her. I suppose we are all waiting for our Godots, but how does she endure the place? She has long lost her farm status and taxes have soared.

She calls to say things in the recyling world have moved on since my father first thought of contributing his billion tires to reincarnation. Melodramatically, she tells me early in the next century I, heir to a woman of no importance, can expect to cash in, provided I hire someone after she is gone to manage the transmigration – sell the tires then sell the land.

'I know you don't want anything to do with the place, mon cher, and I don't blame you.'

'No, you're wrong.'

The provincial government she claims has begun collecting a tire tax of three dollars per tire sold there. This money will be used to finance new schemes to recycle the three million tires junked a year.

'The door is open to you, to make your fortune.'

Door mats, rubber crumb, rubberized asphalt. The world is my oyster.

She says cement plants now burn tires for part of their fuel. This portion could increase with the new technology. She mentions a technique called pyrolysis, and says one day I could find myself in the loop for exports to the States, where they're using tires in power plants.

'Burning, Fin, has come miles since your father tried it. After the big Hagersville fire they had to crack down.'

A heavy rainstorm had helped snuff my father's fire the June I graduated from high school. His burning tires would've lit up the surrounding mountains till Christmas. The smell, in one of those memories accumulated from odourless news clips on TV, reminded me of South African necklaces.

I sang poorly at my high school graduation. I had been testifying at the inquest into Michael's drowning. How an unexpected storm had come up and I thought the wind and rain would make his navigation of the narrows dangerous in the dark.

'Holly Harker,' my mother adds, 'still phones to ask about you.

More than once she's said how much she enjoyed that picnic tu et elle took up Mallard Slough. I *am* sorry to bother you about the farm.'

She is very polite. And despite her despair sounds as healthy as a Holstein.

'Don't be sorry,' I tell her just as politely back. And laugh like a tenor. 'Remember how much I enjoyed bantering with Dad about recyling Goodyears and Michelins? You're dead right about the new technology. I look forward to taking over TIRE MEADOWS when they put you out to pasture.'

Why do we go on talking like this, year after year? To cover the shame of knowing the other knows we're lying? Or are we each in our own way vying for control of the family album?

Just before she dies I'll probably come home and formally announce my engagement to a nice Marin County girl. Deathbed deceptions have their place, I sense, if the diee's doubt can be erased by the deception. At present San Francisco is full of such deceptions, small white ones, partners swearing loyalty to partners who are dying.

Like opera, life seems full of deceptions if you're determined to make an art of it. Ergo the performing artist, in flagrante delicto, the perpetual outsider. Not so bad. Being outside gives him his sound. Each to his place, beholden to a predecessor, Leonard Cohen sounding like Johnny Cash on tranquillizers.

I remember hearing Cash's Folsom Prison album as an adolescent, listening over and over to his rich rhythmic voice. But I couldn't deny my father's voice, breaking through in me as my glands then were like chanterelles. I couldn't deny my genes. How to escape a residency we both regretted, to get outside and be free?

On occasion I will be invited abroad, to poorer countries, for operetta roles in Gilbert and Sullivan, or Strauss, which count for little on my résumé. I've even woken up in Argentina to find myself singing Andrew Lloyd Webber at a breakfast for civil rights workers in hotpants. But these junkets pay for themselves and keep my ego stroked. Stoked? In a provincial town in Brazil, say, I'll receive a kind of baroque hospitality alien to my non-reception in North America. This will match the unexpected nineteenth-century opera house, which is stunning, like the dark skin available back in Rio. It gleams against a jungle. I would love to return some day to sing *Tosca* with Pilar Lorengar, kissing the hems of that old hoofer, as I, Scarpia, lie there dying on the floor of my apartment in the Farnese Palace.

I would kiss Joan Sutherland's hems, too, but she has retired and hung up her size twenty. That doesn't stop me from hoisting my dream sails above the Sydney Opera House, like some reincarnated Peter Dawson, local baritone long dead. Death shapes most stories and mine would have me on board as Germont singing 'Pura sic-come un angelo' to Mrs Bonynge – and, from that same ecstatic scene in *La Traviata*, 'Di Provenza il mar, il suol' to Marshall van Neer. (Where are you, Marshall? You were a wonderful tenor. Have faith!)

I find it perverse Germont is the role I dream myself into heaven with, singing a lament to my son of his fate far from the shining sun of Provence, and how I've suffered since Alfredo departed the joy of our family home. I sang this aria to my father at his burial.

Whoever lives longer can choose to recycle the other's story in theirs. This is the law of the jungle, ignored, I am sure, by French pundits in favour of the absurd. I feel ruthless sometimes, thinking how *I* sing is the highest law of all, how *my* story is the last word in the family album. Like love, a corrupt business of dog eat dog. You sing to be encored.

(Take heart, Mother, this story is for you in case you're left alone without me one day. Pick it up and put it down, where you wish. You will have the last word then. You may even rework the ending.)

– 9 –

No.

The reason I am writing is to explain how the facts that came out at Michael Wing's inquest were opinions and how my father could forgive everything except the truth.

The truth is Michael couldn't make up his mind about me, although *his* version of our wildlife expedition wouldn't have mentioned this at all. Regrettably, his was the version that governed the inquest. The inquest ruled drowning by misadventure.

The version *I* testified to, as the reason for his leaving our tent, was my friend's nagging fear he'd betrayed his parents by not telling them where he'd come – that they'd be worried he hadn't gone home that night. His parents' lawyer countered they *had* known where Michael was and had vigorously disapproved his going. The inquest's story of Michael was of a sensitive, responsible son, whose feelings of responsibility to his parents were acute. Did not drink. Did not chase girls. A good son.

This story should've supported my own.

My mistake was having sworn earlier neither of us had been drinking. Unfortunately, the autopsy showed traces of plonk in the deceased's bloodstream, from a bottle shared over our sausage cookout. Coroner's opinion was I wasn't telling the truth about what led Michael to abandon our tent. In ruling death by misadventure he upbraided me for seeming callous at my friend's 'odd' decision to return to my father's truck. I supposed Michael felt he could sleep more comfortably there, his stomach apparently upset. He was an excitable friend.

But I had lied poorly. Somehow, had failed Michael. My reputation never recovered (whispered suspicions spread like a weedy ground cover) and I was glad to escape into undergraduate life the following September.

I was glad to come abroad five years later. Home had become increasingly exotic to me, as had its shame. My parents were ashamed of me. To return to live in Canada would've destroyed my illusions of the place. To be disillusioned at four in the morning was far worse than to know you had illusions and were still willing to stand by them. Even my father discovered this. Until wandering away from his own illusions, he knew they were everything, when everything else was fading. Corruption was all. Just as central to the map of his brain as rubber to the Trans-Canada. Anyhow, my Canadian driver's licence had expired and I had (have) never renewed it.

Patriotism wouldn't help my career, not at this stage. It would also kill the current relationship I'm in, as my partner has no wish to leave San Francisco and family to live in Toronto or Vancouver. We're content enough. I get to travel, he gets to sleep around. We both sleep around. His father owns three restaurants in Chinatown. We live together in the Castro, in a two-bedroom walkup off Clipper. We maintain a discreet dignity, never compromising ourselves by betraying the other's soul to another partner. Body, yes. In leather clubs on Folsom Street. In apartments as far away as North Beach. Anywhere, really, to keep up the wonderful illusion of romance, especially while young. The curse of desiring to live heroically in a non-operatic age is, of course, the current plague. My father would've approved.

Lately, we hear playing, as a kind of anthem song from the apartment next door, 'Tell Him No' by the Everly Brothers. It seems to be replacing the old gay anthem, 'Chances Are' by Johnny Mathis.

Would I could be so popular. Am afraid my discography is limited to pirated tapes from recitals and performances. These underground masterpieces circulate in the community and I'm cherished among a few for chestnuts like 'Au fond du temple saint ...', singing the role of Zurga with Richard Margison as Madir, in *The Pearl Fishers*. It's like being on the moon when I overhear myself coming out tinnily from some open window in the sunshine. A man inside is dreaming of me.

But where is my role in the great AIDS opera? Who will compose it? Probably a straight shooter from Broadway, some outsider with a mid-Atlantic accent and a mistress, a wife and a soccer team he coaches for his daughter's sake every Connecticut weekend after a papaya breakfast for good skin and a smooth pee. Puccini, after all, didn't need to contract consumption to compose *La Bohème* ... only to create illusion to parry disillusion.

The condition of being in love is what I decided on my eighteenth birthday I'd like for myself. It led inevitably to corruption. I still throw myself into roles that would charm birds from a marsh. Can't help it. And this leads to wounded feelings all round. I desire ecstasy through other men, and while I'm unwilling to pay the price of dying I am willing to live with death constantly in mind.

What else is new? Death death death is the singer's dictum, and everything he performs is an elegy to the temporal voice. Or should be. I tell people what I think they want to hear, that I have/have not tested positive for HIV, in order to enhance their belief in my art. I want them to feel some of the happiness I feel as a baritone even of modest talent, as a lover even of unreliable declaration. Ironic, being in the business of perfection, to have to strive for it with corruption so much on the brain.

Sometimes I wonder in light of my father's auras what lies in store for my own brain. Have begun to wonder on stage if bliss wasn't always the beginning of my end.

To make art of life I find nothing more trustworthy than my conductor's baton, this baton. My instinctive loyalty is to it, confining me to ecstasy and grief upon a fixed stage. My nightmare is I'll fail my vision and discover poltroonery at my centre. So illusion is everything. The collective artifice of librettists, designers, singers, composers and dancing masters – all of us in the bliss business, our gaiety transfiguring all that dread.

Should I expect to experience my father's seizures?

Blackout, heaven blazing into the head.

Some of our friends believe the pulleys, racks and costumes of their S and M machinery are all part of the stage they live upon. I think this illusion the right one. Except their apartments resemble ancient inquisitorial prisons: blindfolds, tit clamps, cockrings ...

Ours favours less impersonal props and more traditional roles. 'You like my weapon? I'm going to shoot you with it.' This excites Richard. It excites me. I talk to him in my husky baritone – Puccini's own voce bruna – as melodiously as I can. I tie up my partner's wrists the way I once tied Michael Wing's, with a scout's half-hitch.

Richard isn't squeamish, doesn't spook if I laugh at his sensibilities. He struggles eagerly to escape. A stage designer, he is used to people walking, so to speak, over him. He's really the one in control. He contains me. He allows us freedom within his three walls (where Michael's sketch of the cook and frying pan hangs framed) and laughs at my thinking a mere stage pistol can be the centre of the action. A big pretend by us both. 'Put your faith in rubber,' I tell him. 'Or die.' Richard has a wolfish laugh. My blue cashmere softens pressure on his wrists.

In our own way, we're happy.

Even my father's directive is ludicrously, prophetically borne out. We've become believers.

Yesterday I found myself on Nob Hill visiting a black and white photo exhibition of AIDS victims in Grace Cathedral. The church was empty. Cool blue light sifted down from the nave's stained glass windows. Birth dates were given, death dates left open or closed, as required. Roommates pictured in kitchens and dens, posing with parakeets or dogs, a vintage Buick, dressed in T-shirts and chinos. Caught before the appearance of Kaposi's sarcoma, with its disfiguring and agonizing lesions.

A note said it's often possible to forget you're infected, because the virus can live undetected in the lymph nodes for up to ten years before launching a final attack.

I felt close to tears. I thought of the mothers who had arrived here from Wichita and Red Deer. And of the ones who hadn't arrived. Of the lovers, themselves infected or not infected, who nursed roommates. Or hadn't and disappeared. I wondered why it took us so long in the early days to shut down the bathhouses and plug the glory holes. We've all immigrated here from outside boundaries we never knew could've saved us from pneumonia and meningitis.

Yet at what cost, compared to imprisonment and falsehood? To risk all in a gamble over a drop of blood, as Sheriff Jack Rance does, hoping to capture the gentle tenor, highway robber Dick Johnson, is to know the value of everything and the cost of nothing. That, I think, is the price of wanting to live operatically: seeing through to the exotic, as Puccini did, and deeming this its own reward. Not a bargain, by any means, killing the thing you love!

Richard claims I am turning into an artistic director.

Afterward, I walked down Russian Hill to Fisherman's Wharf, and along with all the fish-'n'-chippy tourists stood gazing out to Alcatraz across the green salt-smelling bay. It seemed a propitious time to invite an aura: the sky cerulean, the buildings behind me white and Mediterranean, the light crippling. I considered taking the boat tour of the now deserted prison rooted atop the hot rock, something every citizen has eventually to do for a picnic of bread and water. I could see water tanks and windows winking in the sun.

What glory holes over there?

When he was released in 1901, after spending thirty-three of fifty-four years in prison, Bill Miner left California and landed in my native province. I thought now I understood the source of his elaborate façade, his ability to take people in, including my ancestors. He'd been an outsider too. A confidence man. A bandit who couldn't resist the abiding temptation of his nature, of his deceit in love with courtliness, and who ended up in handcuffs and jail, a gentleman recidivist.

Even in prison they couldn't see through him any more than they could through Wilde in Reading Gaol. His true identity resided in the sincerity of his façade. Shame seems quaint now. A performer's curse, Mother. It just gets to the point where it is no longer possible, or desirable, to separate life from its stage.

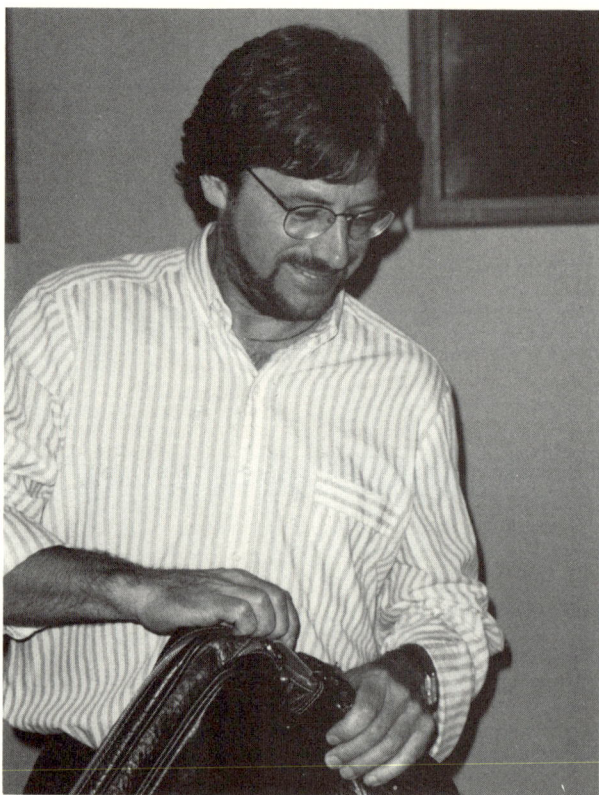

About the Author

Keath Fraser's stories and novellas have been reprinted in numerous Canadian and international anthologies such as *The Art of Short Fiction, Best Canadian Stories, From Ink Lake, On Middle Ground, The New Canadian Anthology, The Faber Book of Contemporary Canadian Short Stories.* He is the author of two earlier acclaimed story collections, including *Foreign Affairs* (Stoddart, 1985), shortlisted for the Governor General's Award and winner of the Ethel Wilson Fiction Prize. His stories have won the Western Magazine Award and the *Canadian Fiction Magazine* Contributor's Prize. His novel *Popular Anatomy* was the 1996 winner of the Chapters/*Books in Canada* First Novel Award.

Educated at the University of London, Keath Fraser returned to Canada where he taught at the University of Calgary for five years before devoting himself full-time to writing. His essays on writing are reprinted in the anthology of Canadian authors, *How Stories Mean* (The Porcupine's Quill, 1993). He has travelled extensively throughout the world and has edited the best-selling international anthologies *Bad Trips* (Vintage, 1991) and *Worst Journeys: The Picador Book of Travel* (1992). He was born and raised in Vancouver, where he lives at present and is a director of Canada India Village Aid (CIVA).

Acknowledgements

These stories have appeared in the following magazines and anthologies, occasionally at variance with their final versions: 'Argentina
My Voice' (*Descant 55*, Winter 1986/87; *The Macmillan Anthology
1*, 1988); 'Damages' (*Prism International*, Spring 1987; *The Macmillan Anthology 1*, 1988); 'The Girl with the White Light: A Soap
Opera' (*Descant 55*, Winter 1986/87); 'Sikh' (*The Malahat Review
87*, Summer 1989); 'Flight' (*The Malahat Review 82*, Spring 1988);
'Memoir' (*Books in Canada*, June/July 1990); 'Foster Story' (*McGill
Street Magazine*, Fall 1996); 'My Honour, Your Honour' (*Carousel
11*, 1996); 'Sturgeon' (*The Malahat Review 116*, Fall 1996); 'Telling
My Love Lies: An Elegy' (*Quarry 45/1*, 1996).

To the following editors may I extend Baudelaire's bouquet: Karen
Mulhallen, Antanas Sileika, Hart Hanson, Constance Rooke, Doris
Cowan, Ron Zevy, Alexandra Soiseth, Helen Walsh, Michael Car-
bert, Derk Wynand, Marlene Cookshaw, Lucy Bashford, Mary
Cameron, Anne Archer, Leon Rooke, John Metcalf: lovers of stories
all, you are the imaginations of your nation. L'état, c'est vous.